I AM CHRIS

By the Author

The Mail Order Bride

I Am Chris

I Am Chris

by

R Kent

2021

I AM CHRIS

ISBN 13: 978-1-63555-904-0

This Trade Paperback Original Is Published By
Bold Strokes Books, Inc.
P.O. Box 249
Valley Falls, NY 12185

First Edition: April 2021

CREDITS
Editor: Cindy Cresap
Production Design: Stacia Seaman
Cover Design by Tammy Seidick

Acknowledgments

Many thanks for encouragement from Steven, Tom, and the rest of the cowboys I work with, laugh with, and learn from. And for turning my "here, hold this" back on me too many times when the lariat wasn't long enough and I was destined to come up short. Good times.

Mike.

Gratitude to Bold Strokes Books, and Rad, for taking a chance on a cowboy in publishing *The Mail Order Bride* (2020) even knowing that the Western dime novel has long since passed. A dream come true for me. Thank you.

Dedication

Mom

Brian

CHAPTER ONE

August 21, 1994

"Chrissy, stop! You can't do it again. It's too dangerous." Lucine clawed at my glove where the tape strangled it to my wrist. "Chrissy, listen."

"Don't call me that." I spun around and shook my fist in her face. The bull rope in my grip flopped like a rag doll. Its bells clanked the ground in complaint.

She was a pretty kid, if she weren't my nagging little half sister. I dropped my fist to inspect the wide tape cinching my wrist. "You want to eat, don't you?" Her eyes grew big. I swear her bottom lip quivered.

"Luce, I gotta do this. You know I gotta." I softened my tone.

"Not for me you don't. I don't need to eat. Chris, please?" She had a pout that was going to melt hearts one day.

But today, it was irritating.

"Let's just go home," she pleaded.

Home. Her mama lost our home. Now we squatted on the edge of a run-down town in a collapsing trailer. All of our possessions and all of our money had gone up that skank butt's nose.

My daddy never approved of drugs past ibuprofen. He didn't even drink but a beer or two during the week. Never on weekends. Never at rodeos. "Drinking or drugging can ruin your balance and timing," he always said. "It'll ruin your life."

Guess my stepmama hadn't taken note. No sooner was Daddy gone than she sucked down enough booze to keep a liquor store in business. Then she snorted everything that wasn't nailed down.

Hell, I once caught her licking the wallpaper in our formal dining room. When we still had a formal dining room. She said it was candy. *Whatever.*

Some man she dated came and went but always left her wanting more—more drugs. I never saw him. I think when the money ran out, she got less interesting. So he ran out too.

"Stay here, Luce." I left her by the pens where I could see her until my ride.

I climbed the chutes with my rope, then eased the bells over the side of the Brahma bull. When the bull felt the rope drop past his heart girth, he tossed his head. Frothy snot blew from his nostrils to splatter the panels. He was a crapshoot—unproven. I was unproven too. We both had a lot at stake.

The only way I even rated a ride at this rodeo was because the announcer, Red, knew my daddy's name.

The hook went through and brought my rope under the bull. I climbed in the chute to secure it around him. After it was set, I got back out because I'd have a wait before my ride.

Everyone behind the chutes moved off to watch a known cowboy. He was the favorite to win, the darling of West Texas. I was hot on his tail with last night's points. But nobody took me seriously. "A fluke ride," they said. Though they saw me take a licking to stay on board for the eight.

"You drew the Bunny," a kid about my age, seventeen, said in a matter-of-fact way. He was below the chute platform looking up at me. His eyes constantly darted toward the next bucking chute over. I could see his face was tense, though he was trying to play it cool.

"Thundering Bunny," I corrected him. "He's badass."

"He's a bit small. No one's seen him buck." He chucked me on my plain, working Wellington boot, making the worn-out rowel of my spur jingle. "Luck on the Bunny," he shouted as the crowd roared.

"Thundering Bunny." I poked a tuft of my hair back under my cowboy hat. "Don't listen to anybody. You be you. You were born to it. It's in your genes." And I didn't know if I was talking to the bull or to myself. Thundering Bunny bobbed his lopsided head and rolled his red-ringed eyes upward, as if the pep talk was all he needed.

Two gates over, the latch was pulled back with a tormented

squeal. The gate was hauled wide. The penned bull made his leap to freedom. I didn't watch. The crowd let me know that the cowboy was making his eight-second ride. The buzzer sounded. Noise grew deafening.

Chute men trickled back toward me.

I straddled Thundering Bunny from the safety of the chute's rails and chewed on my mouth guard. Once I dropped down, it'd be all business.

I checked on Luce. She still stood where I had told her to. I had explained a couple of nights ago that I couldn't worry about her wandering off. Had to keep my head in the game. She knew. She knew quite a lot for a little kid. A lot more than any kid her age should know.

Having a drug-addled mama was making Luce grow up too fast. I was sorry to see her childhood slipping away this past year.

"You taking this ride, son?" the spotter asked like I was scared and might back out.

I wasn't backing out.

I crept down onto the bull. Thundering Bunny lurched, slamming hard enough that the spotter grabbed my vest. I was wearing my daddy's vest. He had been a tall drink of water, like me. And lanky. I looked much like he had when he was my age. Though he matured broader—I could probably fit two of me in his vest. If the two of me were slow dancing on prom night.

I used black duct tape to snug the protective vest to my torso as much as possible. It wasn't tight, but it had stayed put so far. And the black tape didn't show on the black vest, 'cept close up. The spotter looked at me as if he disapproved.

A trickle of sweat rolled from high between my shoulders. My binding absorbed it. I wiggled inside the vest because now the binding felt too tight. *Focus.*

The rope puller held the tail of my rope taut so I could work the rosin. He gave me a smile which looked a bit sad.

Focus. I asked to have more slack pulled out before taking a *truck and trailer* wrap through my palm. That particular wrap did not encircle my hand, which would trap me to this wildcard until I pulled the rope's tail. I wasn't ready to be *that* tied down.

My stepmama always said I lacked commitment. But that was

said about boys. If she only knew I wasn't interested. I was one. I didn't want to date one. And I didn't seem to have time for them anyway.

My stepmama was always pecking at me.

Focus. I tossed my rope's tail over the bull's hump and gave my gloved hand a last punch to tighten the grip.

That's when the announcer, Red, derailed my attention. "Ladies and gentlemen. Getting ready to make his debut win is Chris Taylor."

I was sure no one believed I had a chance. To them, I showed up out of nowhere just last night and had "a fluke ride with a generous score." They were waiting for me to choke on this one. "Never gonna make the eight," I heard repeatedly behind my back.

"He's the son of Buckshot Taylor, two-time champion bull rider." The announcer recited my daddy's winnings and lifetime earnings, which were both considerable. Then he told of my daddy's tragic automobile accident.

Today was the one-year anniversary of his death.

My stomach somersaulted. For a fraction of a second, my head was lost to that night.

Red and blue lights flash in the dark. Sirens wail. The flipped truck burns. My stepmama's see-through, skimpy nightie clings to her every curve as she runs toward the inferno. Firefighters drag her away from the wreckage.

Luce clutches my waist. Her tiny face burrows into my side. She cries. So small. She is so small. And so inconsolable.

No time for my own grief. No time.

My stepmama falls to her knees on the side of the road. Daddy's lifeless body is wheeled to the ambulance. The sheet flutters from his battered face. His hand drapes to the side. Luce climbs me like a suffering monkey. My arms wrap tightly around her. I promise never to let go.

Cowboy up. For Daddy. For Luce.

I would never leave Luce.

"Son?" The spotter hanging onto my vest shot a worried look to the flank man.

"Let's have a big show of support for this young cowboy," the announcer hollered over the loudspeakers. The rodeo crowd loosed their enthusiasm with clapping, stomping, and hooting. They were locals. But I didn't know any of them.

The bull lurched again at the raucous noise. I punched my wrapped hand.

Slide and ride. Winky to my pinky. I got up over that bull and nodded to clear the haunting images from my head.

The latch screeched. The chute flung open.

Thundering Bunny took a huge leap, belying his size. He came down on all fours, stoving my spine into itself. I was sure to be two inches shorter if I walked away.

He spun into my hand. I found the sweet spot. My body took over. That's when everything got real quiet in my head.

Daddy always said, "You could read a bull, but that would slow your reaction time. It's best to feel *of* him."

I set my spur solid. I hoped Thundering Bunny wouldn't come out of his spin.

It worked. For two seconds.

His short back and quick steps allowed his bulk to move around unnaturally fast. I thought I could hang in for the ride, but the revolutions were brutal.

I prayed he'd mix it up before I got sucked down into the well.

I don't know what possessed me, but I took to marking him out with my outside leg. Truth be told, I needed Thundering Bunny to break his blistering spin. I was going to hurl.

So I started pecking at him with my rowel. Much like a petite girl booting a recalcitrant pony.

No. Bulls do not pay any heed to directions. Neither do spoiled ponies.

Somewhere in the distance, I heard the buzzer. I opened my wrapped hand and flew from Thundering Bunny's back. The audience was on their feet. They stomped the aluminum bleachers to a deafening beat.

I'd won.

Daddy, I won!

While the crowd trickled from the arena, I collected my winnings, then sent Luce off to get us a sweet treat. I promised her a special dinner at Mickey D's in town, only after she'd ruined her appetite on something yummy from the rodeo grounds. She ran, delighted. Like a kid should be.

"Red's the name." A big man shoved his hand toward me. "I didn't know ol' Buckshot had a bull riding son." By his voice, I recognized him as the announcer. "Years back," Red continued, "ol' Buckshot had himself a skinny little squirt running around after him. Dragged his bull rope through the grit. He near tanned the hide off of that kid more than once for it." Red pulled his open hand slightly back, as if he were no longer sure he wanted to shake.

He eyed me. "I figured with all of that walloping, it made sense you wouldn't have taken to bull riding. Had to be some reason we didn't see you around the rodeos." He stuffed his hand back out. "Some really good reason you weren't riding bulls on the circuit already."

When I took his hand, he pulled me in close and winked. "Welcome, son. You've got some big boots to fill." He clapped me on the shoulder, which popped the tired Velcro loose, making my vest sag. *I'll add duct tape to that later.*

Luce jogged over carrying way too much in her little hands. "I got them just like you said, Chris. And the man put your change in a paper sack." She peered around the humongous, swirled ice cream cones. They were already dripping in the relentless heat.

Luce lapped at the delicious dribble fleeing over her knuckles. "Oh, hello," she said between licks. "'Scuse me." A dollop of melted ice cream sat on the tip of her nose.

"Well, you two enjoy yourselves. You've earned it." Red tugged my vest up and mashed the patch of Velcro on my shoulder down. It didn't stay. "Okie dokie, then. See you next weekend," he said as if it were a sure thing.

Next weekend was another local rodeo. The payout was bigger but so was the entry fee. If I was careful with tonight's winnings, I'd have money enough to enter. And I was planning to enter.

We walked from the back gate into the parking lot.

The sheriff was waiting for me. His patrol car blocked the front of my truck as if I'd try to get away. I wouldn't. I had nowhere to go.

"Where is she?" I asked when we got within spitting distance. This wasn't the first time he'd hunted me down. My stepmama was always needing bail money or a ride home.

Last week I learned the hard way to let the authorities sort her out before picking her up.

It was near two a.m. that night when I finally found her slumped in a bar across town. The Honky Tonk. As I walked in, two burly men were thrashing out dibs on who was *taking her home.*

I don't think anybody meant to—all I remember is the sound of glass breaking, then a blur slashed across my face. I woke in the hospital as the ER doctor shoved a needle through my swelled cheek like she was embroidering on Grandma's hanky. I'd have a frightful scar marring my face for the rest of my life. Good thing I'm not a girly girl.

I wrapped my arm around Luce, hauled her to me, and held her tight. My bull rope slipped from my shoulder to puddle over our boot toes.

"She's in the hospital." The sheriff had a gleam in his eye that told me there was more to it he wasn't saying. But he was like that. We had only moved to town a couple of months ago and he was already making himself way too familiar with my family. He was way too familiar with my stepmama.

Plop. Luce's soft serve ice cream landed in the dirt. Her thin body shook. She struggled to hold back tears.

"You'll have to come with me," the sheriff said.

I didn't trust him. I didn't like him. It seemed as if he was always trying to run us out of town. Us kids. He threatened to call social services more than once.

There was nothing social services could do. I made sure Luce was fed. And since my stepmama always came home scratching, I was extra careful to keep Luce clean. She always got to summer school on time. I even helped with her homework when she asked. And we still had a parent. My stepmama was no longer a good parent, but I could prop her up to look like something if a social worker wanted to investigate.

The rest of the time, my stepmama could just leave us alone. I took care of Luce now. Without her help.

"I ran those plates. They don't belong to that old heap. What they should be on is a 1983, one-ton dually your daddy owned. I can't quite see how you mistook this antiquated, three-quarter-ton rust bucket for an almost brand new, dual-wheel one-ton." The sheriff walked over to my truck and kicked the dented bumper. It jangled and swung on its coat hanger wire jerry-rigged job. "Piece of crap."

He ought to talk. His patrol car had been in a wreck. One headlight had been smashed out in the past. The entire quarter panel was dented around the new light. The paint was flaking. And the cracks in it were seeing some rust.

Back at the door of his patrol car, he directed Luce to get in. He turned to me and said, "You're not driving anywhere."

I handed Luce my cone and bent to collect my rope.

The sheriff's booted feet stepped beneath my nose. "Before you get up, think real careful about your next move."

Okay, Barney Fife. I showed him my empty hands while gingerly reaching for the bull rope with my fingertips. When I stood, I slowly plucked at the buckles on my chaps until they came away. "I'd like to stow my gear in the truck."

Barney Fife opened the sides of my unzipped vest and made a big show of looking around. "Don't do anything stupid," he said.

Stupid? This entire past year's been full of stupid! And moving to this town? Stupid! I needed to get out of small town idiocy. I needed to get free of my stepmama's insanity. And I couldn't. Not yet. That's what was stupid. This cretin? He was nothing. Soon to be a thing of my past.

The truck door groaned on its hinges when I wrenched it open. An old gear bag waited on the bench seat. I stuffed my bull rope, chaps, and vest into it. Then I tucked the brown sack of change in the glove box. After I stripped my spurs and glove, I slammed the heavy door shut. It wouldn't hold intruders out, but if no one stole my gear, the stuff would stay dry.

"Do you even have a license?"

I don't.

At the hospital, the sheriff escorted us past the emergency room and into the critical care unit. Luce ran toward a bed where her mama lay. The nurse had already prepared us about the coma. Needles and tubes sprang from her arms. Monitors were attached to her chest and middle finger. She had a tube strapped under her nose.

I couldn't work up a tear for her if I had to fake it. Maybe the antiseptic hospital smells could bring on a watery redness, like cutting onions, if I absolutely had to show some emotion. But I wasn't feeling it. Not for her. I felt…relieved.

I mean, for once, I knew exactly where she was. And I didn't have to worry about her wandering off, drug-addled, to somewhere else. The not knowing, and the frantic searching, had been difficult. And then, it was always a surprise as to what I'd find when I found her.

I skimmed my fingertips over the stitches closing the ragged gash on my cheek. To say I was relieved might be mild. I was almost giddy.

It was Luce's sobbing that wrenched my heart. I couldn't stand to see my little sister so miserable. Her face was scrunched in horror. Her nose drooled slime onto her top lip. And spittle ejected from her mouth as she screamed at the nurse to let go of her arm.

I stood in a daze wondering if this was a good time to take up smoking, or some other obnoxious habit to while away the time.

The sheriff crossed his arms in front of his chest and leaned against the doorframe. Monitors beeped a steady rhythm in their boredom. A doctor came and went. Nurses finally gave in to Luce's fight and let her stand by the side of her mother's bed.

Luce's knuckles went white in twisting the bed's blanket. Her wracking cries settled into hiccupping sobs. And all of it seemed a million miles away, like I was watching a movie on late night TV.

Daddy would want me to forgive her. My stepmama. Truth was, I hadn't yet forgiven him. She could take a number. It was going to be a long wait. I'm not the forgiving type.

A deputy stepped in. A woman in a tight skirt and loose blouse trailed after him. She stopped beside the sheriff. She and the sheriff put their heads together whispering.

The deputy plucked a can of Skoal from his breast pocket and thumped it repeatedly on his palm. He must have seen me staring. He offered me some.

I looked into his eyes. They were a pale blue that seemed too clean and too honest to work for the sheriff. His eyebrows were strained with concern.

If my own brows lunged together, they wouldn't affect concern. Their intent would be anger. I pinched Skoal from the proffered canister and stuffed it between my cheek and gum as I'd seen done by the good ol' boys. The deputy handed me an empty Mountain Dew can to spit into. Though I did, I was green in minutes.

"You look like you could use some air," the woman said. Her hands fussed with the handle of a briefcase that she held like a shield in front of her. Her shoulder was overburdened by a heavy purse. "Why don't we step out?" It didn't take much to discern that she was a social worker for child welfare.

My gaze turned to Luce. My little sister had climbed onto the bed and huddled against her unresponsive mama like a mewling kitten. The deputy was slumped in an uncomfortable metal chair, thumbing an outdated issue of *People.* The sky outside the window was black with night.

"Chris, is it?" The social worker touched my arm with chilly fingers that I felt through my long-sleeve button-down. "Chris, why don't you come help me with this paperwork. It seems to show that your mother has two girls?"

CHAPTER TWO

I looked past the pens to where Luce had stood last weekend. She wasn't there. I knew she was safe with the foster parents, but it didn't change the fact that I wanted to see her face. Even if she was highly irritating most times. She was a good kid. She was nine. Irritating came with the age.

Luce didn't enjoy the bulls. Every time she had watched Daddy ride, she gnawed on her bottom lip with too much worry and choked the panel rails with white-knuckled fists. I noticed her doing the same last weekend when she watched me ride. She was happier staying with the foster folks. Still, I missed her.

Thundering Bunny snorted at my approach. He bobbed his lopsided head. He was the only familiar face in the crowd. "Hey, Thunder." I hadn't drawn him. That was a mix of disappointment and relief. He had bucked off a cowboy in less than three seconds yesterday. He had unsettled the guy first when he slammed backwards in the chute before making his big leap out. That was a new addition to his bag of tricks.

"Luck today," I said to him. We were all athletes.

He perked his overlarge ears and watched me intently.

I really like the bulls. I was just as confident in front of them as on their backs.

As cowboys passed by, they slapped me on my vest. The Velcro over my shoulder stayed put under its heavy layer of black duct tape. With worry, I checked it time and again. All good.

My rope hung over my forearm. It was sticky with rosin. A common work glove was taped tightly about my wrist. I'd stove-piped my jeans and tied the shafts of my boots on, then strapped my worn-out spurs to my heels. Having the jitters, I got stuck in a loop of buckling and unbuckling my chaps, over and over again. But I was ready. Too ready.

Sweat pooled between my shoulder blades. I could feel the sticky wetness sop my binding. My stomach lurched at the smell of hot dogs and deep-fried dough mixing with the odors of freshly manicured arena dirt and even fresher cattle manure. I breathed through my mouth.

My draw, Rambo, was loaded into a bucking chute. I climbed onto the platform to dangle my rope down his heart girth. The hook caught hold of it. I cinched it onto the black bull and climbed away. The waiting wasn't long now, but the minutes crept along forever.

Chute men surrounded me with support. My rockin' ride yesterday had gained me some popularity. The seated crowd stomped and clapped in anticipation. Music blared over the loudspeakers. Cowboys slapped my vest or chucked my shoulder. Too many lined the platform to help me. They joshed with each other or bantered about the bull. Their enthusiasm was claustrophobic.

The previous evening, Nuclear had taken me on a wild ride. I barely made the eight. The buzzer sounded in the same moment as I was catching a lot of air between me and that bull's back. The bull's score bumped me high enough to be a threat to the hometown heroes, even if my half didn't rate well. The leading bull riders kept an eye behind them now, with their own mixed bags of feelings for my ascent.

Everyone wanted that prize money. Some for bragging rights. Some for the standings. Some because they'd made bull riding an occupation. But I plain out needed it. I was desperate.

Winning was everything. Anything else was failure. It sure as heck wasn't a game to me. I *needed* to win to live. I had Luce to think of. Foster care was only temporary. And I still had hopes for college.

I climbed down into the chute. Rambo was the biggest, heaviest bull I'd ever seen. He probably tipped the scales at fifteen hundred pounds. A chute man had to shove a two-by-four between him and the panels to lever a space for my leg.

I tied myself on, leaned toward his hump, and nodded.

The gate swung open.

Rambo lumbered into the arena begrudging the fact that he'd have to put exertion into his few seconds of work.

I had anticipated that the huge bull would make a huge exit. So I was too far forward when he stumped out sorry. His head stayed too high to have given his kick massive power. But he swung his mammoth poll up to whiff past the brim of my hat, threatening me to sit back where he could take advantage.

I didn't sit back.

Rambo settled into a gentle spin after a couple of blundering hops.

I pinwheeled my free arm and spurred him in an exaggerated show. At least *my* half of the score would be high for form. Maybe. If the judges didn't tell me to get a circus job. *Can I get an A for effort?*

I made the buzzer. Inertia, equivalent to a slow mudslide, slung me off when I opened my hand.

Bull riding wasn't supposed to be easy. Everyone would be doing it if it was. But my kid sister could've stayed on this Rambo. He wasn't headed for a big career in the business. Any of Daddy's homegrown bulls would have put this Rambo to shame. I think we even had a Rambo who was more keen to the work. After that movie came out, everyone seemed to have a Rambo. We might have even had two.

My daddy bought bucking bulls to practice on. He'd coach me after his rides. But I was never going to make a bull rider, being born as a girl.

My wandering attention was reined in as I heard a latch squeal and thunk. The bull rider to beat was gripped onto Thundering Bunny as they vaulted into the arena. If that cowboy made his eight-second ride, it wouldn't matter the score. He'd be the winner. He already had the points he needed.

Thundering Bunny went out with a fury that fueled his spring-like jump. He shot straight into the air and caught a lot of breeze beneath his toes. Thundering Bunny landed on all four hooves simultaneously. It was his signature move: tight, straight legs hammering down hard.

I'd already been acquainted with that spine crunching shock.

In less than four seconds it was over. Buck off.

I moved into first place with no other bull rider near enough in the points to threaten me.

Rolling my winnings into a wad, I wandered back through the chutes. Thundering Bunny blew snot and pawed the ground inside his pen. He was the only genuine friend I had at the rodeo. If he was a friend at all. We had talked. Well, I'd talked. He was a good listener. And we knew where each other stood. We were opposing wrestlers. So no hard feelings.

That was friendly enough for me.

"No big score on Rambo," I said to Thundering Bunny. "He kinda wandered out of the chute." I scraped at my gloved hand with a wire brush to remove old rosin. "I did my best to make a good showing. I spurred him when he tucked into a spin."

Thundering Bunny watched me. His ears swiveled in my direction. He bobbed his head and snorted. I'd like to think he approved. I dared hope he'd be proud to know me one day. *Proud of me.*

I wished my daddy were here. But then, I wouldn't have been riding the bulls. He would've. With me watching. And wishing all the time Daddy'd seen me as man enough to compete.

Daddy knew. He was pretty torn up about it. During summers, he liked having a son to train with him on bulls. But fall would come and he'd ship me off to boarding school as a girl.

It didn't matter now. *He* didn't matter now.

Thundering Bunny's pen gate rolled open in the back. With another bob of his head, he turned and climbed onto a stock trailer.

I nodded in agreement. *Yeah, I do kind of feel like I won this one by default.* But heck, it wasn't *that* easy. "If it was easy, everyone would be doing it," I repeated to no one.

I wiped my feet before climbing the couple of steps to the foster parents' house. I shucked my boots off on the covered porch and hollered, "Hey, I brought pizza." Then I stuffed the tip of a big slice of cheese and pepperoni into my mouth as I went in. The screen door threatened to slam behind me. I was extra careful to ease it closed.

"Pizza! Pizza!" Luce came dancing down the stairs in the front hall. She was full of energy this past week. Her cheeks were pinked.

The sallow look she'd been carrying had melted away. She brimmed with health and enthusiasm. "Pizza!"

"Well, don't I get a shout out?"

Luce slammed into my midsection and wrapped her skinny arms around my waist. The two large pizzas teetered on my palm as I raised them from her crash. "Did you win again, Chris?"

"Sure I did. The next one's an even bigger payout. I'm telling you, Labor Day weekend is my event. You'll see." I took my cowboy hat off, propped it on the banister's post, then finger-combed hair out of my eyes.

"Maybe they'll keep us," Luce said as she let go of my waist.

And I could only hope. For her sake. It was a good place—small, but good. Luce and I shared the attic room. In fact, we shared the bed. Nothing new.

"Chris, did you hear me? Maybe they'll keep us cuz we've been here a week and they're nice like grandparents and they don't care if you go to the rodeo and the sheets are clean and there's food. We sit at the table for family dinner. Real family dinner. Like when Daddy—"

"Luce." I didn't want to hear it. "Take a breath."

They weren't our grandparents. They could get rid of us at any moment. As enamored as they were with Luce, they couldn't quite accept that I was part of the package.

I was doing everything I could to ingratiate myself for Luce's sake. The foster parents were nice. But I didn't know how long they'd put up with me. Foster parents didn't sign up for teenagers. I was trying, though. I was really trying. If I wasn't a burden, maybe we could stay.

My monkey girl raced down the hall and set a stack of plates on the table before I got there. She fussed napkins from the lazy Susan and dashed to the dish drain for cups.

"It's not seemly," I heard Margaret, the old lady caring for us, say in exasperation. She and her husband liked to sit in the backyard late evenings. They'd watch the sun go down. "A teenage boy should not be sharing a room with a nine-year-old, little girl."

"He's a good boy," Rupert said. "He mowed the lawn early this morning before going out to that rodeo. It was no easy job, mind you. That dang lawnmower's been broke since last year. He had to fix it first." His chair creaked. I heard him sigh.

"Just for another few days?" the social worker pleaded. I wasn't sure it was solely on my behalf. "It's difficult to find a placement for the two of them together."

"What will the neighbors think?" Margaret gasped.

"He's a good boy," Rupert reiterated.

"But he must go. Tonight." Margaret declared my departure with a finality that wouldn't be argued further.

He must go. So they'd be willing to keep Luce.

I dodged from the kitchen as Luce wrestled a milk jug from the fridge.

"What's wrong, Chris?" she called in my wake.

In our bedroom, I slapped the few things I'd had into a green garbage sack. I'd go. I'd go willingly. For Luce. She deserved nice things. She needed a proper home. And folks who could offer her stability.

"No," Luce shouted from the doorway. "We can't go." Her face got red. She was on the brink of tears. "I like it here. I like Mrs. Margaret and Mr. Rupert. I want to stay."

"You will stay. But I have to leave."

She marched over and began emptying my trash bag of clothes. I caught her by the hands and hugged her to me. "Hey, I want you to do me a big favor." Her breathing was short and rapid as if she'd just run a race. "Will you keep hold of the winnings? I know it's a big job—"

"I can do it, Chris." She yanked away from my embrace. "I can do it." Tears burst. They ran over her red cheeks. She clutched my roll of cash to her heaving chest.

We walked down the stairs to where Margaret, Rupert, and the social worker were already waiting. I kept my hand on Luce's shoulder. I'd miss my little monkey. We hadn't slept a night apart since Daddy's death.

I dropped my garbage sack to the floor then squatted. "Look, Luce, I'm going to see you real soon. Hang tough."

"Daddy used to say that," Luce said as her tears started again.

"That's right. And what do you say back?"

"Be dangerous." Luce lunged on to me, almost toppling us both to the floor.

I sprang up, carrying her with me. "It's okay, Luce." But it wasn't. None of it was okay. Not since Daddy was killed. I buried my face in her strawberry-blond hair. She smelled of the apple shampoo that she insisted on using "so horses would like her."

I had told her over and over that there was nothing and no one that wouldn't like her.

The social worker wrapped her claws around Luce's skinny arms and attempted to pry her from me. "I think it's best if we get going," she said to me.

"Don't make a scene," I whispered in Luce's ear. "You're Daddy's girl. Buckshot Taylor. The greatest bull rider there ever was. Hang tough."

"Be dangerous," she replied into my shoulder where her tears and runny nose had already sopped my shirt. When she hit the ground, she turned to cling to Rupert's waist.

I stuffed my hat on, then ruffled her hair. "I love you, monkey. Don't forget." I picked up my trash sack and walked to the street to get into the social worker's car.

My heart pounded in my chest. It felt like a fifteen-hundred-pound bull was sitting on me. I couldn't breathe. I clenched on to the plastic sack and twisted it in my fists.

"I love you, Chris," Luce screamed like a scalded cat. Margaret held her from scrambling after me. "I love you!" Through her jagged crying, she shouted, "Don't forget"—she struggled on a gulp of air—"me."

I wanted to get out and run back to her and scoop her up and keep running and never ever stop. I wanted to protect her and keep her safe and never let anyone or anything hurt her ever again.

But I couldn't.

For that, I felt like I'd failed her.

My heart shattered in a million pieces. I didn't turn back to look.

We drove into the night.

"Chris, you're seventeen." The hateful social worker spoke to me like I was something to be scraped from the bottom of her shoe.

"If your stepmother recovers, she won't be out of her mess before you're eighteen. We can petition the court to emancipate you as an adult now. You can get your GED and a good job in town. I hear the grain store is looking to hire."

"No. I'm finishing high school and going to college. It's what my daddy wanted."

"Be reasonable. Your daddy is gone. He might have changed his mind about college. And I think you should too."

She was truly hateful.

"No," I repeated and hugged my garbage sack to my chest.

In the dead of night, we turned off the highway and meandered a long driveway to a sprawling run-down ranch style house. Back in its heyday it could have housed the herd of cowboys that ran roughshod over thousands of acres of ranch land. Now? It looked like a haunted institution on the set of a horror movie. Its windows were dark. A spider web stretched across the top of one window. The web had been undisturbed so long that the spider might add a second floor to its domicile. I shuddered.

A small porch light flickered with the yellow glow of an ancient bulb. COUNTY BOYS' HOME was printed in large black letters on a peeling white sign nailed to the right of the door.

Boys. That might be a problem. I mean…it didn't bother me. Me being a boy felt right. It felt natural. It was exactly who I was.

The buzzer sounded like a bug zapper frying a gargantuan fly. Three different locks were tortured before the solid wooden door opened a crack. A bloodshot eye peered through the slit. Then the door was thrown wide. "This couldn't have waited until a sane hour?" A glowing cigarette bobbed as the man spoke.

"Sergeant," the social worker rebuked him.

"Your bag," he prompted me with a flapping hand.

I swung my sack from my shoulder and held it toward him.

He jerked it from my grasp with one hand and jammed a clipboard at the social worker with his other. "Sign him in."

Pleasantries done, the social worker pushed me forward and left, without another thought, I was sure.

The man slammed and bolted the door. "Turn out your pockets." He upended my trash sack on a table in the hallway.

"What?"

"Turn out your pockets."

"Why?"

He lifted his hand as if to strike me. "Don't ask questions."

A ghost of a boy leaned around a doorjamb behind the man's back and shook his head.

I rummaged pitifully little from my pockets. If the old drunk was looking to get rich, he'd be disappointed. I only had small change and a clip-on knife with me. He confiscated my scant hoard anyway.

The man pawed through my belongings and jerked out a small pajama top. "Is this what you're in for, boy?"

I grabbed for the pink shirt emblazoned with a white unicorn jumping over a rainbow. "That's my sister's."

He held it to his nose. I heard the snort of air struggle up his nostrils. He then stuffed Luce's pj top into his pocket.

My jailer plucked the cowboy hat from my head and shoved a stack into my arms—blanket, sheet, pillow, towel, toothbrush, soap, and a roll of toilet paper. "In there," he barked. He jammed my hat on top of the pile in my arms, then pushed me. "Give over your shoes. You'll get them tomorrow before school."

The room was nothing more than a glorified broom closet with a cot. I'd seen bigger prison cells on TV shows and movies. "What? There's been a mistake."

"No mistake." He flipped through the papers on the clipboard. "Chris." When he shoved my chest, the backs of my knees buckled on the cot's edge. The thin mattress sank almost to the floor from my landing. Worn springs stretched nearly to their breaking point. They strained to maintain their grip on the metal frame of the cot.

I shucked my boots.

He grabbed them and dumped my pillaged bag of belongings to the floor.

The door closed with a bang. A lock clicked shut.

I jumped up and tried the knob. "Wait," I yelled, pounding on the solid wooden door. "Wait."

Too early on Monday morning, we arrived at West High School for orientation day. I was one of a half dozen new boys from the county's juvenile halfway house. Others had attended last year and were acquainted with the school.

"Chris?"

I stepped forward when the vice principal called my name.

"I have your transcripts here, but there must be some mistake." The vice principal shuffled the paperwork that overfilled a brown folder. "Academic excellence? College prep courses?" He looked at me with a stern expression.

"Um, yes, sir." I finger-combed strands of hair off my forehead to stuff them under my hat. Then I stared back without flinching.

"Okay." He slapped my folder closed and handed me a class schedule. "Devyn will take you around the school to orient you to your classrooms and locker. He'll acquaint you with our policies."

I turned with my hand out.

"We've met," we said in unison as we shook hands.

He had a solid grip, as I'd suspected.

Devyn was the bull rider kid I'd seen at the rodeo. He was a twitchy kid. Wound as tight as a racehorse packed into a starting gate. You could just feel him waiting for the bell to go off.

Hair fell over his eyes. He ran his fingers through its blond lengths. The strands settled properly to the sides once again. The top of his head looked like a parted mushroom.

Devyn was broad shouldered and square jawed. He was ruggedly handsome. He hadn't shaved for a few days, affecting a perfectly disheveled look. I wondered if that was on purpose. Then I wondered if anyone would notice that my own chin didn't sprout even a dusting of peach fuzz.

"…and if you play on an extracurricular sports team, you don't need to take gym class. And you still get the credits."

Gym class. The locker room.

We walked through the school and peered into each of my classrooms. It was all much smaller than the preparatory school I'd spent the last three years at. I'd miss the Autry Academy, but I was a girl there. Here, I had a chance to be a boy—to be me.

"Well, that's your locker. Mine's right next to it." Thankfully, Devyn's tour was brief. I wasn't paying full attention anyway. He jerked open the metal door to my locker. A combination lock waited within. "They give you a plastic tag with the numbers on it, for your key ring."

Devyn paid way too much attention to the locker details. It was obvious he had something else on his mind. "Okay. That's about everything," he said.

"Cool. Thanks, man." I waited.

"Hey, maybe you'd want to try out for the rodeo team?" He shuffled an orientation pamphlet around in his hands. "There's a lot of guys at practice, but the school only sponsors the top few for each high school rodeo, in each event. I'm sure you'd make the final cut. You're like, already winning money." Devyn handed me the wrinkled pamphlet. "We could use a guy like you."

A guy like me. A ripple went through my chest. *A guy...like me.*

"Colleges are looking, ya know," Devyn said. "I mean, I heard you were college prep."

"Yeah, cool," I said. "I'd like that."

I slammed my empty locker and turned to leave. I had to make it across town to hide my truck in a more convenient location. If I could find one before the County Boys' Home bus came to pick us up.

"There's a party at my house Wednesday night," Devyn said. "We have Thursday and Friday off for the Labor Day weekend rodeo. That rodeo is a big deal in this town. Bull riders come in from all over. Tourists too. The town makes a lot of money on that rodeo." He scribbled an address on the crumpled paper in my hand. "Wednesday night. Come early. Say, eight."

CHAPTER THREE

The next morning, the Sergeant threw open the door of the bus before it came to a complete stop. If the vehicle had been equipped with ejection seats, I swear, he'd have launched us out. He was in a foul mood. Rumor was, daylight hadn't caught him sober in all of the summer months.

As the navy blue County Boys' Home bus pulled in front of West High School's main entrance, students stared. The bus looked like a transport from the state's mental institution.

Maybe I'd have stared too.

I shuffled into the bus's aisle. A couple of jerks knocked me back onto the bench seat. I wanted to pound them. Instead, I choked my bag lunch into a rumpled mass like it had insulted my daddy. Squashing it didn't matter. It had already been mashed by a County Boys' Home punk with a mullet. He wanted to make sure I knew my place as a newbie.

I wasn't planning to settle into being their newbie. I wasn't a juvenile delinquent. I wasn't going to be at the County Boys' Home long. The social worker promised that the Boys' Home was only a temporary placement—until she found foster parents willing to take a teenager.

I was hardworking and honest. Someone would want me.

I trudged off the short bus last. The door slammed behind me. The engine belched a hasty departure. And the whole of West High stared.

Freaks on parade.

I stood on the curb and clenched my ruined bag lunch. The mob was blocking the entrance. I smoothed my rumpled hoodie over my bound chest and pulled my hat lower over my eyes.

'K. Show's over.

The county's boys scattered like scurrying rats. I wiped the tops of my dusty boots on my jean-clad calves in trying to look more presentable. It was hopeless. I was never going to fit in. Not like this.

Move along. Move along. These aren't the droids you're looking for.

The muck-stained Pro Rodeo Wranglers hugging my thighs were hideously outdated, and totally out of style. Loose-fitting jeans were in. The baggier, the better. Oversized flannel shirts worn as jackets proved that the iconic checkered warmth wasn't just for rural farmers anymore. And the Polo shirt had made a comeback from the eighties. *Gag.*

The first bell rang.

Luce. I should have taken her shopping for school clothes. I should have bought her a new outfit for her first day of school. I don't know why I hadn't thought of it. Maybe because we had always worn uniforms. Or maybe because we were separated. Or maybe because school shopping was her mother's job.

I mentally kicked myself. New school clothes might have spared my little sister the playground ridicule she was sure to suffer this day.

Kids can be cruel.

Luce didn't deserve cruelty. She didn't understand it. She was too soft. Too sensitive. Too kind.

Each year, at calf brandings, she cried as the "baby calves" were roped and dragged for vaccinations, castration, and branding. She fed penned bucking bulls corn husks by hand and climbed the rails to stroke a curry over their backs. Luce didn't understand that their bucking wasn't a meanness to take out.

Genetically bred to buck, the bulls broke her heart over and over each time they did their job.

Last year, Daddy's death destroyed her. Then, we'd lost our ranch, our home, and our community. Now, with her mama in a coma, Luce had had enough upset to last a lifetime.

And this was the first year we didn't have our picture taken together on the first day of school. Daddy had always insisted on a picture to mark the milestone. He'd squat on the lawn with his Nikon SLR in hand. We'd hold a dumb sign with the year scrawled on it in crayon.

In anticipation, Luce hid under the covers with a flashlight the night before, to draw and color the damned sign. She'd have tried on her new uniform ten times or more in making sure it was perfect.

I'd climb into her bed and wrap my arms around her in the height of darkness. The only way she'd fall asleep was if I hugged her to me.

Maybe if the foster parents had run her clothes through the washer last night? Laid them out flat? Maybe she'd look okay. Maybe Rupert had an old flannel to tie around her tiny waist?

But who would have held her until she finally fell asleep?

I'm sorry, Luce. Tears burned behind my eyes. I twisted a wad of sweatshirt over my heart, willing myself not to cry. Boys don't cry.

I wouldn't. Not here. Not now. Not ever again.

Students clogged the halls of the high school. Their packed mass was unassailable. I drifted in their wake and tried to steer toward my pitifully empty locker. I'd dump the nasty bag lunch in it attempting to look as if I had purpose.

Guys strutted like bantam roosters. They looked sharp in their crisp Izod "throwback" shirts. And knew it. They shoved each other, knocking notebooks and pencils to the floor. Then they'd laugh. Girls stole last glances in compact mirrors and freshened their lipstick. Coiffed heads jounced through the hallway like bobble-headed dolls on a dashboard.

When I spun the lock open, my locker door jumped. It was overburdened with school supplies. Notebooks, pencils, and pens threatened to leap to the floor. I rocked back and knocked into Devyn.

"Hey," Devyn said with a bright, shiny smile. "Come on." He slammed his locker. "Grab your books. And, um, take off the hat."

I stuffed my crumpled sack lunch to the back of the locker, then fished out a couple of notebooks and a pen. "Thanks, man." I closed my locker with the suspicion that Devyn had been the one to fill it with school supplies. He didn't seem the type. But I didn't really know him at all.

"Hat, Chris," the vice principal said in passing.

I tugged my hat off and smoothed the bangs back from my forehead.

During the day, kids gawked at me, but no one actually said anything. No one talked to me either. Just as well. I had to concentrate on my bull riding if I was going to earn enough money to get Luce out of foster care and go to college. I didn't have time for friends. Only bull riding.

At the last bell, I blew a sigh of relief. Everyone else erupted in enthusiasm.

I was quietly thrilled to have made it through the day. I had kept my head down. Nothing seemed to have gone wrong. I had skipped gym class, knowing that that was bound to catch up to me eventually. I'd have to take the detention or whatever.

"What time's that bus picking you up?" Devyn asked as we both stuffed books into our lockers.

"Not till four thirty," I mumbled.

"Good. See you at practice." He slammed his locker with exuberance, then breezed off to join the cool kids. Their new clothes were barely off the rack. *Jealous much?*

Yes. I was jealous.

I was jealous because they were all confident in their own skin. I had never felt like the real me.

They each knew who they were. They fit with one another. And they were popular. I'd never won any popularity contests. And having been a loner hadn't kindled a sense of belonging to any class of '95.

From beneath the brim of my hat, I watched the guys punch each other's arms while heading toward the locker rooms. I watched Devyn.

He had a genuine smile and easy laughter. His broad shoulders tapered to a lean waist. His muscular thighs strained a pair of stonewashed jeans. He could have been the poster kid for the All-American boy. Handsome. Homegrown. Wholesome.

I smoothed strands of my hair from my forehead, then jammed my tired straw hat on. I headed for the front doors. Rodeo team practice didn't start for a half hour. I'd run to grab gear from my hidden truck.

I bent over at a fenced clump of trees outside the school's livestock arena and huffed and puffed. I dropped my heavy gear bag to the ground and liberated my vest. The roll of black duct tape eluded my search at first. When I found it, I fumbled my arms into Daddy's old protective vest and hoped I'd get the tape wrapped tight enough over my heaving sides.

Three bulls were moved through the pens into bucking chutes.

I slapped strips of tape onto the vest's shoulders. *It'll have to do.* My hands shook as I dug my bull rope out. I was never nervous about bulls. Those high school guys scared me to death, though.

Would I fit in? Would they see I'm not like them?

The bells on my rope clanked their peculiar sound.

Devyn looked in my direction from tugging rosin along his rope.

I lifted my hand, then thought better of it.

What was I thinking? I didn't belong here. I didn't have time for this. I didn't have the outfit.

All of those guys had official bull riding gloves. I didn't own one. Their new protective vests were form-fitting and perfect. As were their starched and ironed ProRodeo Wrangler jeans.

I picked at the tape on my ill-fitting vest and watched the guys parade around in their new, colorful chaps. Mine had seen better days. My bull rope was worn thin—*probably shouldn't put too many rides on it before the Labor Day rodeo.* It only had so much life. Shouldn't waste that on a practice ride. The dented bells had been crushed when a bull had stepped all over them during Daddy's last event. I had done my best to pry them open and hammer them back into shape. They weren't shiny new.

My bells had a distinct and peculiar clank that was easily recognizable. I loved their odd clank because that was the sound of my daddy's happiest moments. Daddy had said there were only two sets of hand-hammered, riveted bells with their peculiar clank. His had been a gift from a family friend who still possessed their match. But I'd never heard the others sound off.

Devyn waved me in. He held his hands to his mouth and hollered, but the stale breeze carried his words away from me.

No matter. I collected my gear bag and walked away.

Wednesday went much the same. I tossed another ruined lunch into my locker and kept to myself. I skipped gym class and finished all of my homework in study period. At the last bell, I ran to my truck before the County Boys' Home bus picked us up.

I had time to brood on getting Luce out of foster care. Or at least in a same foster home as me. When I got one.

The only difference was that I had avoided Devyn at all costs today.

What to do about his party tonight?

At the County Boys' Home, I skulked in my stifling, eight-by-eight cell until dinner. None of the others bothered with me. For one, I was the newbie. The other reason? I was older and taller. The pack of hyenas wanted to size me up before they took me down. Wasted effort on their part. I wasn't planning to be here when they got the courage to gang up on me. The social worker was going to get me a foster family.

I was counting on her. Though she didn't seem all that interested in me.

When a bell clanged, I went to dinner and hunched over a plate of mystery meat. How was I going to get out of this place for Devyn's party? It was locked tighter than the cool kids' clique.

After dining room chores, I scurried to my cell. I had a plan.

I stood on my cot to reach the window. The window wouldn't budge.

Devyn's party. I had to go. I owed him an explanation.

"You ever been locked up before? Cuz you're not very good at it."

I turned around and jumped from the cot.

Beneath an overlarge Toad the Wet Sprocket concert T-shirt, a ghost of a boy folded his arms across his thin chest and leaned against the doorframe. He wore tan shorts, two sizes too big, that showed off his startling white chicken legs.

"Why won't the window open?" I asked him.

The kid rolled his eyes in an exaggerated manner. "Uh, duh. We're all baby cons in here, right? Convicts? Next gen crims?" He pulled a Phillips head screwdriver from a side pocket. "Watch the door."

We switched places. He pecked away at the paint and putty that hid the heads of two screws. "The name's Michael, in case you're wondering." He twisted the screws from the window and pocketed both. "I procure things." He jumped down and said, "Put toothpaste in those holes. It'll dry white like the paint. No one will be the wiser unless they're looking closely."

I stepped onto the cot and squeezed my toothpaste into the holes and smeared it flat with my pointer finger. "I don't suppose you could get a hold of my boots?"

When I turned around, Michael was gone.

I raised the window ever so slowly because it threatened to squeal.

With it all the way up, I stuffed my hat on and escaped the County Boys' Home. My trash sack of belongings was over my shoulder. I carried everything I'd arrived with. *Minus my boots.*

I padded along the dirt driveway in holey tube socks, constantly checking behind me.

Michael's face appeared in the open window. He waved, then shut the creaky, wooden window.

My truck coughed and choked like a ninety-year-old chain smoker on the last square-inch of lung. "C'mon," I urged it. "C'mon." It fired to life with an angry growl.

I reached behind the seat for my bull riding boots. *Gone.* They were gone.

The worn-out spurs had been taken off of them. They were left behind, as if someone was sorry they'd had to steal my boots and wanted to make amends by not depriving me of more.

Leaving my spurs wasn't enough, damn it. I need my boots.

What else was taken? I panicked. My bull rope. I ripped the zipper open on my gear bag, then pawed through its gaping maw. *Phew. All there.* If I had lost my bull rope I'd be out of business.

I jammed the stick shift into first. The gears ground in complaint, but the three-quarter-ton Chevy rolled from behind the back alley dumpsters of the local grocer.

On the outskirts of town, I crept toward the interstate trucker route. It ran past the high school, past the playing fields, and past the school's huge livestock arena.

Seeing the school's vast, after-hours emptiness reminded me of *Red Dawn*. That movie that had been released in 1984. *Ten years ago.* I sighed. Had it been that long?

It was a total favorite of my daddy's. He and I used to watch it on VHS when I was a kid.

In that movie, Soviet soldiers parachuted onto the high school grounds of a small town to begin an invasion of America. A bunch of teenagers, led by Patrick Swayze, escaped the massacre by hiding in a national forest. They rallied to fight back. *Wolverines.*

I'd like to think I'd survive against all odds. I'd like to think I'd have the guts to join a guerrilla force that harried a greater enemy. I'd like to think I'd fight to right wrongs. I'd like to think I had grit—that I too would be a Wolverine.

The biggest problem with that movie? Most of the good guys died by the end.

From the address scribbled on the crumpled orientation pamphlet, Devyn's home wasn't far from the center of town. It was desolate. But not far.

I turned at a rusted mailbox. Parallel goat paths ran between two barbed wired fences. These were the only marks that a driveway existed. Those and the dried length of feed grass that had been toppled from the sweep of an occasional car.

My truck rumbled along the strips as I drove, jolting and jarring, over erupted boulders. Nothing it wasn't used to.

Hidden from the road by massive clumps of overgrown brush was a single-family ranch house. It was the size of a double-wide trailer. It could have been quaint with an old-fashioned porch on the front. But the sagging wooden steps below the door suggested its owner was too tired or too broke for building up or adding on.

Opposite sat a two-car garage. The garage doors had been flung open. Chairs were placed in several meticulous semicircles. Flanking muck buckets bulged with ice.

I rolled past the setup to park where a painted sign indicated, then climbed out and slammed my groaning truck door.

"Come on over." Devyn waved from the garage. "I'm lighting the coals."

A fifty-five-gallon metal drum had been torched in half to

make two large BBQ grills. Grates were spread across each. When I joined Devyn, flames were already devouring the lighter fluid. Gray tendrils of smoke danced on the hot breeze.

"Hey." I held my hand out to him. I really wanted to chuck him in the arm like the others had, but I didn't think our familiarity went that far.

Devyn slapped my palm. It was less formal than a handshake. That was promising.

"Cool place," I said.

"Take a look around." He pointed into the garage with a long set of hot dog tongs.

I wandered in and immediately headed toward the practice barrel. Mattresses of different sizes were strewn on the floor beneath it. "This is awesome," I said.

I stepped across a mattress to toe the massive spring spiraling its way to supporting the belly of a steel barrel.

"Thanks," Devyn said. "I put that together in metal shop sophomore year." He tossed the hot dog tongs on a cooler then picked up a can of beer and joined me. "The drop barrel on the other side is my pride and joy. That one I built as my junior year project."

His garage was a Disney World for bull riders. Bull ropes hung from the rails of a pen panel that was secured to the side wall. Gear bags lounged below as if exhausted from their rodeo adventures. A long Gatorade banner hung above. A bench seat, created from pillaging a truck, sat in front of a small TV with a VCR. They were surrounded by heaps of VHS tapes. The labels were hand-scribbled as to which rodeos, riders, and bulls were featured.

My daddy used to watch his own rides on tape. He had said that studying was key to becoming the best. *Working hard is first and foremost, but study promotes excellence.*

"I want a mechanical bull for my collection next." Devyn swigged the beer. "So far, my mom says no. She's always seeing folks get hurt on the mechanical bull in the Honky Tonk. That's where she works. She's the bartender. 'Mixoligist' is what she calls herself. Like she's got some doctorate of adult beverages." He held his can up in salute.

I padded to the drop barrel and gave the bar a push. The rig spun in a circle, rising and dipping, just like a bull in slow motion. "What's the weight for?"

"That's the best part. Counterweight. And I can add or subtract weights to let me practice balance and form by myself." Devyn looked questioningly at the holey socks on my feet.

I wiggled my toes.

"I'm not gonna ask," he said.

I shrugged, stuffing my hands deep into my pockets.

"Hey, that reminds me. I have a bunch of stuff around here that I've outgrown. I was thinking, since you're skinnier than me, maybe you could use it?" He upended the last swallow of his beer.

"Well, thanks. But I have stuff." I didn't need charity. "In my truck...I have stuff."

Devyn looked at my feet again. "You want a beer?" He dug through the ice and plucked a can.

I shook my head.

He snapped open the tab, then sauntered to the back wall of the garage and whipped a massive curtain aside. The cubbies and hanging space would have made my clothes-queen stepmama cry.

I plunked down on the truck bench seat. I was awed by Devyn's massive collection of bull riding gear.

"Wood shop. Freshman year. The boxes." He pointed. "I built the boxes." Devyn took a long swig of beer. "Well, wood shop was just the beginning. I came home and stacked them for what I call my open closet." He ran his fingertips along a shelf of boots. "I'm guessing you're an eight?"

"Seven, actually."

"Ah. Here you are, then." He tossed a set of yellow boots at me.

"I can't," I said.

"I know, huh! Those were from my *Mork and Mindy* phase. I watched every episode there ever was. Reruns. Mork had those rainbow suspenders. So I had to have those yellow boots with the rainbow stitching when I saw them in a catalog."

"Heads up." He spun a black felted hat at me like it was a Frisbee. "Get it? Heads up?" Devyn slapped his knee and slurped that next can dry. "I crack myself up." He crushed the aluminum can in his palm, then hauled down a protective vest. That too was thrown.

It smacked me square in the chest. A puff of air whiffed my hanging bangs out of my eyes.

"I can't pay you for all of this."

"Didn't ask you to." He made a show of tossing the can toward a bucket. "You'll owe me one."

Cars rolled in. Too many kids tumbled from each as if they were sneaking their numbers into a drive-in movie.

I didn't like crowds. I didn't like people. Not close up. I pulled on the yellow boots, swapped my straw cowboy hat for his felted one, and stayed sheltered inside the garage. Parties weren't really my scene.

Actually, I'd never been to one.

At some point, I wandered toward the grills. Guys were playing football with water balloons. Girls acted all indignant if they got splashed. The hot dogs were burning. My stomach growled.

I skulked within the garage's haven not knowing what I should do. And not feeling comfortable in doing anything else. Finally, I resigned myself to leaning against a wall. I propped my battered straw cowboy hat on an end post of the panel, then jerked the black felted hat low over my brows. I didn't know anyone.

"I was dropping my kid sister off and I saw you mysteriously lingering in the shadows. How're your stitches?" She was tall, with raven-black hair and deep brown eyes. We had met before.

I traced the line of neat embroidery over my cheek. "Um, good. Yeah. Fine." I squirmed at being recognized.

"Well, you're one tough..." The doctor from the emergency room hesitated. "Cookie." Right then, I knew she knew.

I could imagine my look of horror—a deer in the headlights just before the car smacked into its fuzzy little face. She knew. She had to have known. I was unconscious on arrival at the ER from the bar. I woke up with monitors taped to my chest. My binding had been cut off. Someone, or several someones, had pawed all over me. I wondered how many people in this town knew. Or would soon find out.

"Taylor? Chris Taylor. Any relation to the Taylors of this town? Sheriff Taylor?"

Do I look like a backwards Neanderthal? I rolled my eyes. "Taylor is a common name. Like Smith and Jones." I stood from leaning then crossed my arms in front of my chest. "I'm relation to *the* Taylor. Buckshot Taylor. The best bull rider there ever was. Two-time champion…" My thunder fizzled. *Dead. He's dead.*

"There are a lot of Taylors around here. And relations to Taylors. You'll get to know them, I'm sure."

No. I won't. I'm only here for the school year. After I graduate high school, I'm collecting Luce and heading to college somewhere else. Anywhere else. Just me and Luce.

The doctor lady bumped my shoulder with her own. She smelled clean and fresh, like Ivory soap and summertime. "If you ever need to talk, I'm around." She turned to leave then turned back. "And come in to have those stitches properly removed. I know how you kids are. Pocket knives in the mirror like you're popping pimples." She smiled showing beautiful straight white teeth. Her face was naturally pretty. Kind of perfect.

Get control of yourself. It's not The Dating Game. *She's too old anyway.*

"My kid sister's right over there." She pointed to a girl who looked like an exact younger version of herself. "Laney. She's in your class."

CHAPTER FOUR

The parched ground was damp with dew in the predawn hours of Thursday morning. A thin streak of pink seared the gray sky. It was enough light to see by. I hid my truck, shucked my yellow boots, and hoofed it back to the County Boys' Home. My socks sopped moisture, which chilled my feet. My big toes played turtle with every step. They peeked out of the socks each time my foot slapped the dirt.

The window of my room threatened to squeal as I shoved it open. Slowly, ever so slowly, I inched it up. Inside was as dark as a bear's cave. I struggled through the tight opening and plunged onto my cot. A mounded lump broke my fall.

Jump back, Jack. I rolled, hitting the floor on my hands and knees, ready to spring.

My new cowboy hat had flung off. I scanned the darkness for it, but my eyes hadn't adjusted. *A black hat in blackness? Not a chance.*

I crouched against the wall, then I strained to hear.

Silence.

I watched the dark for shifting shadows.

Nothing moved.

I mouthed a silent prayer, then reached to prod the lump in my bed. I hoped it was nothing. No one.

What if someone *was* lying there?

I hesitated. Could I scramble over them to escape out the open window? Could I shove them out of my way? Could I punch a person for real?

I'd never been in a fight. I fainted in the bar when I got my face slashed. So I didn't know if I could defend myself. And to what end? Surely the commotion would bring the Sergeant slamming through the door. He'd see the opened window.

My body tightened like a compressed coiled spring. I poked at the lump.

Pillows.

Phew. My shoulders collapsed as if my entire being sighed in relief.

I flipped the blanket back and sat on the edge of the bed.

I made a fist. Daddy had taught me how to hold my hand, but he preached to "turn the other cheek." I punched the padding. No reaction. What was I expecting? Pillows didn't run crying for their mama.

I peeled my wet socks from my bruised feet. The socks hung heavy from my fingertips. *What a delight. Not.*

I wiggled my liberated toes and let myself slump into the pillow.

My head hit a brick of hard plastic. The gray haze of burgeoning dawn crept through my window enough to make out a Walkman tape player. I reached for it. As I turned it over in my hands, I squinted for the buttons.

Rewind. Play.

Snoring assaulted my ears.

My hand flew to my mouth to stifle a burst of laughter. Too late. I lunged to check the door. Of course it was locked. With my ear pressed against it, I listened for any noise. All was quiet.

I lay down on the cot. I don't remember falling asleep, but I woke as a jangle of keys tormented the lock. With a clunk, the door opened.

First things first. I needed a shower. I grabbed my towel, soap, and toothbrush, then lumbered toward one of the bathrooms. It was strange there were no boys clambering in the halls for dibs at a shower. But there was no school today.

I cautiously pushed open one of the bathroom doors. Empty. I flicked the light on, then set my toiletries on the sink and shoved the door to close it.

The door burst inward before it latched. I tried to block it with my foot. I grabbed hold of the knob.

Three boys bullied their way through. Their hands clawed at

my shirt. One gripped over my mouth. My lips were crushed to my teeth. In a knee-jerk reaction, I scratched at the hand clenching my face. It stunk like the kid had forgotten to wash after he'd wiped.

They shoved me into the tiled shower stall.

It was that first blow that rocketed me into action.

I had wondered how it all worked. Fighting. Would I have time to make decisions? Time to come up with a plan? Girls were vicious, but they formulated a long game and came from behind, perpetuating damage felt for years. To chicks, fistfights were seen as unsophisticated and beneath them. I hadn't learned a girl's way of scheming. But I hadn't brawled either.

The tiny bathroom was too small for a full-on assault from three pimple-faced teenage boys. The one holding my mouth pressed his shoulder into my chest and pinned me against the cold wall. I heard the snaps of my shirt give way in a blurp of ripping.

A second kid socked me in the ribs. My chest binding did nothing to soften his knuckles. I cringed around the blow.

My brain didn't have a second to take in the pain because the third grabbed for my hands.

Fear blasted through me. *My hands.*

I balled them into fists and brought the pinky sides smashing into the ears of the short, stocky boy that shoved into me. I felt him jerk from the impact, right before my own body jumped from another sock to the gut.

Again, I slammed him. And again. He buckled from me.

The next boy stepped in to take his place. I jerked my knee up, impaling his groin. As he doubled over. My elbow caught his cheek.

That third kid hesitated. He was the punk with a mullet who had ruined my bag lunches. He eyed me as his friends nursed their pains. I could smell his fetid breath and unwashed clothes. In contrast, his dark wavy hairdo had been fluffed and coiffed with a blow dryer. I swear he'd used his grandma's Aqua Net hairspray to keep it puffed in place. His short cap of hair looked permanently lacquered. And the lengths behind his ears stiffly scratched at his shoulders.

He swung at my face with his right. I blocked the weak attempt, only to fold around his left as it walloped into my gut. *Left. Didn't see that coming.* I should have been aware of a potentially stronger left hand. I too was a southpaw.

I bent over and gasped for air, then lunged with my head. It buried in his torso. I drove him backward. He tripped to fall over his buddies' hasty departures. When he recovered his footing, he scrambled out after them.

They were gone.

I slid down the tile wall, and sucked short, quick gulps of air while clenching my belly. Pain exploded into my brain.

I knew it was coming. *Whatever.* Fistfights were a boy's rite of passage. I just had mine.

In the hall, feet trampled a retreat. But other footsteps came toward the door.

I still struggled to breathe as I gained my feet. I truly didn't think I could fend off another attack.

"Oh my God," Michael exclaimed. "What the hell."

My shirt hung open. I saw the question in his eyes. I saw the worry too.

"I've got them on the run," I said as I lurched to find my feet like a drunk on Saturday night.

Michael helped me to stand, then helped me to my room.

Propped on the edge of my bed, I began snapping my shirt closed.

He pointed to the wraps of Ace bandages engulfing my torso. "You're hurt. Do you need a doctor?"

"I'm fine," I barked.

Michael flinched as if I'd tried to strike him.

"Sorry," I mumbled. "I had these on before the beating."

Smoothing my shirtfront, I channeled my daddy by lowering my voice to his deep timbre. "Bull riding is a dangerous sport."

Michael spit in laughter. "Yeah, that voice doesn't fit you."

"No?" I eyed him with a big grin.

He dropped onto my cot, sitting too near, like we were best buds.

I didn't want to disappoint him, but I wasn't looking for any friends.

"Shoot," I said, "you'd think the Sergeant would have come running." I tucked the tails of my filthy shirt into my jeans as best I could. Movement shot pain through my side. I winced and reminded myself to take shallow breaths.

"I could stand outside the door for you." Michael stared at his knobby knees. "I mean tomorrow. Or sometime. There's no lock. So I could stand watch outside the bathroom."

He was all of one hundred pounds soaking wet. No, he had to be less than that.

"Yeah, man. Thanks." *No lock?*

Michael cracked a grin with only one side of his mouth. "Anyone can do anything here. Except leave." He plucked at a loose thread on his shorts. "Torment. Maim. Kill. The Sergeant doesn't care. He just needs to show a body count if anyone official comes inspecting." Michael stuffed his hands into the pockets of his baggy shorts. "The Sergeant's not going to lift a finger. Not unless the sheriff tells him to." His grin fell.

"There's your real problem," Michael said. When he looked at me, there was something haunting about his washed-out green eyes. "Sheriff Taylor was born in this town, raised in this town, and now, runs this town. He gave the Sergeant the job of babysitting all the next gen crims of this county. Why? I can't fathom. It's not like the Sergeant's qualified to be a role model." His hands never stilled. Even in his pockets. "The two of them are as thick as thieves," he said.

I fished the Sony Walkman from beneath my pillow, then placed it in Michael's lap.

He took his hands from his pockets to turn the tape player over and run his fingers along the row of push buttons. "He's a Vietnam veteran, ya know." He pushed rewind. "The Sergeant. He's a decorated veteran. People say he came back with a screw loose." Michael shoved the player into his pocket. He rubbed his palms on his shorts. "He had a wife once. She left him."

"How long have you been here?" I asked. I was way less interested in the Sergeant than Michael apparently was.

"It seems like I've been here all my life. But really, it's only been a couple of years."

Years?

Michael stood, fidgeting like he was guilty of something. He probably was. Why else would he be in the County Boys' Home? *For years.*

"Don't fight him," Michael said. "The Sergeant. Never fight him. He likes it."

I jerked my filthy socks from the floor, then shoved my feet into them. My big toes quickly peeked through the holes.

"What are you doing?" he asked.

"I'm not a criminal. I don't have to be locked up. And I have a rodeo to get to."

"You can't," he said.

"Have to." I checked the hall. My room was closest to the front door. It was only a short waltz to freedom. I grabbed my hat, then went for it.

The Sergeant's overlarge, sweaty body loomed behind me as I tried the knob to the County Boys' Home's front door.

"Going somewhere?" The Sergeant's ripe breath fogged the air.

Before I had a chance to answer, his meaty hand encircled the back of my neck. The Sergeant wrenched me from the door to slam my face to the hall wall.

My cheek slapped violently against the cracked, peeling paint. I clawed at the Sergeant's fingers. They were like overstuffed sausages greased with oil from the frying pan.

I felt the tip of his nose run through my hair. His long intake of breath moved stale air past my ear. And his fat, sweating body pressed the length of my back.

"You smell good," he said.

Michael peered from my room. He shook his head.

The door's buzzer erupted like a bug zapper sizzling a nest of hornets. The Sergeant staggered his weight off me. He released his grip from the back of my neck, then smoothed tendrils of oily hair from his forehead and tugged his shirttails down.

The buzzer crackled another complaint.

The Sergeant disengaged all of the door locks.

I slumped against the wall, thankful that the peeling paint held me upright. And I was truly thankful for that maddened door buzzer.

"I'm here for Chris."

Devyn.

"There's no one here by that name. Go away."

"In a house full of boys? You have no Chris?" Devyn shoved at the solid wooden door. "I know Chris is in there." The door smacked short on the Sergeant's work boot. "He's on the rodeo team. And the coach already called to have him released for this weekend."

The Sergeant's back stiffened. He rocked away from bracing the door like he'd been slapped.

"I'll just head off without Chris. Coach will come collect him. You can explain it all to him."

"Hold on," the Sergeant growled.

I shouldered the Sergeant off balance and tugged the door wide.

Michael's half-grin beamed from my bedroom doorway. "Come with," I mouthed.

He shook his head and slunk back.

I fled through the door.

My truck.

"Dude, the visor? Anyone could have found the keys and taken your truck." Devyn tossed the keys to me and wrenched the passenger door open. "Your gear bag and a trash sack are in the back."

I crammed the stick shift into first. The clutch clunked. I stomped on the gas. Gravel sprayed the driveway as I spun the battered old truck around.

"Woo-hoo!" Devyn shouted. He smacked the dashboard. "Go! Go! Go!"

We fishtailed our way to the road.

The rodeo grounds were crowded for a Thursday night. We parked in the competitors' lot among livestock trailers, vans, and trucks. I climbed into the truck bed and rummaged through the sack for a clean pair of socks and a shirt. I'd needed to change, but not in front of Devyn.

The binding over my chest was loose. It had started to slip. I reached into my gear bag and found the roll of cloth tape used to secure my glove to my wrist. I stuffed it into my back pocket.

Devyn watched cowboys file into the arena in the distance. I dropped his gear bag over the side of the truck bed. It hit the ground with a clank of his bells. A puff of dust billowed into the air around it.

I sat on the rusted running board of the truck, then rolled my holey socks off. After I'd replaced them, I pulled on the yellow-topped boots. "I'll see you in there. I need to find the can." I flopped my clean shirt over my shoulder.

"So pee here," Devyn said.

I gave him a look.

"Bashful? I won't watch."

"Look, I just need to go to the can."

"Ah. Number two. Coulda said so." He jerked his gear bag from the ground. "Don't get lost." Devyn threw his bag over his shoulder and headed toward the arena.

I ran through the rows of trucks and vans toward a row of empty stock trailers. A couple of two-horse trailers were parked tightly next to one another. They offered the best shelter. I squeezed between them, ripping the snaps open on my dirty shirt as I went.

Behind the trailers, I rolled the Ace bandage from my torso. Oppressive, hot air rushed onto my skin. I rubbed the red, wrinkled lines that were made from the slipped binding. Pain blasted through me. I sucked in a huge breath. Another stab of pain from my ribs reminded me not to. A colorful bruise had blossomed over my side.

At the front of the trailers, footsteps scuffed the dirt. "I'll kill that scrawny kid. Dead as his daddy."

Several men stomped to a stop.

I hastened to replace the bandage around my chest. My hands shook.

I dropped the roll of tape. It escaped beneath the trailer.

Crouching, I patted the ground for the tape. Nothing. I crawled lower to peer under the trailer. I saw two sets of boots. There wasn't anything particular about the boots. One was a set of cowboy boots. The other were untied work boots. The tongues of which hung out like those of a pair of panting hound dogs.

But there was one thing particular. And familiar. The stripes on the outside seams of one set of pantlegs were particular to the sheriff's department.

"He's standing in the way of what's mine." One of them spit a gob of brown goo to the ground. "It'll look like another accident."

I grasped the tape and carefully, quietly, tore off strips. I plastered them to my Ace bandage, then pushed my arms into the sleeves of the clean shirt. My trembling fingers had trouble with the buttons.

The two men went quiet.

Did I make a noise? Are they now listening for me?

Another glob of spit smacked the dry ground. I heard their footsteps scuff the hard-packed dirt.

Are they coming around the trailer?

They moved off.

I blew a sigh of relief. Really. I deliberately blew a sigh of relief.

Behind the chutes of the arena, Devyn rosined his rope. He bobbed his head to me then tugged even more furiously. His face was pasty. His jaw was tight.

I set my rope on the rail nearby and ferreted gear from my bag. It was a strain to buckle my daddy's old chaps to my thighs. They had stiffened this past year with disuse. I think they had grown weary of the work. I just about lost my struggle with them when a dry leg strap tore off.

I cut a piece from the leather ties I used on my boot shafts and ran the short length through the last hole on the strap to its buckle. It would hold.

Bulls were being loaded into the bucking chutes. In the arena, bullfighting clowns performed calisthenics. The crowd roared. The announcer, Red, rattled his spiel. *The voice of bull riding.* There was something familiar about him. I'd think on that another time.

I had drawn Bluff for this ride. He was a powerful, buff-colored bull that always tried to hook the rider with his stubbed horns. The threat of his horns slapping at his rider's face could set a guy back. Slide too far back and that bull owned the ride. It'd be over in a split second. And that's what Bluff counted on.

I meandered over to the chutes and climbed to the platform.

Bluff was cool as a cucumber. I dropped my bull rope past his heart girth. *Easy peasy.* He rolled an eye to look at me and flicked an ear in my direction as if to say "c'mon, boy, you're taking too much time."

I climbed down and got busy. The spotter still had his hand in front of my vest as I checked back with the flank man. I stuffed my hat lower over my forehead and nodded for the chute to open.

Bluff came out big. He blew snot in the air. It slapped onto my vest. Then he went to haulin'.

I stayed up over him to keep away from his powerful hindquarters as he kicked and twisted to rid himself of me. Then he spun into my hand and I thought I had him.

That's when he threw his head.

One of Bluff's horns hit the brim of my hat. It flipped into the air.

I slipped back.

The hat tumbled to the ground in front of Bluff.

Luck was on my side. Bluff dropped his head and tracked my hat. With his massive forward leap after it, I got my winky back to my pinky, then hung on until the buzzer.

I made eight seconds, but it hadn't been pretty.

Not one cowboy had made their ride look pretty today. The bulls were rank. They dropped riders every which way until it was all over. Just saying, none of it was pretty.

There were forty-two bull riders for Friday night. Devyn and I were among them.

I had lost track of Devyn. He knew everyone. So he had wandered off. I think earlier he said he'd go congratulate some girl on her barrel run. I didn't expect to see him again tonight. I didn't expect to see anyone I knew.

"Luce," I hollered at the crowd.

She filed from the arena. Rupert held tight to her hand. I scrambled over the panels. Her strawberry-blond ponytail bobbed as she shuffled within the packed assembly.

"Luce," I hollered again. But the exiting crowd swallowed her.

When I clambered to the main entrance, she was gone.

I searched for an hour or more. But she really was gone.

I slumped into the dirt behind the chutes. *I'm not going to cry. I'm not going to cry.* I wrapped my arms around my legs and rocked. She was my sister. I missed her desperately.

I was tired was all. I got up and grabbed my gear bag. It felt too heavy. It was a torture to drag it to the truck. I swear my right arm had been stretched two inches longer, or more. My side groaned. All I wanted was to curl into a ball on the vinyl bench seat of my truck and try to sleep the night away. In the morning, I'd figure out what to do about food and washing.

"You're driving," Devyn said when I got to the truck. He raised a beer in my direction, then jumped from the open tailgate. "Here." He handed me his can and jammed the gate shut. "Don't spill any. I'll get your bag." Devyn lifted my bag and tossed it like it was full of feathers.

He plucked the can from my hand. "Get your own," he said, then climbed into the passenger's side. I opened the driver's side door. He pointed to a cluster of cans slouching on the seat. "Vroom, vroom. Let's go."

He leaned back and shoved his feet through the open window. "Extra points if you do those whirlies." Devyn took a last swallow from the can, crushed it, then dumped it in the foot well. "I got a six-pack. Let's see if you can make it to my house before I start drinking your half."

CHAPTER FIVE

"I didn't know it was your birthday the other night." Devyn and I fell into a relaxed camaraderie. Relaxed? More like bone tired. It had been one long weekend of nonstop rodeo so far. And it wasn't over yet. I understood the addictive fever for the fervor, but geesh. How would either one of us drag our battered butts to the short round tonight?

On the other hand, it was over after tonight. It was Monday. Labor Day. I'd be in school tomorrow like nothing happened.

"Eighteen years old," Devyn replied. He was plastered over the bench seat in his garage. An ice pack draped over his bare thigh. Yesterday hadn't been kind to him. His performance had been stiff and clunky. The bull had been slow and methodical.

Devyn got hung up in his rope after the buzzer. When he shook loose, he landed under the belly of the bull.

That bull tap danced around Devyn's ears. Devyn tried to stay real small. If not for those bullfighters working overtime to draw the one-ton wrecking ball off of him, he might not have crawled away. It was crazy that he'd only been nicked by a toe.

To add insult to injury, a low score reflected his rigid ride.

I handed him another beer, then peered under the ice pack. "Good one." The egg had swelled to the size of a baseball. An impressive purple bruise blossomed through the center of the cherry red lump. It wasn't clear how he'd get his jeans on over that mass, never mind ride.

"Hey," I said, "I found you something. For your birthday." I twirled a turkey's tail feather in my fingers. "It's a thing."

"Well, I can see it's a thing. But I'm not sure what I'm supposed to do with it."

I plucked the hat from my head and stuffed a matching feather into the hat band. "My daddy used to wear one. For luck. It's a thing."

A huge grin split his face. "It'll be our thing." Devyn took the feather, then swigged on his beer. "It's like we're twinsies. Matchy matchy." His face lit with genuine appreciation. Otherwise, I'd have thought he was kidding on me.

A twinkle returned to his eyes. Devyn jostled the feather, then stuffed it to sit over his ear. "Now help me pee in a can," he said. He rolled to his side without upsetting the ice.

"Get your own peeing done. I'm going to the house for a shower and to check the laundry."

His mother was pulling double shifts for the bar she worked at. The Honky Tonk. We had passed each other in their house twice this weekend.

Once, she was in a pink fuzzy robe, hunched over a cup of coffee that she escorted back to her bedroom. The next time, she had blown through while I was in using the bathroom. I had heard her collapse on her bed.

She had practically lived at the Honky Tonk all weekend. In fact, the entire town was awake round the clock for their coveted Labor Day Rodeo. I don't think anyone noticed my whereabouts.

More like, no one cared.

Well...that wasn't true. Red, the announcer at the rodeo, cared. He played me up over the loudspeaker like I was the next Professional Bull Riding champion coming through the ranks.

After showering, I brought a plate of scrambled eggs and bacon to Devyn. He was fast asleep on the bench seat. The turkey feather was still propped over his ear.

"Wakey wakey. Eggs and bakey."

Noon was coming on fast. We were due back for the final round of riding bulls—the short go.

We pulled into the parking lot. Red, white, and blue flags snapped on the breeze. Cattle trumpeted from in their pens. Horses whinnied to one another. And competitors hooted howdies to each other.

A muffled roar erupted from the stadium crowd. The loud-speaker crackled with excitement. "Darn," Devyn said. "I promised Laney I'd watch her run. Barrel racing. I totally forgot."

Out past the clamor, I shut the truck engine down. It gasped with relief. The dented doors creaked and groaned like an eighty-year-old man climbing out of bed. My body felt the same way, but the sights and sounds perked me to not noticing.

I could smell pine shavings on the slight breeze. The scent reminded me of our workin' horses, long ago. Daddy would stall the cow ponies in the barn at the first sign of lightning moving fast over the flat miles of range. When they were all put up in fluffy shavings, the horses would quietly munch on feed. We'd throw extra hay bales into the aisle to sit on, anticipating the splendor of the storm.

He and I had watched as jagged streaks lit the dark sky like fireworks on the Fourth of July. The breeze outside the barn had hummed with electricity, but the unconcerned horses chomped on hay and stomped in fresh shavings. The scent of pine had filled the sizzling air around me.

The smell always reminded me of Daddy.

I closed my eyes, inhaling the scent of shavings. My chest warmed.

"Nothing like it, huh?" Devyn asked.

I opened my eyes and stared at Devyn.

"To be a part of something so raw, so wholesome, so American? Cowboys. Livin' the dream, dude. Livin' the dream." He said the words with enthusiasm, but his face was deadpan. I wasn't sure if he was trying to convince me or if he was trying to convince himself.

"Fried dough," I replied. I tugged our bags from the truck bed. "You ever tasted fried dough with way too much powdered sugar dumped on top?"

"Seriously? That's what you got? Fried dough?" He shook his head as if he'd given up on me. "I'm talking American icons. Legends. And you got fried dough."

"Yeah. C'mon. I'll get us each a slab." I hoisted my gear bag over my shoulder and made sure to walk slow while Devyn gimped alongside.

When we came around to the crowded midway with its rows of food and games, I brushed the back of Devyn's hand with the tips of my fingers before I'd realized what I was doing. When my daddy was competing, Luce and I weren't ever allowed down the midway without holding hands. She was like, four. I must have been thirteen. Daddy didn't trust the carnies—the guys that traveled with the carnival. They were a mean looking bunch with their greasy ropes of hair and unwashed jeans. Not all of them. But those couple of bad apples spoiled the bushel.

I jerked my hand away, thankful Devyn hadn't seemed to notice my slip.

Glass shattered inside the beer tent. My hand flew to the scar marring my face. I traced the ragged line over my cheek.

"What are you looking at, boy?" one of the rednecks in the beer tent asked.

I hadn't realized I was staring.

Devyn chucked me on the shoulder. "Dude, those are locals. *Locos.*" He beamed a broad smile at the locals and nodded. "That herd of rednecks are bigoted, backwards, judgmental turds," Devyn said through his grinding grin. "If you're going to live in this town, you'll have to get used to them."

Avoidance, sounds better.

As we made our way behind the chutes, I carried two slabs of powdered fried dough. I dropped my gear bag to the arena dirt and eyed each pen for Thundering Bunny. He wasn't in any of them. Even though Devyn stood right beside me, I felt a loneliness creep through my body. It was stupid—looking for him. He was just a bull.

"There's been free pizza in the locker room," Devyn said as he grabbed a fried dough from my hands. "You haven't been back there once."

"I like my space." Stuffing fried dough into my mouth kept me from having to explain further. It was true. I did like my space. Regardless of the locker room being full of men in various states of undress. *Maybe I'm bashful.*

It was a struggle for me to be social. I was too nervous around people. I didn't know how to start a conversation. I'd try too hard. Which made me sound like a crazed, chattering squirrel scolding a nut thief.

I didn't know how to carry a conversation. My jokes fell flat. Others saw me as weird. I know they laughed behind my back.

And I didn't know how to end a conversation.

I'd wind up not saying anything. And that gets even more awkward.

Kids at the Autry Academy thought I was creepy.

"You go," I said with my mouth full. I sprayed powdered sugar into the air as I spoke.

"I'll stay." Devyn bit off a hunk of dough and unzipped his bag. His leg was bothering him. He stood with most of his weight on the uninjured one. His usually swarthy face was as white as a ghost.

I set my dough down, then grabbed his bull rope and hung it for him.

"Who'd you get?" he asked as he opened his rosin.

"Tornado Alley," I said.

Behind the chutes, that bull was known as "the homewrecker." A bad draw in the short go. He literally preyed on tired cowboys. Tornado Alley tested for fatigue and weakness before he settled on a plan to make his rider come apart.

"Tough draw," Devyn mumbled. He caught himself. "Hey. No problem for you, though. You're a fly by the seat of your pants kind of guy. You've got this. Just waltz him for eight seconds."

Tornado Alley tossed in the chute when I set my rope to him. His furious power both unsettled and exhilarated me. I tucked the tail of my rope under the rigging, climbed out, and resigned myself to the wait.

I was the last rider of the day. My legs felt like jelly. I'd never been more nervous.

My heart hammered in my chest. I bent over, gripped above my knees, and reminded myself to breathe.

I started to feel ill.

My stomach churned. Bile threatened. *Breathe. Breathe.*

Time ticked too slowly. *If only I was the man they thought me to be.* I hauled myself upright. *I have to be the man they see. Can't go back now. Luce needs this.*

I need this.

My daddy always prayed at this point. Many, many times over

the years, I'd seen him bow his head, close his eyes, and move his lips in prayer. I knew he asked the Lord to protect him and watch over him. I knew he asked it for all of the athletes—two-legged and four. He'd kiss his cross, then lift his eyes to heaven.

God and I weren't on speaking terms lately. Or rather, I wasn't speaking to Him. Which I felt was justified. He took my daddy from me. And He hadn't listened to any of my prayers.

If He'd had a plan for me, it was shit so far.

Tornado Alley lunged upward in the chute as I stood over him. My feet gripped the rails. His bulk shoved my legs against the steel.

I waited for him to settle.

He was a deadly serious bull. I needed to get more serious. I needed to commit. I decided to change my wrap on this ride.

The pressure of the event seeped into me. My head swam with too many what-ifs, and too much second-guessing. It wasn't my confidence. I'd been riding since I was a little kid.

It was the fact that I was an impostor.

I didn't have the right to be in the company of these cowboys. I wasn't one of them. They'd never accept me for who I really was if they knew. I'd never be allowed to compete if they knew.

Because I didn't have what it took to be a real man, I'd never live up to any of their expectations. Regardless of ability.

Why isn't it about being good at riding bulls? Getting the payoff? It should only be about that bull between your legs. But it was about that other thing that was there. *Or isn't there.* If the rodeo officials found out about that one missing body part, I'd never compete again.

This town was looking for a local cowboy hero. Bull riding fans counted on me as a Cinderella story. The announcer promoted me as the next bull riding sensation. Cowboys slapped me on the back in passing. Chute men were quick to help. Heck, young kids stuck Sharpies under my nose, wanting me to sign their hats. And I didn't want to disappoint any of them.

I didn't want to make a bad showing. I didn't want to come off before eight seconds. I wanted to be all that they saw, and hoped for, and cheered for.

But I was still an impostor.

I heard Daddy's chant in my head. "Focus, damn it. Eye on the prize. Dollar bills. Focus."

Below me, Tornado Alley slid back from his leap like a receding ocean wave. I gingerly dropped onto his back to get to work.

Visualize the outcome. Don't overthink the ride. Go with the bull. Jump for jump. "Focus," I whispered. It's what Daddy always told himself. I'd like to think that's what he'd tell me.

I wiggled my fingers and squirmed my hand open inside the handle to seat the bull rope tighter. *Perfect.* I ran the rope across my palm and closed my hand. The *truck and trailer* stopped there, shy of a full wrap.

I hesitated.

Tornado Alley lunged for the top of the chute rails again. My spotter gripped the front of my vest and anchored himself to the side steel rail with his other hand. The music blared, but the crowd went deathly quiet.

When Tornado Alley retreated to all fours, there was a collective sigh of relief from the stands.

I decided to commit my hand into an encircling wrap. It was a bold move for me. I wasn't a bold person.

I gave the rope a couple of twists on the backside, then came around my hand to add a couple of twists on the front side too. That gave some curvature for my hold. I opened my hand one more time to lay the rope in. It felt good. I was ready.

I flicked the tail of the rope over Tornado Alley's hump. I checked in with the flank man, then the gate man. I slid my feet forward on the rails. *Good to go.*

Winky to my pinky. I dropped my feet down, got up over Tornado Alley's front end, straightened my back, and nodded.

The chute ripped open.

Tornado Alley took an honest leap out and turned into my hand. He bunched beneath me and surged with power.

Too much thinking shot through my head. *If he did that, I should do this. If he does the other, I could do that.* But thinking only got in my way.

My neck snapped back. My hat flew. I slipped a hair off the timing.

That's when the mighty bull figured he had me. He switched his moves up.

My foot shifted out of position. It slid behind my bull rope. I reset it to his heart girth in the next jump but felt off balance. My arm strained because my legs faltered as my base. I chunked onto the gummy guard in my mouth and willed myself to get down into Tornado Alley.

In the last seconds, he settled into a blistering spin. I barely held myself out of the well. But I was able to set my spur. I made the buzzer.

That was the best ride of my life!

When my scores came in, the lights went out and the pyrotechnics shot off.

Under the roar of excitement, the stadium trembled like a waking volcano. Feet stomped the stands near to collapsing.

I'd won.

I spit my mouth guard into my palm and shoved it into a pocket on my vest. I unzipped the vest and let it fall from my shoulders. *I'd won.*

A spotlight crashed onto me. Music blared through the loudspeakers, especially loud. My heart pounded. *What song is playing?* I wracked my brain but couldn't come up with the answer.

All of a sudden, my mind felt as if someone had packed it full of cotton.

Oh no. Not now. Please not now.

A tightness crept over my chest. My mouth went dry.

The nurse at the Autry Academy had called it social anxiety. She said it "manifested" in different ways for different people. As a haze descended over my brain, I heard her in my head, ticking off the entire list of physical symptoms associated with the disorder.

My palms grew clammy. I scratched at the sweaty wetness with my fingertips.

In excited tradition, two cowboys doused me with a cooler of leftover Gatorade. The spotlight panned the arena. Three riders galloped past. The Stars and Stripes flapped high above the middle horse.

I slapped at the ice cubes clinging to my shoulders.

Devyn gimped toward me in a rush. His face was contorted. His cheeks were flushed.

"What?" I barked above the commotion. My question was swallowed by the riotous world around me. My eyes darted everywhere and nowhere.

In the dim light, Devyn slammed into my chest. His arms encircled my torso in a fierce bear hug.

That's when exhaustion overtook me.

I leaned on him.

In response, he held me tighter.

I wanted to go limp. I wanted him to hold me up completely. I was done.

Burning fatigue washed over me. I was done.

My knees shook. Unshed tears stung. I needed to vomit.

"The Labor Day Rodeo is the biggest attraction this town's got going for it all year," Devyn screamed in a high pitch like an excited girl. "Tuck in your shirt. Wipe off those boot toes. And prop that hat on straight. You're the new bull riding champion of podunkville." His words vibrated my inner ear. "Heck, the mayor will probably give you a key to the town."

I rolled my eyes and clung to him. *God, I hope not. Just the check.* "Will it take long?" I hollered back. I was tired.

I was scared.

Why? This was all I had wanted. The payout would be huge. I wouldn't think any further than that. But I hadn't imagined I'd become a public spectacle.

I shivered. Maybe it was from the iced Gatorade. It soaked my rodeo shirt. The cold, wet shirt stuck to my body like a second skin.

My shivering intensified.

Devyn let go of me. He shirked from his jacket, then held it out.

I stared as if I didn't know what it was.

Congratulatory smacks stung my back and shoulders. I was suddenly missing the protective padding of my vest. Where had it fallen to?

Devyn wiggled the jacket in his hand and said, "You can take that wet shirt off."

"As if," I yelled over the raucous noise. "This is now my lucky shirt!"

He stuffed his jean jacket over my wet shoulders. I went through the motions of shoving my arms into the sleeves.

"You've got this," Devyn said. "Being a Taylor only makes this a bigger win for the town."

I'm not one of their Taylors though, am I? I'm not from here. I only just moved to town. I heard the hushed whispers of my daddy's name on too many lips. The murmurs swarmed like droning bees.

Devyn ate it up.

Most of these cowboys had been competing for years—I wasn't sure I even deserved to be here.

The spot blinded me in white light. A grossly oversized cardboard check and a shiny silver belt buckle lodged into my hands.

I don't remember the rest.

When did it end? How did I get away?

In the parking lot, Red clapped me on the shoulder. "Your daddy would be proud of you."

I hoped so. I doubted it. I mean, I wanted him to be proud of me. Would he get over the fact that I was deceiving his fellow bull riders? I didn't know. Theirs was a camaraderie that I'd always felt went deeper than him and me.

Red's wide palm was comfortably heavy as it remained on my shoulder. "Your daddy won his first buckle right here. Back in his high school days." His big smile was warm and welcoming. It had a smidgen of awe in its delight. "There will be no stopping you now, son."

Had he known my daddy well? Red looked a lot like my mother's side of the family.

I had pored through her albums, memorizing the face I'd hardly known. Her family was full of redheads and blondes. Apparently, my daddy had a thing for blondes. I don't know what he saw in their fair hair and baby blues, but it would never be enough for me.

"So you'll be bringing stock back to the ranch, then? The old place could use a breath of fresh air." His gray-flecked bushy eyebrows jumped and jolted like two spiky caterpillars doing a happy jig. But his washed-out eyes spoke of seriousness and concern. "What does your uncle think of—"

"Congratulations, Chris." The social worker burst between us. She peered daggers at Red but dropped her eyes as if she were hiding something. Her thin fingers clutched at my upper arm. She squeezed and tugged me to leave with her. "I'll take you to Lucine. You can tell her all about winning. And maybe we'll stay a moment to celebrate."

She tugged, but my feet hadn't been convinced enough to move.

"She'll want to hear your big news."

Luce. "Can we pick up pizza?" I asked. "Luce loves pizza." For a second, I forgot about Red. I forgot about Devyn. He had grabbed my gear and told me to meet him at the truck. I forgot about everything happening around me.

I wanted to celebrate with family. I wanted desperately to share my news with Luce. I wanted desperately to see her. She was my only family. *Isn't she?*

I turned around. "Do you really think Daddy would be proud of me?" Red was gone.

"Come on, dear. Let's get that pizza." The social worker's icy fingers pressured my arm.

"What about a foster family—"

Sheriff Taylor stepped in front of us. "Not tonight." He clenched my other arm in his fist. I swore his grip would leave bruises. "You're going back to the County Boys' Home. Where you belong." His grunt was filled with fury.

Who kicked his dog?

I half expected him to foam at the mouth as rabies took hold.

"Madge. Evening." The sheriff bobbed his head in greeting. He was too familiar with the social worker.

She batted her lashes in a flirty manner.

Eww. Gross. How could anyone be attracted to an oil slick like the sheriff?

"A celebration is in order, Bubba. Don't you think?"

Bubba?

Sheriff Bubba Taylor slapped my back hard enough to knock me forward. His hit jolted the air from my lungs.

I coughed.

The sheriff's meaty paw squeezed the nape of my neck.

I winced from the pain. My temples pounded. My face grew hot. It felt like too much pressure built in my head. I didn't know whether to pop or drop. All of a sudden, I got dizzy.

"It's a school night, Madge."

Madge released my arm. As she stepped away, she seemed relieved to have me off her hands.

The sheriff jammed me into the back of his patrol car and slammed the door. He oozed into the driver's seat and adjusted the mirror to keep an eye on me. The engine growled to life. Sheriff Taylor watched me in his rearview mirror with squinted beady eyes.

"Your daddy may have been Mr. Big Shot, but he's gone now. And you'll never be anything more than trailer trash. Even with your fluke win."

"You don't know me," I retorted through gritted teeth.

"I knew your daddy before you were even a mistake."

Chapter Six

"Don't you wonder why he's out to get you?" Devyn asked.

Rodeo team practice had been canceled for a well-deserved rest after the Labor Day events. We sat on the high school's arena bleachers soaking up the sun. Devyn propped his sore leg up.

"He's not out to get me," I said. "He's just a dick."

"Who's a dick?"

I turned. She had hair as black and iridescent as a raven's wing. I knew who she was, even without staring into her deep brown eyes.

My stomach leaped into my pounding heart. Or my heart dropped into my stomach. Either way, just looking at her felt like a roller coaster ride. *Oh, man.* She was tall and athletic and beautiful.

And taken. I'd seen her with Devyn before. From a distance.

"Laney. Chris. Chris. Laney." Introductions over, Devyn asked her, "You're not still mad at me, are you?"

She ruffled his hair, then dropped her armful of schoolbooks to the aluminum bleacher. Laney flopped next to him. She asked me again, "Who's a dick?"

"Sheriff Taylor," I mumbled. Heat rose into my cheeks. They'd be bright red in two seconds. If they weren't already. I pulled my hat lower over my eyebrows and feigned interest in an old bleached crease running up the front of my Wranglers. Starched and ironed jeans were a tradition of old-school cowboys.

"Sheriff Taylor? A dick? Yeah, well, no surprise there. And I heard he's particularly interested in *your* family. Must be about Taylors who aren't the *founding* Taylors. I don't think he likes competition. He's working real hard to make you all disappear."

Disappear? I doubt it.

Laney continued. "He's already got *you* locked away. He's trying to get your poor mother committed to the state hospital. Never to be seen or heard from again."

Stepmother.

"And he's petitioned to have your baby sister put up for adoption before you turn eighteen and can rescue her." Laney draped over Devyn's shoulder. "And what's with that? I thought you Taylors all stuck together."

"Laney—" Devyn quietly rebuked her.

"Hey, Dev, don't shoot the messenger."

"Why you gotta to be like that, girlfriend?" Devyn asked.

"If *I've* heard it, you better believe others have too." She ran her fingers through her silky hair, twisted the lengths, then spiraled it onto the back of her head.

"Let's focus on me," Devyn said. "'K. So last year, in business class, I worked on this model for making it rich as a professional bull rider. Of course, I'm going to college and don't need to know all that. Buuutt, it got me thinking." He dragged a backpack from under the bleacher seat and unzipped it slowly, like he was a Chippendale dancer teasing his clothes off.

I giggled.

He jostled his eyebrows up and down.

"What I was thinking was, we could really use that plan now." Devyn reached a hand in and paused, as if expecting a drum roll. He shook his head. "Nothin'?"

I shrugged.

"Sponsors." He drew out two folded, plastic-wrapped shirts peppered with logos. "Black for you. And of course, blue to match my eyes. Sponsors are going to pay our entry fees. And you can get that new rope you desperately need, Chris. Cuz that thing you're dragging around is gonna leave you faster than a racehorse out of a starting gate."

"How—When—Who would give you money?" I stammered.

"Read 'em and weep." He handed me the black shirt. "Sal's Auto Emporium was the first to sign on. Sally paid a premium for her logo over the left breast pocket. After that, I didn't have enough shirt to fit them all." He dug around in the backpack as if he'd lost something. "Patches. For the vests."

Laney plucked an embroidered patch from Devyn and looked closely at it. "Good for you, Dev. Entrepreneur in the making."

Devyn said, "Folks had cash and enthusiasm from the long rodeo weekend. It was just a matter of collecting on their enthusiasm to get their cash, then trotting their logos to the embroiderer. I already had the shirts." He half zipped the empty backpack and tossed it under the bench. "The embroiderers were done by two p.m. Free of charge. Their logo runs along the back of the collar."

He smacked a stack of patches on top of the packaged shirt in my hands. "I made it back to school to hear the last bell of the day. So it's not like I played hooky *all* day."

I ran my fingertips over a raised embroidered logo. My heart skipped a beat. Then it quickened. *Sponsors.* This was the real deal. *But am I?* I couldn't look at either of them.

"Dude, all of the townspeople believe in you. And I skipped classes for you." He held his fingers to the side of his face as if speaking into a phone. "Hello?" he squeaked in a higher pitch. "Yes. I'm calling to let you know my son, Devyn, will not be in school today. He's hurt his leg."

Laney broke out in giggles. "You didn't." She threw her head back and howled.

Still tracing a logo with my fingers, I glanced at the two of them from beneath my hat brim.

Laney squeezed Devyn's shoulders and gave him a shake. "Well, I don't think that's what your mother sounds like," she said.

Devyn prodded my knee.

I looked at him.

"Well?" He shrugged. Devyn was completely thrilled with himself.

I stared at the decorated shirt on my lap. I couldn't look at him. "I don't know how I'll ever repay you." My eyes burned. I was afraid he'd think I was crying.

"That wasn't what I was asking." He leaned his forearms across the blue shirt resting on his uninjured thigh. The plastic crinkled. "You like?" he asked softly.

"Is that your short bus?" Laney pointed to the front of the school. The bus swerved to a stop at the curb.

"Oh, shoot." I jumped to my feet. "You'd better hold on to

these." I shuffled my shirt and patches on top of his, then darted down the aluminum bleachers.

"I could give you a ride," Devyn shouted at my fleeing back. "I have a truck."

"*My* truck," I yelled without stopping in flight. "Might want to get it registered proper."

Spitballs pinged off the back of my hat as I rode in the front seat of the short bus.

At the County Boys' Home, Michael was waiting just inside the main entrance to jump me. He pinched my shirtsleeve. "Follow me."

We hiked to the end of the long hall. Michael peered both ways, then ducked into a janitorial closet.

It was weird. I thought twice about going in after him. But I did.

As soon as I stepped inside, Michael pushed the door closed behind us. The small room went black.

"Give me a second," he said in the dark. A flashlight clicked on under his chin like he was preparing to tell a ghost story around a campfire. Then, Michael started to climb the metal shelving units. The light's beam swung chaotically around the tiny room. It reminded me of a seriously faulty disco ball at a lame middle school dance, back in the day.

He grabbed a string that pulled down a hidden ladder. The ladder unfolded. He climbed it. As I added my weight behind him, it creaked.

When I reached the top, the brim of my hat hit the edge of the ceiling's opening.

"The Sergeant knows I study up here," Michael explained with a quavering voice. "He doesn't ever climb up."

I doubted the fat drunk could.

Books lined shelves in neat rows. Notebooks waited patiently near a craning lamp on a makeshift desk. Pencils stood sentinel in a Campbell's soup can.

I trailed my fingers along a plywood countertop nestled on milk crates. A toaster oven with its guts showing was plugged into an outlet. The receptacle sat loose inside a metal junction box nailed to the roof joists. All of the exposed wires looked like an electrical fire waiting to happen. But I had to hand it to Michael. He had constructed a cozy home away from home in the attic crawl space.

He busied himself at the counter as I looked around. The toaster oven tick, tick, ticked behind me.

"How'd you get all of this stuff?"

"When you guys are in school, and, like, the Sergeant drinks himself into a stupor, I go out."

He saw the question in my eyes.

"It's all from dumpsters. I didn't steal any of it. People throw totally cool things away." Michael hop-skipped sideways to the louvered shutters at the end of the attic. With a snap of a latch, the shutters flung open. Block and tackle hung from a track overhead. "Getting it up here is the fun part." Michael leaped onto the hanging ropes. He flew out the opening and swung back in.

"Sweet." I turned in a complete circle and took measure of his hideaway. "You rigged all this up? Even electricity?" He was a genius.

Michael's cheeks glowed bright red in the lamplight. "Sit." He pointed in invitation.

Vinyl beanbag chairs, their rips covered with silver duct tape, were tossed on a fake oriental rug. The rug's garish designs were too fancy and too out of place in the attic secrecy.

"Why don't you go to school?" I asked, lowering myself to a beanbag chair. A stained Chutes and Ladders game board lay open on the corner of the rug. I picked up one of two "game pieces." It was a plastic Army man posed in a belly crawl.

"That's the Sergeant." He stooped to the board. "This is me." He pointed at a blue monkey. The kind that came from a plastic barrel and could hook together by their arms.

A ding sounded behind me. Michael jumped up.

"Where's the rest of the game?"

"Dunno. Thought I'd collect pieces and make it up as I went along. I've never played any board games. I don't know what's missing." He fussed at the counter as he talked. He returned with his hands full. "Here." Michael offered me a balled, lumpy napkin.

I took the crumpled lump. Steam rose from within. "Whoa—" I jounced it from one palm to the next. "Hot."

"Oh, yeah, careful." He flopped onto the opposite beanbag.

Michael set his napkin down then squirmed like he was having a fit. From his pocket, he plucked a tiny ceramic figurine. "Almost forgot. I got this one today."

It was a brown bull.

"This one's you," he said. "These ceramic ones come in this old lady's carton of tea bags. She throws them out. I think cuz she's collected all of them. They sit along her kitchen windowsill." He put the bull on the board. "I saved up a pouch full of them once. But I gave them to this little kid in the trailer park. I wish I could have given him marbles. The other boys picked on him cuz he didn't have marbles."

Neither one of us spoke for a moment.

Michael asked, "How do you like it?" He picked up his rumpled napkin and bounced it in his hand.

I took my first bite of what looked like a crumbly biscuit. "Mm," I said with a smile. The texture was…different. Dry on the outside. Doughy in the middle. I mashed it around in my mouth, afraid of what would register on my tongue.

It's good.

He saw my expression of surprise. "Moon rocks, I call them. Bisquick powder, water, that grated cheese in the shaker bottle, and sugar. I like to add butter, but it's hard to get before the refrigerator and pantry are padlocked. Without anyone noticing, that is. It doesn't keep either. Butter. I can't keep it up here."

"My compliments to the chef." I raised the napkin in salute. Michael was a weird kid. And I was afraid I had an admirer. Worse—I might have another friend.

He ducked his head a smidgen and stared at the floor. A smile played on his lips. "So is it true?" Michael asked. "I heard you won the bull riding at the Labor Day Rodeo. Is it true?"

"Yeah. It's true. With that win, my friend, Devyn—I mean, I think he's my friend—I kind of look up to him because he seems to have his shit together. He's like, older. But only by a year. We're in the same grade. His name's Devyn. Well, he got some sponsors so we can keep competing." I stuffed the last hunk of moon rock in my mouth and chewed. "I need to get a new bull rope."

"Didn't you win, like, a lot of money?"

"Yeah. But I have a kid sister. I'm going to save up and take her away from here. Get to college. You know. Make something of myself."

"Ah." Michael picked at the rug. He traced the designs with his finger.

"How old are you?" I asked.

"Fourteen." He squirmed in the beanbag chair. "And you're seventeen. You're like the oldest kid here," Michael said around his mouthful of moon rock.

"I'm not *like* the oldest kid. I *am* the oldest."

"Well, yeah, that's what I meant. But *why* are you here? You could be emancipated. Get a job in town. You could get your sister. Have some money to go out on Saturday night. Meet girls."

"Is that what you'd want? Money to spend on Saturday nights?"

"Just getting out sounds good to me. Besides, it's all I'll ever have. The County Boys' Home isn't a posh, preppy boarding school preparing me for a white-collar future."

"Why don't you go to school?"

"I'm home-schooled. It's totally sweet. I'm three grades ahead of where I would be in a traditional school. I used to get in trouble in a classroom setting. I don't fit in. And I get bored easily." He tossed the last bit of moon rock into his mouth. "At least here, I get to go at my own pace," he said around the crumbly biscuit. "Study what I want. Learn what I want. Build what I want."

His face brightened. "You should see all my cool projects. I like electricity. I'm not thinking any public school is going to let me experiment with live electricity to wire stuff."

The dinner triangle clanked. It called everyone from their hidey-holes to the community meal.

Raucous running, laughter, and screaming, not normally allowed, warned me before I reached the dining hall.

Oh my God. "Where's the Sergeant?" I asked Michael in a whisper. The scene inside the kitchen was havoc. Michael scurried away.

In English class, at the Autry Academy, we had studied a book that came to mind now. *Lord of the Flies.* It was about lost boys surviving on their own. Without adult supervision, and free from civilized structure, the boys were disastrous at governing themselves. With the wrong direction, they became brutal savages.

The dining hall was cut from the pages of that novel.

A smaller kid was held flat to the long table. A large kid sprayed whip cream into his mouth and nose until he gasped and choked for air. Tears streamed from his reddened face. His hands were clenched in fists, but his arms were restrained at the wrists.

"Who rang the dinner triangle?" I asked, taking a wide stance in the doorframe. I tucked my thumbs in my front pockets. *Obviously, no dinner.*

The self-appointed king, Mullet-head, wore the Sergeant's ring of keys on a shoestring around his neck. He scooped ice cream into his laughing mouth from a dripping carton. Vanilla drool ran the length of his T-shirt. His eyes gleamed with delight at the torture of the boy pinned to the table.

"Who rang?" I asked again.

Mullet-head flopped his spoon toward the squirming boy. "The Mex kid."

I could walk away. Turn a blind eye. Not get involved.

I stood there. It was a risk with so many of them. *If that was Luce on that table?* I sucked in a long breath of air, then breathed it out in a heavy sigh.

I could choose to do nothing.

But I wasn't brought up that way.

Daddy always said to turn the other cheek when someone riled me. But he never did abide bullying.

I walked to the table, then stuffed my palm over a kid's face and shoved him off of the restrained boy. He stumbled backwards to fall on a chair behind him.

I pushed the next kid in the chest with force. He slammed into the counter.

The prone boy scrambled up. He spit whip cream from his mouth, blew out his nostrils, and wiped at his face.

Mullet-head watched. With a flat tongue, he licked the spoon in his grubby hand. "What are you gonna do? Take us all on?" Melted ice cream puddled on the floor between his feet.

"No," I said. "Just you."

"Well?" He eyed each of the others individually.

I clutched hold of his lower jaw.

"Just you," I repeated. I dug my fingers into his cheeks until he focused on me. I worked the shoestring of keys over the back of his head and onto my wrist. The keys swung lazily from my arm.

My fingernails broke his skin.

The bucket of ice cream hit the floor with a plop. The spoon tinkled and chinked as it bounced along the cracked linoleum. His hands clasped my wrist as he attempted to break my hold.

"Chris, look out," Michael yelled from the doorway.

I swung Mullet-head around by his jaw. He was stiff in my grasp. I had to twist the front of his shirt in my other hand to keep him from tripping.

It wasn't as easy as the saloon fights on television made it look.

A whipped cream can struck Mullet-head's skull.

I shook my head at his buddy. "Clean up this mess," I growled with as much authority as I could force into four words.

Everyone stared at me. Their faces twitched with indecision.

Mullet-head bashed at my forearm. His pale cheeks flushed brightly. His eyes began to water. Blood seeped from his scratched skin to pool around my cuticles.

"Now."

Michael jumped for the fallen carton and can. He sent the refuse sailing to the trash barrel. Others followed suit, righting chairs and gathering utensils into the sink.

Mullet-head stopped struggling. Good thing. I could keep hold of his jaw all night long with my riding hand. He didn't buck half as hard as a romping bull. "Get some proper dinner started," I said in a calmer tone. "The Sergeant?" I asked Michael.

"He's alive. He's in his rooms. Passed out." Michael switch gears from cleaning up to leading me down the hall.

Mullet-head scrambled backwards as we walked together. Well, I kept hold of his jaw and directed him. It wasn't like we *walked together*.

The Sergeant had a small apartment midway along the row of cell doors.

"Call nine-one-one."

"He's breathing," the kid on the floor reported. He was crouched over the Sergeant. He had rolled the Sergeant onto his side.

"I didn't do it," Mullet-head said through my strangling grip. "I didn't do anything to him. Found him like that." He huffed from his nose.

"He could be telling the truth," the kid on the floor offered in a weak voice. "The Sergeant choked on his own vomit." The kid opened the Sergeant's mouth and shoved a pen between his teeth. "That'll keep his airway clear if he pukes again. He'll drool it out." The kid's eyes darted toward the door like he was a trapped animal seeking an escape route. "Had to do that for my pops every time he shot up."

"Call nine-one-one," I repeated. Mullet-head's eyes wandered around as he tried to get a look at what was happening on the floor.

"You can't call the ambulance," Michael said. "You can't call anyone." He stepped too close behind me. I felt his wispy breath tickle the back of my neck. It was only for a split second, but I wondered—

"We'd all get sent to the juvie jail. No matter who you are or what your involvement was. Or wasn't." Michael stuffed his fidgeting hands into his pockets. "No matter how bad this place is, juvie is way worse."

The kid on the floor still squatted next to the Sergeant. He nodded agreement. "I'll watch him. I do it for my pops." He sank onto his butt and patted at the Sergeant's gray face. "Just don't forget to send me some dinner."

I slammed Mullet-head against the wall. "We done?" I envisioned Clint Eastwood in my head, playing Dirty Harry. It took a lot of restraint not to add, "punk" Totally badass. *We done...punk?*

Mullet-head attempted to nod within my merciless grip.

I let him go. Maybe the Sergeant would sort him out when he came to.

"Somebody's got to feed that new kid in segregation," Michael said. "He's a big one."

"I'll do it." I flipped the ring of keys into my hand and headed to the kitchen.

Several dozen scrambled eggs were hissing in two frying pans on the front burners of the stove. Bacon sizzled on the back. The table was set. The serving counter was laid out. I nodded appreciation to the cooks. *They might make capable wives one day.*

Mullet-head wandered in behind me. "I ain't sitting with a bunch of pussies."

"Don't." I grabbed a plate from the serving counter. "Better hope they don't spit in your food."

One of the boys cooking slopped a heaping dollop of eggs onto the plate in my hands. A wide grin plastered his face. The other set a glass of milk next to the plop and winked.

Down the hallway, I opened the newbie's door. He was already standing there, sneering. Yes, he was a big bugger. He was taller than my five foot, six inches. And twice as thick. His beefy build was all muscle, as if he'd had nothing to do in his entire life but work out. His pale blond scuzz made him look bald. Bald was not fashionable in these days of blow dryers and big hair.

"Scrambled eggs? For dinner?" His eyes were trained on me with disgust. His pock-marked face scrunched, reminding me of the similar gnarly texture of the scrambled eggs.

I stuffed the heaping plate at him. "Yup." I hauled the door closed and locked it.

"I heard we got us a Mex in here," he hollered through the door. "I love me a little chili dippin'." The door shuddered as he kicked it with a stocking foot. "Hey, I gotta go to the can. Hey. Hey, you. Skinny twerp. Let me out. I gotta take a dump."

Chapter Seven

It had been a long week. Boys in the County Home scurried along the corridor in silence, like rodents running in a sewer passage. The kid with the scuzz cut had his head together too often with the Sergeant. And Mullet-head patrolled the County Boys' Home every day like he was in charge.

Growing up, I was taught to mind my own business if things didn't concern me. That went with "turn the other cheek."

TGIF. Thank goodness it's Friday.

When the lock clicked open in the dead of night, I rolled from the cot, stuffed my hat on, and grabbed my plastic garbage sack.

"You bringing that sack with you?" Michael asked in a strained whisper.

I shrugged, which was totally lost on him in the dark. "I'm not leaving my stuff here all weekend," I mumbled. *What if I get a foster home and never have to come back?*

Metal scraped against the floor in one of the rooms. That could only mean someone else was out of bed. But the doors were locked. No one could've escaped their room into the house at night.

I just did.

Michael scampered silently through the hallway. I padded quietly behind.

It was midnight. The day had come and gone in a scream of monotony, like the rest of this past week's days. School was exceedingly easy. The Autry Academy had had higher curricular standards. I had been buried by constant homework and had to study every waking second at the Autry Academy. Now? I was bored. That made me restless. I lived for the weekends.

Rodeo time. Bull riding. I couldn't quit the addictive high any more than my daddy could have—any more than any other cowboy riding. Bull riding was like an incurable disease. Once it got into the blood, it was there to stay. The only treatment was the next bull ride.

"You ever think about quitting? Seems too dangerous." Michael asked as he closed us in the closet and climbed the metal shelving to pull down the attic ladder.

"Never." I pointed the flashlight toward the ceiling. Michael disappeared into its gaping maw. When he peered back down, I handed my sack to him. "You ever think about getting on a bull?" I asked.

"I'm used to riding those quarter horses at K-Mart. Fall off one of those and I get a couple of scrapes from the cement. They don't chase me. And I don't get stepped on."

From above, we folded the ladder to haul it back into place. The attic hideaway was sealed. Michael flicked on a dim bulb. He plugged the toaster in, then started mixing what I hoped was a batch of moon rocks.

My stomach growled. I walked to the far end of the attic and snapped open the latch to the louvered shutters. They flung wide. Crisp night air blasted the stale attic. Its clean chill wrapped around me. I shivered.

The sky was blacker than my stepmama's lost soul. The stars twinkled like a million diamonds. I shucked my hat to jerk the hood of my sweatshirt over my head. It was a comfort thing.

When I tugged the rug and beanbag chairs in front of the opening, Michael raised his eyebrows in question but said nothing.

I plopped down and stared out at the vastness of the expansive sky. It was peaceful. I released a sigh through my pursed lips like blowing out a candle. It was supposed to help release tension.

Michael plodded over and handed me a can of warm pop. "You know the sheriff's got his hands in drugs and other illegal activities?" The toaster oven dinged.

Okay.

Michael continued. "He controls people with his drugs. Doles them out to get them hooked. Then has them in his pocket. The Sergeant will do anything Sheriff Taylor says. Anything."

Michael descended cross-legged to the rug. "The point is, the

Sergeant can't help it. He's an addict." He handed me a paper towel with a steaming moon rock on it. "They say he drugged his own parents. Sheriff Taylor. They say that's why his father died."

"Why would the sheriff kill his parents?" I asked.

"Maybe he got tired of them?" Michael laughed. He picked at his moon rock and tossed a piece into his mouth. "He's got a big old family ranch. Near to a thousand acres. I hear it's all run down." Michael pushed another clump in and chewed with his mouth open. "Barns are falling down. Weeds are growing up inside the pens. Fences are sprung. Barbed wire runs in rusted coils on the ground toward leaning poles that still have staples refusing to let go. A real disaster. But there's no stock left out there to starve or anything."

"Sounds like you've seen the place," I said.

"I hear the sheriff just squats there. Doesn't repair it. Doesn't take care of it." Michael swallowed, then stuffed a last crumbly lump into his mouth and talked around it. "If I owned a place, I'd fix it all up."

I crumpled the paper towel and chucked it at him. "Maybe he doesn't know as much as you about fixing things." I sucked down the can of pop and squirmed onto my side to let myself get engulfed by the bag of beans. "Those stars are amazing," I said.

Bean stuffing rustled under Michael's slight weight. "Amazing," he repeated quietly.

At some point, I must have drifted to sleep because I startled awake at Michael's whisper.

"I'm gay," he said.

I remained very still.

"I've never told anyone. So I don't know how my father had figured it out a few years back. But when he did, he kept me from school as if I could spread a disease to the other kids. We moved away shortly after." Michael sniffled. "He hates me. But I think he's always hated me. Even before." His beanbag chair jostled.

"I wish I were more like you," he said. "I wish I had your courage and strength. I wish I could stand up to others. And be exactly who I am. Most of all, I wish I had the confidence you have. If I did, I'd tell you about me, even at the risk of losing you as a friend. But I can't. I'm not very brave. And I'm tired of being alone."

I squeezed my eyes shut. I was none of those things. *Courageous? Strong?*

I lived a lie. Too many lies. Courage and strength were found in truth. Lies were a coward's way no matter what I told myself to make it all seem okay.

I wasn't worthy of Michael's praise.

Minutes of silence passed. Michael's breathing grew heavy. He began to snore softly. My mind drifted with his rhythmic peacefulness. Finally, sleep took me.

Red and blue lights flash in the dark. A single officer is illuminated in the strobe. He flips a broken car part from the road. It rattles the brush.

Flames from the flipped truck lick the night sky. Dual back wheels rotate slowly in the smoke-filled air. Sirens wail. Daddy's lifeless body is covered by a sheet.

Bright daylight stings my eyes.

I run to my three-quarter-ton truck.

The dented door groans in complaint as I wrench it open. A lifeless body sits behind the steering wheel. The sun washes over his pale face. I yank him by the sleeve. He falls into my arms.

He's coming for you.

Thundering Bunny lines me up in both eyes. He charges.

I curl into the fetal position. I can't move.

I jolted awake.

Dawn was peeking through the attic opening like a blossoming gray-purple bruise. I rolled from the beanbag chair and accidentally thumped into Michael. "Sorry."

"It's cool." He yawned. "You okay?"

"Yeah, fine," I said. "I just realized what time it was is all. I've got to get going."

"You'll have to use the rope. I'll help." He yawned and stretched, flailing his arms out like a gangling colt taking its first steps. Michael cracked open the top of a warm pop. He sucked a slurping gulp, then offered me a swig.

My face scrunched in revulsion. I shook my head.

"Grab hold. I'll lower you down."

It was actually thrilling. The block and tackle creaked and squeaked. I swung on the frayed rope and slipped slowly to the ground. When I triumphantly jumped from dangling in midair, I did a five-second rendition of the Macarena.

Michael laughed. He tossed my trash sack out. I caught it, waved, then scrambled along the dirt driveway in my stocking feet. I was headed to my first high school rodeo ever. It was a shortened venue, but excitement still coursed through my veins with every beat of my heart. Nothing could bring me down.

I had to pee. I darted into a clump of brush.

Devyn was waiting at the end of the long drive. Shaking his head at my filthy socks, he said, "I won't ask." He handed me a thermos. "Lots o' sugar. Lots, in that. The brew is nasty, but it does the trick." He shoved his balled fists to his hips and posed like Superman. "Look at me. I'm invincible now."

I sniffed the steam streaming into the way-too-early morning air. "I'm game." I swigged gulp after gulp of the strongest coffee known to mankind.

Devyn punched the gas pedal and spun the tires. The rear wheels kicked gravel behind us as we roared onto the roadway.

"What's the plan?" I changed my socks and pulled on the yellow boots from behind the bench seat.

"Hitching a ride with Laney. She's trucking her barrel horse to the event."

"Laney, huh?" *Laney. Woo-hoo!*

C*onfidence. Have confidence. Michael believes I have confidence.* I did have confidence as a bull rider. I could muster confidence with a girl—a hot girl.

I think.

I mean, I know she's hot. I think I could muster confidence.

I grinned. I could do confidence. Like a swashbuckling pirate, I had swung from the rigging of the highest mast at dawn. Like an old west bank robber, I had escaped a rickety jail. Like a WWII French Resistance fighter, I had dodged the enemy's inky shadows in the early hours of light. Now I just needed to win the girl. *Laney.*

As I tossed my gear from the three-quarter-ton truck into

Laney's rig, I blurted, "I hope you're wearing your sunscreen cuz it's about to get hot." I settled in the middle of the bench seat, then licked my thumb, hiked a cheek, and pressed it to my back pocket. "Tss. Hot."

Too corny? It was also totally too cocky. Not my usual style.

A bull rider had to be overconfident to ride. Probably shouldn't be cocky, though. Cocky could get a cowboy killed. There was a thin line between the two. I was walking that line this morning. Odd. But it was happening.

Laney rolled her eyes as she clambered behind the steering wheel. "Donuts?" She shoved a box of Krispy Kremes onto my lap and stuffed the truck into gear. We all munched in silence for the entire ride.

At the rodeo grounds, Devyn jumped from the slow rolling truck. "I'll sign us in." He headed toward the looming arena.

"Alone at last," I said. *'K, that was stupid.* But I beamed a disarming, and hopefully charming, smile at Laney. I wanted her to like me. I mean, *really* like me. I liked her.

I can't believe I said something so dumb. It's just that Laney made me nervous. I'd never talked to a girl before. Like, *a girl, wink wink.*

She looked at me as if I was being a smart-ass. It wasn't the look I was hoping for.

Laney rolled the window down; a breeze tossed the lengths of her raven-black hair. She brushed the strands from her face.

I stared like a schoolboy watching a swimsuit model. *Yup, probably creepy.*

"Look," she said, "I'm not Devyn's girlfriend. I'm not his type."

Good to know. Did I have a chance? Cuz I'm thinking she is sooo my type.

Her shapely brows furrowed toward her petite nose. "He doesn't have a girlfriend. The girls crush all over him, but he's never more than friends. He's had a one-track mind to go to college." Laney pulled through the parking area to a secluded patch and stopped. "Until you."

Her full lips pressured into thin lines. "You've got him all worked up." Her cheeks pinked with anger.

I didn't know why we had to talk about Devyn. Especially if it upset her. I mean…if she *wasn't* his girlfriend.

"You're heartbreaker material." She slammed the shift on the steering column into park. "I don't want you messing with my best friend."

I'm heartbreaker material? Is that good? Does she like me?

"Earth to Chris. Are you listening to me?"

Every dripping word from your gorgeous lips.

"He needs that rodeo scholarship. He needs out of small town USA."

Devyn yanked open the passenger side door. "Could you park any farther from the arena? I practically had to hail a cab."

Devyn unloaded Gold Rush for Laney, then brushed and booted the mare. Laney stuffed her arms into a spangly fringed shirt. I tossed the pad and saddle onto the mare's back. It felt like old times. It felt like home.

The smell of leather and horses. The creak of a saddle. Sunshine warming my face in the crisp morning air. I sucked a breath in through my nose and slowly released it in that blowing-out-a-candle deal. I reached under Gold Rush to bring the cinch into her heart girth.

"I'll do that." Laney gently bumped me out of the way with her hip. "I like to cinch her myself. That way I know she's comfortable." Her nimble fingers went to work. "Thank you for throwing my saddle. You looked like you knew what you were doing."

"I had a horse. My daddy had horses." *I had a horse? Really? Ugh. Everyone has a my-pony-and-me story. Everyone. Ugh. What a dweeb thing to say.*

She beamed a toothy smile, shoved her toe into the stirrup, and vaulted like a gazelle.

"Good luck," I said, resting my palm on her leg.

She pointedly stared at my hand. "I'm not your type. I see how you look at Devyn. He *is* your type, by the way."

You are my type. "Wait. What?" Did she just out Devyn? Was Devyn gay?

Laney rolled her eyes.

The national anthem blared over the loudspeakers to open the rodeo events. Laney and Gold Rush jogged toward the arena.

"Your shirt." Devyn handed me the black shirt and stood waiting.

"What? I'm not going to put it on now. I'll get it dirty."

"Suit yourself." He stripped out of his button-down and donned the blue shirt.

My jaw dropped. Devyn was ripped. Heavy pecs overshadowed six-pack abs. I wished I looked like that.

His open shirt flapped in the slight breeze as he climbed the side of the truck to retrieve his gear.

"Um, you may want to wipe the drool from your chin," he said as he dumped the bags and jumped. His grin couldn't have gotten any wider. He hefted his bag to his shoulder, then walked away. His shirt was still wide open. The tails flapped in the breeze.

When I eventually got behind the chutes, it was business as usual. That didn't stop me from scanning for Luce. She wasn't anywhere around here, of course. I knew she wasn't here. But that didn't keep me from the hope of seeing her clutching at the pen rails to watch with her eyes closed. I missed my monkey girl.

"Who'd you draw?" Devyn asked on his way by.

"Slap Happy."

"Chute three. Better head over." He stopped mid-stride. His complexion was ashen. Every muscle in his face was tense. His jaw was clenched. He spoke through gritted teeth. "The shirt looks good on you. Luck on Happy."

"Slap Happy," I retorted to his back as he walked away. "Good luck to you too," I shouted after him.

Inside the chute, Slap Happy dug his nose to the ground as I set my bull rope. No amount of prodding was getting him to keep his head up. That was a problem. I climbed out to wait.

When I hunkered onto his back to tie on, a chute man was cradling Slap Happy's chin with a rope. It kept his massive head from ducking too low.

But in the one split second at my nod, Slap Happy shoveled his head to the ground. When the gate flung open, one of Slap Happy's stumped horns hung up on the way out.

With his horn caught, his one thousand pounds of bulk rammed into his bent neck. I flailed to stay upright on Slap Happy as his hind end escaped the chute first. When he jumped backwards, his rampage was on.

I stuck with him like a bloated tick on a dog, but that was all I managed to do.

At the buzzer, I let go, landed, and ran.

A bullfighter took a hit meant for me. The three bullfighters then closed their triangle around Slap Happy until he found his way out of the arena.

The re-ride flag was thrown.

Behind the chutes, the doctor lady was immediately at my side. She flashed a light past my eyes and asked if I knew my name.

Of course I knew my name. I attempted to wave her away as I kept walking. I tied my rope on a rail to work at the rosin.

She leaned against the panels and crossed her arms. "Talk to me. Are you sure you're okay? You took a pretty good hit to the cheek."

I lifted my fingertips to the healed scar that would forever mar my face with its white, ragged line. An egg swelled below it. "I'm fine. Have you seen Laney? I didn't get to see her run the barrels."

"You like her, don't you? My sister."

What wasn't there to like? Laney's hot. She's smart. She rides like the wind. A real cowgirl. "Yeah. I guess. I mean, we're friends." *I think. I hope. I want to be more than just friends.*

"Yeah. Friends." The doctor lady pushed off from the panel and slapped the back of my vest as she walked off.

My re-ride, True Grit, leaped into the arena like he was trying out for Olympic pole vaulting. He inverted his back and still managed to swing his muscular hind end. When he landed, he stumbled. True Grit crawled forward on his knees. I hiked my legs up so as not to touch a boot to the ground and disqualify.

That's when True Grit lunged straight in the air from his powerful hindquarters.

With my knees just about at my belt buckle, I slid too far back. True Grit slingshotted me off.

When I came down to earth, I caught his hoof in my side.

The re-ride flag was thrown for his stumbling.

I gimped behind the chutes while clutching at my gut. The protective vest could only do so much damage control.

"Unzip," the doctor lady said. "I'm going to have to take a look at that one."

My vest was constricting me, which meant something was swelling. "No. I'm all right. Just got the wind knocked from me."

"Unzip or you don't ride."

I opened my vest and slid the tails of my shirt from my jeans. I scrunched the shirt only to the bottom edge of my binding. That was high enough. I wouldn't go any higher. Not for anything. Not even to ride. Or I'd never ride again.

The doctor lady prodded. I winced. My binding kept the swelling from creeping higher, but a red and purple bruise leaked through my entire lower side just above my hip.

"Doesn't look like anything's broken. X-rays when you leave here tonight." She rummaged a wide Ace bandage from her emergency kit. "You're used to this." The way she said it didn't seem friendly. "Deep breath. Tighten your stomach." The doctor lady wrapped an Ace below my binding. "X-rays," she repeated. "Zip up." She grabbed her bag and left.

I was tucking in my shirt when I felt someone hovering behind me.

It was a creepy feeling. The hairs on the back of my neck prickled.

When I turned around, I didn't recognize the sheriff. He wasn't in uniform. He wasn't in *his* county. "How's that brat sister of yours?" Sheriff Bubba Taylor sneered.

I tried to leave.

He blocked my way.

So I pushed past Sheriff Bubba Taylor. He followed me.

I tied my bull rope on a panel then searched my gear bag for the wire brush to scrape rosin from my glove.

"What is she? Nine?" He shoved my shoulder. "Look at me when I'm speaking, boy."

I stood toe to toe with him in a staring contest.

The sheriff's eyes were shot through with red. Acrid fumes from his breath nearly singed my eyebrows.

He poked a finger to my chest. "Be a shame to lose her in the system. Be a shame to lose her for good." He thumped me with that finger. "Maybe she gets adopted. It's a big state. Not easy to travel. Maybe you have no rights to ever see her again."

"What do you want?" I asked *Bubba Taylor*.

"I knew you were a smart boy." His prodding finger dropped from my chest. "I'm losing money. But you're gonna help me get it all back. And then some." Stuffing his hands on his hips, he leaned toward me. "You're gonna buck off on this re-ride."

He took several steps to leave, then said, "You are a smart boy. Not a word of this to anyone."

I was spitting mad. I didn't know what I was going to do.

Luce.

I was also exhausted.

My head wasn't in the game.

I didn't need any of this.

My next re-ride was bull number three. *That's just insane.*

My muscles burned. My biceps shook with fatigue. My thighs felt like jelly rubber.

From the look of my third bull, Mountain King, he had been first to the feed trough every day of his life. He was huge. And he was all muscle.

Cowboy up.

No sooner was I tied on than I nodded.

Mountain King came out to the right, then went to the left.

He hammered into my hand, then jerked my side. My legs barely held. I was no more than a flea perched on an elephant. *Do elephants get fleas?*

Mountain King set me back with his next giant leap.

As he moved forward around the corner, I never did get back up front. And when a bull rider gets behind, there's just no chance.

Buck off.

Devyn caught up with me as I fled the arena. He slammed the heels of his hands into my vest. I rocked backwards. "What the hell was that, Chris? You tried to muscle that bull. You lost your timing and balance. You sat down on your pockets. You had no finesse. What the hell?"

"Leave it alone." I walked away. I didn't need him, or his anger.

Devyn swung around me and got back into my face. "No! I won't leave it alone. You were muscling down through your arm." He grabbed on to my vest. "You could have ridden that bull in your sleep."

Who was he to judge? Who was he to tell me how to ride?

"What's it to you? Did you lose a bet or something?" I viciously shrugged from his hold then walked away again.

"High school rodeo? The team? The school needs a win. Ya know, scholarships? Don't be stupid." Devyn shouted at my back.

I didn't care. I had bigger things to worry about. What sense was getting out of this podunk town on a scholarship if I had to abandon my sister?

Devyn continued hollering, "Not to mention sponsors, dumbass. We just barely got a good thing going and you're working hard to screw it up? For what? Too tired to win? Out past your bedtime?"

I spun around then covered the distance between us in four long strides. "What the hell's your problem? I can't win every time. Why don't you win one?" And that wasn't fair. Devyn had only ever tried to help me.

But he couldn't help me with this.

At Laney's truck, I threw my gear into the bed and ripped my sponsors' shirt off. I stuffed my arms into a plain button-down then sat on the running board to unwrap the string ties from the yellow shafts of my boots. I jerked them off and tossed each one up and over my shoulder, into the bed of the truck.

"Um, Chris?"

The voice was small and familiar. *Michael.* I stood. He was held at the back of his neck by that big kid with a scuzz cut. A smiling scowl contorted Scuzz-cut's face.

Out from behind them stepped the Sergeant.

"Chris, lovely boy. No need to scurry from your home in the dead of night." He sniffled and wiped at his filthy nose with a filthier hand. "We're going to ensure you get to all of your competitions. But it's time to come home with us now. You're done for this weekend."

The Sergeant bobbed his head to Scuzz-cut. Scuzz-cut squeezed Michael's thin neck.

Michael winced and started to buckle at the knees as the Sergeant and Scuzz-cut turned to walk off. Michael flopped and staggered in Scuzz-cut's grip as if he were a ventriloquist's dummy.

I followed.

"Let him go," I demanded while trailing behind in stocking feet.

Scuzz-cut spun to face me. "No," he said. "The sheriff doesn't want you hurt—yet. A shame really. Cuz I like hurting little boys. So I'll keep a hold of this one." The tips of his fingers dug into the side of Michael's neck.

Tears pooled in Michael's clenched eyes.

CHAPTER EIGHT

"Why'd you leave the competition last weekend?" Laney shouted at me as she marched over to where I leaned against Devyn's garage opening.

She had avoided me at school all week, and now she wanted to yell at me?

Devyn fussed under the hood of the broken-down three-quarter-ton. On a glance, I saw him wince. "I called her," he said with a look of guilt. "We need a ride."

The truck had gimped its way from the school's parking lot to his house like a wheezing geezer whose heart was giving out. I wasn't mechanically inclined. All I could do was watch Devyn tinker under the hood. Our gear waited at my feet, resigned to going nowhere fast.

"Because you lost the first round, you left?" Laney crossed her arms over her chest and inhaled a deep breath. Her bosom plumped. I snapped my eyes away from ogling.

"Laney, we could use a ride." Devyn tugged a frayed belt from the engine and held it up. But Laney was a dog on a bone.

"That's not how we play as a *team*," she yelled.

I stared at her. I just stared.

I used to think she was beautiful. I used to really like her. I used to want her to like me. But now? I wanted her to leave me alone. I bit onto my tongue. The tension that plagued my face tortured the tender lump beneath my scar.

"Laney?" Devyn rubbed the length of her upper arm. "He's sorry. Let it go. We need a ride."

Devyn sat in the middle. I plastered myself against the passenger side door. The pulled muscles over my ribs screamed as the armrest poked into them with every jounce. It was a relief to see the arena and surrounding carnival rides loom in the near distance.

I jumped out at the main gate to sign us in. Escape from my friends was a blessing today.

I worked my elbow as I walked. My upper arm was tight. Last weekend it felt like its length had been stretched until my knuckles dragged on the ground. Now my arm seemed too short.

I knew injuries were prevalent in the sport, but I hadn't been competing long enough to have had experienced their detriment before this.

I didn't like it. I didn't know how my daddy kept going in his last year. He had suffered one injury after another, and still he rode.

The fairgrounds were alive. The midway was packed like a raucous cattle car hauling bawling feeder calves to market. A Tilt-A-Whirl swung its riders around in sickening circles to their laughing delight. Screams emanated from the highest points on a Ferris wheel. Darts popped balloons. Bells dinged. Hawkers wailed. Lights crackled on poles, awaiting dusk.

The air around the huge arena vibrated with tense excitement, as if the arena itself was holding its breath in anticipation. Fried dough, apple pie, and those gargantuan sausages tantalized my nostrils. My mouth watered.

A little girl in braided pigtails bopped by with a large candied apple—*Luce.*

"Luce!" I pushed through throngs of people to catch up with my kid sister. She was handing change back to the social worker. "Luce?"

"Chris!" She flung herself around my waist and buried her sticky face in the buttons above my buckle.

I grabbed her like my life depended on it. "So good to see you," I whispered as I lifted her into a bear hug.

Sheriff Taylor emerged from behind the social worker like a bad smell.

The social worker wrapped her claws around my sister's arm. "Come on, Lucine, sweetie. Let's go find our seats so we can watch Chris ride."

Luce slid from me. "Hang tough," she said. She let the woman lead her away but remained twisted around in my direction. She waved her candied apple.

"Be dangerous," I said as the crowd swallowed her.

Sheriff Taylor shoved me in the chest with the tips of his fingers. He pushed his face to mine. His breath was sour with stale alcohol. Weeping sores that weren't there a week ago drooled around his neck. He scratched at them. His forehead was riddled with plump zits.

"You know what you have to do," he said. "I'll be in the stands with your sister." He turned, then hustled to catch up with the social worker. When he did, he placed his hand low on her back.

I spun on my heels. And smacked right into Devyn.

I didn't utter an apology. My thoughts were in a furious tangle.

Devyn flipped a hand in Sheriff Taylor's direction. "What was that about?"

"Nothing. It was nothing. They brought my kid sister to watch me ride."

"Cute couple." He tugged his hat lower over his eyes. "So that was your baby sister?" Devyn chucked me on the upper arm and said, "Hang tough."

In a knee-jerk reaction I replied, "Be dangerous."

"I like it." He swung his arm around my shoulders and marched me into the back of the arena.

I bucked off. I could have held on. My feet were set east and west on a southbound bull. The bull was just swapping ends. I could have rode him all night long. But for Luce.

I scanned the crowd. There was no way to discern one face from another. I thought Luce's familiar freckles would stand out like a beacon. I looked for her pigtails and that bright candied apple. I wanted to tell her I could've rode that bull. I wanted her to know that I only did what I did for her.

I didn't find my kid sister. So I went in search of Devyn. Laney was right. We were all part of a team.

Red, *the voice of the rodeo*, sidled up to me, a steaming cup of coffee in his hands. "Son," he said with a drawl, "you probably want to take a hard look at which family you need to be loyal to." He bounced his cup in a salute and exchanged his furrowed brow for a kindly smile. With a slurping sip of his hot coffee, he moved off.

Cowboys dropped from bulls like sprayed flies. The audience alternated between gasping and cheering.

Devyn stood on the platform. He waited to lower himself into the chute. I grabbed his boot shaft from below the staging and offered encouragement. When he looked down at me, his face was as white as a sheet. I thought I felt his leg tremble.

"Who ya got?" I held on to his leg with a hope to steady him. Was it excitement? The thrill of the ride? I didn't want to imagine fear. Not Devyn.

"Tumbleweed." He spit the answer through gritted teeth. The little muscles flexed alongside his clenched jaw like he was grinding his molars.

"He's a pussycat. You've got this."

Devyn smiled a tight-jawed grin and said, "Hang tough. Right?"

I nodded and slapped his boot shaft. "Be dangerous."

Tumbleweed came out hard and fast. After a huge leap, he turned away from Devyn's hand. That caused trouble.

Devyn got off balance. But luck made Tumbleweed throw Devyn back to the middle. He got up over Tumbleweed again. As the hairy carnival ride tossed and turned, Devyn hung on for eight.

The buzzer sounded. Devyn yanked the tail of his rope.

"Woo-hoo!" I waved my hat around like it was me who had ridden. "Woo-hoo!"

Devyn climbed over the panels and fell against me. "Seventy-six! I'll take it. Seventy-six!" He squeezed me in his muscled arms and lifted me off my feet. My spine crackled. If I ever needed chiropractic work, I knew who to see.

When it was over, back-slapping and beer-cracking followed our escape from the arena. Devyn was well-known and well liked. He'd ridden bulls since he could walk. Maybe even before. Rumor had it that he was trained to be a champion from the crib. And the local enthusiasts were elated to see him win the round.

I was happy to see him win the round too.

Back at the garage, Laney helped me pour a very drunk Devyn over the bench seat. "Good luck with that," she said. "He hasn't had a win in a while. Let him enjoy it. But make sure he's ready to go in the morning." She jumped into her truck and ambled down the driveway.

I tugged on Devyn's boots to extricate his stocking feet as he languished over the bench seat. "A little help here? Like wiggle your foot or something."

"You're a pretty boy, ya know?" He twisted his ankle from each boot.

"Hey, now," I said, "I was going for ruggedly handsome." I dropped his boots to the floor at the end of the bench then sat down beside him.

"I mean, you're not as good-looking as me, of course," Devyn said.

"Of course," I repeated.

"I've got all the girls chasing me." He swigged the last of his beer and crushed the can in a fist. "But I don't want all of the girls." Devyn made a three-point toss into the trash barrel. "I want a pretty boy."

My mind was instantly on fire. A flurry of emotions rocketed through me. My thoughts were jumbled. I'm not sure what he read on my face. Shock? Fear?

"No, I mean it in a good way." His words were garbled.

I squirmed in discomfort, then went stiff. A forty-watt bulb overhead struggled to light a hundred-watt space. Dark shadows resided around the myriad of training equipment. I wished I could slink into one of them.

Devyn's eyes grew hazy. He could have been drifting in that dreamy stage of half-sleep. "You look like an elf. A fantasy, fairy elf. Your rides are magical. The way you thrust into the center of those bulls with each hop."

"Okay, man," I said. "I think you should get some sleep."

He smoothed my cheek with his palm then let it slide to lay flat in the middle of my chest. His eyes stared into mine. For those seconds, he didn't seem all that drunk. I harrumphed and tried to move away. His palm fell to my thigh.

"Chris? We could do this together. You and me."

"We are doing it together."

"I mean professionally. We could chase the rodeos together. Leave this town."

"I can't ever be a professional bull rider," I said.

"Why not? If it's cuz you think you're not good enough. You are."

I remained silent. I picked at the callouses on my palms for something to do and somewhere to look. I couldn't look at Devyn.

"Why not, Chris? We could go on the road together. You and me. A lot of young guys do it at our age."

"I'm…" *I'm physically female.* "I'm going to college. And I have my kid sister."

"What if you didn't? What if you didn't go to college? You could bring your kid sister."

How do I explain myself? I couldn't. I shouldn't. Not one word. I scrutinized my fussing hands. "I need to go to college. You need to go to college."

Devyn's face slackened. There was a sadness in his eyes that ran too deeply to be altered by his one win tonight. It seemed he was hoping for something epic in life.

"It's taking too long to get out of podunkville," he said.

"We're seniors. Besides, I just got here. Our time will fly. You'll see."

"You're a beautiful boy. You make me feel like I could conquer the world if you were by my side. Or at least conquer my demons." Devyn reached to gently take my face in his hands. Some part of me reasoned that it was a guy thing. A normal buddy buddy deal.

Some part of me knew exactly what he was doing.

Some part inside of me screamed to pull away.

Not a hair on me actually moved.

Most of me wanted this.

I wanted his lips on mine. I had never felt the touch of another person's mouth pressed to my own. I was hungry for my first kiss. Even if it was with Devyn.

Even if it wasn't fair to Devyn. And it wasn't fair. I liked Devyn, but not *like* liked him.

His thumb smoothed over my closed mouth. The pad of it was too gentle, too slow, too soft, too caressing.

I squeezed my eyes shut. Nothing else mattered. I wanted to feel his kiss. He was handsome and kind and sensitive. Why not let him give me my first kiss?

Devyn's breath tickled my cheek just before his lips met mine. I leaned onto them. I couldn't stop myself. The sensation was... pleasant.

I withdrew. There were no fireworks. His kiss lacked those fabled fireworks that were supposed to explode in my head. I wanted the fireworks.

I sat back from him. "You don't really know me. You wouldn't kiss me if you knew who I was."

"I'd kiss you if you told me you were a troll who lived under a bridge."

"I'm a female." The words came out in a rush. They sounded like one single, solitary, garbled word. *Imafemale.*

After a split second of disbelief, resolute disappointment washed over Devyn's face. His shoulders rounded. He slouched into the bench seat. Something in his expression told me he had known already, but he hadn't wanted to know.

He had to have known. Hadn't he?

I watched his Adam's apple bob as if he had just swallowed too big a lump.

And I hated myself. I had hurt the only guy who truly cared about me. *But is it me he cares about? Or only that me he wants to see?* And that wasn't fair, because I'd been the one portraying a lie. "I'm a boy. My mind is a boy's. My body doesn't match who I want to be, who I truly am." He should understand. I prayed he'd understand.

I shook my head, disagreeing with my next statement, even before it slipped from my lips. "I was born a girl."

Devyn sank deeper into the bench seat. His hands fell to his lap. "Yeah, okay." He swiped across his mouth and nose with the back of his hand. I thought I heard him sniffle.

"Devyn?"

"Yeah. No worries. I'll take your secret to my grave."

"I'm sorry. I never meant—" Loud snoring interrupted my sentence. I thought his snoring was a little over-the-top, but at some point, as I sat next to him, it became real.

I shucked my yellow boots...his yellow boots and stuck them under the bench. I plucked the black felted Stetson from my head then brushed the dust off its brim. Then I liberated the turkey feather from the band. "I really am sorry," I whispered. I flipped the hat upside down and left it next to the yellow boots.

I'd messed everything up. I rolled the socks from my feet and stood, then padded to the panel where my battered straw hat perched. *A turkey feather always looks good on straw. It always looked good on Daddy's straw. Where is he when I need him desperately?*

I pushed the feather under the band. With a last look at Devyn, I left.

At the end of the driveway, where the dirt met the asphalt interstate, I balled the socks and shoved them into the front of my jeans. It looked right. It felt right.

But it's all wrong.

The full moon lit the dead of night like a cloudy day, making visibility possible. I stared at the bulge in my jeans. I'd only recently figured it all out. Why I took up being a boy. Why it came so easily to me.

I'm a freak.

If only Daddy hadn't left me to fend for myself. To fend for them.

How do you think I can take care of them? I can't even take care of me.

Growing up, I had always known who I was supposed to be, for him. His oldest daughter. Honor student at the Autry Academy. Bound for college as a business major. He loved me. I would have kept living *his* expectations. We were a family.

This was all his fault. He shouldn't have left.

I didn't mean it. I didn't mean to be Chris.

It's who I am inside. It's who I've always been. It's who I have to be. It's me.

And if Daddy were alive, I'd never have been me—a freak.

He left me. This is his fault.

"I don't want to be all messed up inside," I shouted to the heavens. "This is your fault. You left me." I felt the stinging trails of hot tears on my cheeks. I wiped them away with my shirtsleeve. I had once said I'd never cry again. I sucked back a sob. I wouldn't cry. Crying was for girls.

An oncoming vehicle's lights shined in my eyes. I stepped from the road to let the truck pass. It pulled over instead.

Laney leaned across the seat, then pushed the passenger side door open. "Where are you going? It's like, two in the morning."

I didn't know. I tucked my chin to my chest and looked at my cold toes. Life was blowing up in my face. Did it matter where I went at this point?

"Hop in. At least it'll get the chill off you."

Silence stretched for far too long.

Finally, Laney asked, "Are you going to tell me what happened?"

My daddy died. Now I'm Chris—the man of the family. And I like it. It's who I am. And it's all wrong. Daddy died. I couldn't keep my stepmama from the drugs. I couldn't keep my sister from strangers' arms.

Life isn't going well lately.

"I really like you," I said to Laney. I didn't expect her to say anything in return. Maybe I expected her to pull over and toss me back onto the interstate.

Laney swung through the gates at the rodeo grounds without commenting on what I'd said. "There she is," she shouted. "Who's she with?"

I recognized his silhouette as Laney pulled to a stop in the parking lot.

Sheriff Taylor and I made eye contact. If it was pleasant, it would have been "a moment." It wasn't. I wanted to kill him.

That realization socked me in the gut. *I want to kill him.* I sneered at Sheriff Bubba Taylor. *I want to kill him.* It felt good—No, it felt powerful to imagine hurting him.

"Have you been drinking?" Laney blurted at her sister.

"What of it? I'm old enough."

"Our mother is worried about you." Laney chastised her sister in a haughty manner. "You didn't come home. You didn't let anyone know where you were." Her voice grew cold and distant. The disapproving edge to it was disturbing.

"I'm a big girl. I don't need a babysitter. Besides, everyone knew I was working the rodeo. I *always* work *every* rodeo." I swear the doctor lady's words were slightly slurred.

The sheriff kissed her on the cheek, then whispered something in her ear that made her giggle. He walked off.

"You're part of a family. You have responsibilities. Get in. I'm taking you home."

I was crammed between the two of them. The cab was warm. The atmosphere was tense and uncomfortable. The doctor lady's head lolled along the glass of the passenger side window as Laney drove. I thought she might have fallen asleep.

Laney reached into my lap and took my hand. Her grip was warm, and soft, and strong.

At Laney's house, her sister quickly climbed from the truck and slammed the door.

We sat in the dark inside the truck's cab. Just Laney and me. Neither one of us spoke. I didn't want to move because Laney held tight to my hand. It felt good. I felt incredible. I didn't need a Tilt-A-Whirl or Ferris wheel to flip my stomach into my throat with a thrill. Her touch did that and more.

The doctor lady yanked open the driver's side door, then jerked Laney from me. "I called Sheriff Taylor to pick you up." She jammed the door closed so I couldn't come out after them. "I was willing to play along with your little sham. It was interesting to watch how far a girl could get riding bulls against the men. But you've gone too far. I won't have any misguided lesbian infecting my sister with perverse filth."

Laney looked from me to her sister and back at me. Her face was full of shock and horror, disgust and accusation. She clasped her hands over her mouth and ran to the house without saying a word. The screen door squealed as she ripped it open.

"Laney!" I yelled.

The door smacked closed behind her.

The doctor lady climbed the porch steps in Laney's wake. She stood with her feet apart and arms folded across her chest. She eyed me as vigilantly as a guard dog.

The sheriff wailed up in his squad car. Blue lights spun. Gravel spit from the tires as the vehicle skidded to a stop.

CHAPTER NINE

Too early in the morning, my cell door blasted open. Scuzz-cut shoved Michael in like a mutt tossing a rag doll.

I leaped from the bed and lunged around Michael to stand nose to nose with the biggest, ugliest kid ever born.

"The name's Skull." His pocked face had broken out in a layer of angry, weeping acne. "I'm supposed to stick real close to you." He withdrew a toothpick from his teeth to point it at my nose. "You don't shit without me knowing how, when, and where."

I ground my teeth on purpose to make the muscles on the sides of my face bulge. I hoped my jaw looked square and rugged. "I'll call you Scuzz-cut."

Mullet-head snickered from behind Scuzz-cut. His Aqua Net hairdo jounced in one solid mass as his shoulders twitched and twittered. When I stared him in the eyes, he looked to Scuzz-cut.

"Try it," Scuzz-cut said. A canker on his bottom lip cracked and bled. "Just try it." His tongue darted out like a lizard's. He licked at the blood on his lip. Sores at his buzzed hairline drooled over his temples. Pustules wept on his forehead. He grinned, showing gray, translucent teeth.

"Don't taunt him, Chris," Michael whispered from behind me. I heard the feeble springs of my cot complain.

Scuzz-cut stuck the toothpick back between his teeth. He lowered a finger pistol at me and pinched his thumb hammer down. With a wink, he left.

I peered into the hall in their wake and asked Michael, "What's with those sores?"

"Meth," Michael said. He drew a tortured breath that audibly sucked air through clenched teeth. "Hallucinations while tweaking make them scratch their skin off." The springs squeaked again. "Crank bugs," he mumbled. "Meth mites. The sores get infected."

I pushed my door mostly closed, then turned. "Oh my God. What happened?" Michael's favorite T-shirt was torn. The gap exposed an angry red ring around his neck.

He rested his chin on his chest as he slumped forward. His shoulders rounded toward his knees. Bruises ran the length of his arms. Welts blossomed on his lower legs.

"Did he do this to you? Scuzz-cut?" I was horrified. I was angry. "Did he do this?" This was my fault.

I gently shoved Michael upright. A blackened eye was swollen shut. He lowered his head and wouldn't look at me.

"I'm supposed to tell you this will continue in direct consequence to any disobeying Sheriff Taylor." He peered up at me with his one good eye. "He's making money on you, Chris." The corners of his mouth were cracked. His lips were enlarged. "Money to buy more drugs. Put more people in his pocket. Like he's done before to others."

Michael curled into the fetal position on my cot. He wrapped himself around my thin pillow and closed his good eye.

The breakfast triangle clanged. I sat at the foot of the bed and ignored its summons.

As I rested my hand on Michael's bare ankle, I listened to the County Boys' Home's inhabitants grinding through their morning routine. Two hours, and the cacophony finally died as everyone shuffled from the building to the bus.

No one looked for me.

Skipping school would be the easy part. Skipping practice?

I hadn't wanted to let my friends down. If they were still my friends. I'd given them too many reasons to be angry with me lately.

What did it matter? I mean, it had. They had mattered. Aw heck, there was no real money in high school rodeo anyway. I needed big winnings that bull riding professionally could offer. I needed the money for Luce.

Devyn might be right. I'd have to chase the rodeos.

Was I man enough for that next step?

The idea of going to college was slipping away.

That steady job at the grain store in town looked better and better. Could it provide for both me and Luce? I'd have to give up my hopes of leaving this small-town-nowhere-ville. I'd have to give up my dreams of a college education bettering my lot in life. But that's why they're dreams. Dreams are often unattainable. Dreams are something you let go of, for the greater needs of those you loved.

Michael snored quietly. I covered his cold feet with the end of the blanket, then stepped into the hallway. My working Wellingtons slouched against the wall. I jerked my boots on and abandoned the County Boys' Home to hike into town.

My truck was parked outside the grain store. A new license plate stood out on the dented bumper like a lighthouse in a tempest. The doors were locked. The cab had been cleaned.

I peered through the windowed front of the store. Devyn perched on a stool inside. He was hunched over a wooden barrel that held a checkerboard tabletop.

As I entered, a bell ding-a-linged overhead. Devyn didn't look up.

I peered over his shoulder. My eyes widened.

"No," I barked.

Devyn was filling out a job application. I snatched it from him. "Hell no," I said.

He spun around and stood. The abandoned stool clattered over. His eyes were bloodshot. Stubble peppered his jaw. His usually manicured hair was unusually disheveled. And he still wore the same jeans he'd rodeo-ed in over the weekend.

"Oh, hell no." I held the paper from him as he grabbed for it. "You're not doing this."

"Who the hell are you to tell me what I can and can't do."

"Someone's got to. And I'm the one standing here." I ripped the page in half.

He took a swing at me.

I ducked.

The bell above the door complained as the owner of the store shoved us both to the curb.

"You're going to college," I shouted at him.

"I am not. I'm never getting to college." Spittle sprayed from his lips. His eyes were large and furious and wild. "I need a full scholarship for college. And I'm never going to get that." He wiped his mouth on the forearm of a clean button-down shirt. "I'm not good enough. When I win, it's *his* doing."

"What are you talking about?"

"You're the one with the real talent." He looked away. He looked thoroughly defeated. His shoulders slumped forward. "And how many times did he make you buck off?"

My mouth dropped open. "You don't understand."

"Over the weekend. Did I win because the Great Chris let go?"

"You don't understand," I said again, this time in a raspy whisper.

"I do. Don't you see? I was you." Devyn punched the side of the truck. A sickening crunch followed. "I was you. All I ever wanted was to quit riding bulls. I'm scared to death every time I get on. I don't want to be this scared in life. I shouldn't have to live like this."

"Why do it?" I asked.

"At first, because I was a pawn in Sheriff Taylor's twisted games. Then somewhere along the way, I realized it was the only means of leaving this town." Devyn cradled his injured hand. "Your daddy made it. Big time." His wild eyes calmed with the thought of hope. "Since him, every kid around here who's wanted more out of life has looked to the rodeo." He drew a long breath in. It puffed his chest.

"The sheriff did me a favor." Devyn shrugged. "He didn't mean to. But he made me look like a winner. For a time." The skin over his knuckles was turning bright colors. "Being a winner could have saved me." A tear rolled from the corner of his eye.

"There's only one way out of this town. Bull riding." Devyn held out his arms with his palms up. "I mean, look around you. This town? High school? Even my garage? It's all about bull riding. Even my absentee father—"

Devyn's shoulders slouched. "At least my father stopped sending me more bull riding equipment this past year. Maybe he knows I'll never make it. Maybe he doesn't want to waste any more money on a son who can't live up to his high and mighty expectations." He hugged his injured hand to his chest. His butt hit the side of the truck as he leaned against it for support.

"And what's with that? I've never heard of any famous bull rider named Langdon. So I'm not following in my father's boots. He doesn't have any. I'm shit sure he doesn't have to risk his life riding bulls. He's got to be far away from podunkville because he's never stopped by to visit. I'm sure he has a new family. Probably a new kid. Or two." He sniffled back a sob.

Devyn stood from leaning against the truck. His face flushed as anger surged through him again. "I have bull riding." He shook his head. The motion swung down to his toes. It forced him to plant his feet wider apart. "Or do I?" Spittle drooled from his bottom lip. He squinted his eyes to slits and thrust his square jaw forward. "Sheriff Taylor can make you or break you. One is just as crippling as the other. I've been there. You don't think I know what's going on?" Devyn's knuckles were blooming into a single bluish-purple bruise. His fingers started to swell.

I plucked the hanging key chain from his pocket and opened the truck door. When I grabbed a fistful of his shirt and shoved him into the truck, I had hoped to have tormented a few of his blond chest hairs. It'd serve him right. "Move over, I'm driving."

The entire week hopped at a snail's pace. I divided my attention between Devyn by day and Michael through the nights.

I ducked from Laney every second. If I stayed out of her sight, I'd stay off her mind. And Luce? I knew Sheriff Taylor wouldn't trot her freckled face in front of me until he wanted me to dance like a marionette. She was safe in her foster home, for now.

Friday after school, I climbed into the three-quarter-ton. It was no high school rodeo for me this weekend. I'd chase the big money.

Devyn was more than willing to come along. We hadn't talked. Not about that night. Not about the kiss. I don't think guys talked things out. Girls chatted, gossiped, and hounded subjects into submission. Guys? A slug on the arm and we were off and running again.

Yeah, I didn't know where Devyn and I stood. I did know he was being overly good. Overly perfect. Not just toward me.

Devyn had presented Laney with a white carnation. He was teacher's pet in every class. And every day, he worked in the school's main office, filing papers during his study period.

A freshman was bullied in the hall? Devyn stuck up for him.

Rodeo practice? He coached younger bull riders. And Devyn talked endlessly of what he'd cook his mom for dinner before she doggedly did her shift at the Honky Tonk each night.

His homework was always done. He aced every test. He did everything but help little old ladies to cross the street. That was only because there weren't any little old ladies crossing the street.

Friday, after school, we climbed into the immaculate truck for a two-hour drive.

"You left your boots and hat under the bench in my garage last weekend." Devyn pointed to the yellow-shafted boots standing guard in the passenger side foot well. "You'll be wanting those."

I wrestled my working Wellingtons from my feet to pull on the bull riding boots. "Thanks, man." I didn't deserve his generosity. I didn't deserve his friendship.

Guilt niggled my mind. I felt horrible. I wished he'd yell at me some more. I wished he had socked me in the mouth. Maybe I wished he hated me. Anything but his gush of niceness.

Devyn knocked the black felted hat from the dash. "Go ahead, man. It's yours. I gave it to you. It wasn't a loan."

I plucked the feather from my straw and pushed it into place on the black felt. I didn't know what to say.

We drove in silence.

When we arrived, it was a rush through the gate, and a hustle into the arena. I worked the rosin on my rope, then made my ride. Devyn made his. I expected he'd hole up with his beer-drinking buddies the rest of the night, so I gave him space.

I went in search of Laney. Well, not exactly in search of her. I wanted to know that she got Gold Rush here okay. Devyn said she too was competing this weekend. I wanted to know she was all right. I wanted to see her. Even if it was only a glance from a distance.

At the end of one of the long, competitors' horse barns, Laney was grooming Gold Rush in the aisle. I slouched against a stall wall close by, thinking to be noticed, and at the same time, hoping she wouldn't see me.

"You're deceiving everyone," Laney said. She didn't look up from her work.

"I'm not deceiving anyone. This is me." I rolled from leaning on one shoulder to flattening my back against the wall. "I can ride any bull that's run into the chutes." I stuffed my hands into my front pockets. "That's no deception. This is me, Laney."

"Did you simply wake up one day and decide to be Chris?"

"There was nothing simple about it." *Daddy died. I scrounged to feed Luce. Riding bulls is all I have. And it's dangerous. Not simple.*

I sighed on purpose to disturb the tense silence Laney left me to hang in. *My stepmama is a deadbeat. She's now in a coma. My kid sister was taken from me. And I'm in the County Boys' Home.* I bit my tongue between my molars.

There's nothing simple about any of it.

"I am Chris. This is me. I've always known. Somewhere deep inside, I've always known. But I didn't really get to be me until I stopped trying to be everything for everyone else." *It wasn't until Daddy was gone and I had no one's expectations to live up to. Survival dictates I play to my strengths regardless. But I am Chris.*

"This is who I am. I am Chris."

The stretch of silence ran on and on until my nerves frayed. I stood to leave. I shoved my hands deeper into my pockets and walked past her. She hadn't even looked at me. I doubted she ever would again.

At the doors, I paused. "You can never let anyone know. Please, Laney." Asking her to keep my secret was a long shot. I'd hurt her. I had no right to ask for any favors. *Yeah. And didn't she out Devyn to me? Her keeping my secret is a long shot at best.*

"Folks will find out," she said behind me. "It's a small town. Too many people already know."

I didn't look at her. I didn't turn. "But not from you. They don't need to hear it from you. Not now. I need time. I need money. For my kid sister." I kept my back to her. I let my head fall forward in defeat. "Then I'll leave. I'll leave and never come back. You'll never have to see me again."

Outside the barn, under a struggling flood light, I fell against the wall and slid down until my back pockets planted in the dirt. I scrubbed at my face with calloused hands. I wouldn't cry.

My eyes stung. My face burned. But I wouldn't cry.

It took me a minute to realize who sniffled. It wasn't me.

"I like Chris," Laney said from the aisle of the barn. "Oh, Rush. Even knowing, I'm still attracted to him."

A brush thwacked into a bucket. The grooming tote rattled. Laney sniffled again. "Does it matter?" Gold Rush's halter jingled with the shake of her head.

"Would I still feel this way about him if it did?"

The soft clip-clop of Gold Rush's hooves told me of Laney's departure.

"I'm sure Sheriff Taylor would be interested in your little secret."

I sprung to my feet like a jackrabbit caught in the sights of a jackal.

The doctor lady's length of raven-black hair lifted from her shoulders on the slight, autumn breeze. "I'm also sure you don't want him finding out." She tugged at the brim of a white Stetson.

"So here's what you're going to do for me. I don't want you near Laney. You're going to stay far, far away from my sister. If I catch you near her, see you near her, or even hear you've been near her, the sheriff and everyone else in this town will know all about your ruse." She stuffed her hands into the pockets of her Carhartt chore coat. "Understand?"

I understood. I glared and said nothing.

When I wasn't bullback through the rodeo weekend, I made myself scarce. I walked the midway. Gawked at the carnival rides. Ate too much fried dough and way too many Italian sausages. I won a basketball in a game of chance. Then practiced my balance during the long hours by standing on it. Mostly, though, I curled up in the cab of the truck and slept.

Nights were cold. Days were hot. And none of it mattered. I was riding for the money. That's all that mattered.

Sunday night rolled around with the fanfare and hoopla of the rodeo's finale. The stadium seats were packed in anticipation of the bull riding event. Twenty-six riders had gotten through. Devyn and I were among them. I was ranked second going in. Devyn was fifth.

In the pens, Thundering Bunny stood stock-still. He was as cool as a cucumber—like he was in a deep freeze and had no pulse.

His beady eyes were the only things that moved. He trained on even the slightest motion around him and watched it with a detached, lofty stare. He looked like he was calculating physics in his head. He was that serious.

"Hey, Thunder." I was glad to see him. I had a soft spot for Thundering Bunny. He was always a good listener.

Thundering Bunny hadn't gone to work yet this weekend. The stock contractor was, most likely, keeping him fresh for the finale. That's what I'd have done.

Thundering Bunny had become a big commodity. With his signature moves and an outrageous learning curve, he had his own fan club.

No one had ridden the small, short-backed bull to the buzzer since I had. Fact was, I was the only one to make the eight on him. Gossip said that my ride had been a fluke. It was a qualified ride, but folks said it would never happen again. And definitely not by me.

The bull was talented. Word had it that he was becoming unpredictable with his never-ending bag of tricks. *That* was said as if it were a bad thing. *Isn't bull riding supposed to be unpredictable?*

"Chris."

I hardly recognized Sheriff Taylor. He had lost a lot of weight in one week. Black rings shadowed his eyes. The zits on his forehead had opened wide. He looked gaunt and hungry.

Sheriff Taylor brushed the dust from my vest. To any onlookers, Sheriff Bubba Taylor seemed like a doting well-wisher. "You're gonna buck off. I'm betting on you. More specifically, I'm betting against you. Buck off."

If I bucked off tonight, I'd be out of the big money. *Why am I even here? Why bother to show up? I risk my life every ride. For what? For whom?*

Squinting my eyes into slits, I glared at the sheriff until he walked off.

"Your biggest fan?" Michael pointed to the retreating back of Sheriff Taylor. His face was tense with hate and pain.

"What are you doing here?" I wrapped my arms around him in a quick guy's hug, slapping his back twice.

Michael brightened into a big smile. "I brought you socks.

They let me in cuz these aren't just any socks. These are your lucky socks." He winked. "Can't possibly spur a bull without your lucky socks."

I'm sure my face betrayed my confusion because Michael broke out in laughter.

He tossed the balled socks onto my gear bag. "I'm betting on you to win this weekend, Chris." Michael stuffed his hands in the pouch pocket of an Air Force hoodie, through which he clung to the waistband of a baggy pair of jeans that were threatening to slide down. "I'm not just saying that. I've bet *a lot* of money on you."

"What are you talking about? How did you get here?"

He raised his thumb in the air. "The global way of travel." Michael cracked an enormous smile.

That's when I noticed his face. Makeup expertly concealed most of the grotesque coloring. With makeup, Michael's flat cheekbones were angular. His pale cheeks had a blush. His thin lips were lusciously lined and moist. And his normally washed-out eyes popped.

Previous bruises had covered his cheeks in sickening browns and greens. His eyes had been ringed in a deep purple, almost black. And where there wasn't coloring from abuse, his skin was pasty pale. But all of that was hidden now.

"You look fantastic," I said.

"You like?" He framed his face with his hands and cocked his head to the side. Long eyelashes fluttered like doves dipping on a wind, graceful and beautiful.

"I really do. Good for you." I rubbed his upper arm. Something I had seen Devyn do to calm and support Laney.

"Aw. Thank you. Now, don't disappoint me. Get out there and win this hoedown." With a flair I hadn't seen before, Michael marched toward the stadium stairs.

Win? Michael knew what would happen to him if I won.

Anger crawled into me. I was angry that my family and friends had been held hostage, ensuring my cooperative behavior. I was angry about being manipulated and used. *Win?*

If I made the buzzer and scored seventy-six or better, winning was possible. *I could do it. Should I do it?*

The crowd was on their feet when Thundering Bunny was

loaded into a chute. I was on my feet—on my tiptoes to be exact. A bull rider hovered over him. I didn't recognize the guy. The crowd stomped and cheered. I gripped a panel rail just like Luce had each time she watched me ride. Onlookers forgot about the performance happening in the arena in anticipation of what was about to happen.

At every rodeo, I'd ignored the crowd's excitement. But I wasn't the one riding. And their fervor shook the stadium to its foundation tonight. That one last rider ahead of me was up against Thundering Bunny.

When the gate latch squealed, Thundering Bunny went three feet in the air, barely clearing the chute. The game was on.

In a split second of hang time, Thundering Bunny arranged his muscular body for his big, signature move. When he came down to earth, he landed on all four hooves simultaneously. With his stocky legs straight and tight, Thundering Bunny pile-drove into the dirt. The move sent a spine grinding shock through his rider. And it was over. A backwards jump let Thundering Bunny slip from under the bull rider's shaken grip.

The bull rider went down.

The crowd went crazy. Their exhilaration ripped through me. Adrenaline rocked my world.

When I tied onto Two Steppin, I knew I'd take him to the buzzer.

The gate hauled open. Two Steppin lunged.

Around to the right. Back to the left. Two Steppin couldn't decide which way he wanted to go.

The bull was trying to find his game. As he went up and down, I rode from leap to leap. He came out of my hand for an instant as he whirled in the other direction. I clambered back to Two Steppin's sweet spot, then stayed right in the middle, tracking him in front of the bucking chutes.

I waved to the crowd in perfect form. *Not really. Not the wave anyway.* But I felt perfect.

I was on fire.

The buzzer sounded. I took a few more hops with Two Steppin before I plucked the tail of my rope and stuck the landing.

The crowd was on their feet. I punched the air, then danced in a circle.

A standing ovation stomped the aluminum bleachers to a thunderous beat. Smoke guns shot into the air. Sirens wailed. The rock song over the loudspeakers was drowned out by applause. Lights lowered. Strobes panned.

I'd won.

CHAPTER TEN

"What do you do with your winnings?" Devyn asked.

I listened for any inflection in his voice that'd warn me if he was upset. I thought we were okay from last week, but then there was last night. He had been upset again.

Upset about what? Maybe because he came in second over the weekend? Maybe because I had torn up his job application and he stoved in his knuckles over it. I knew his knuckles were causing some pain. But maybe he was mad because I wasn't the guy he thought he'd crushed on? I shrugged to put an end to my endless guessing. Devyn was just moody lately.

And I was worried *I'd* have PMS. Ha.

After the last bell rang, we met at the truck in the school parking lot to grab our gear for practice. As he unlocked the doors, I stole a glance at him for any clues as to which Devyn I was dealing with.

His face had softened.

I pried the wad of winnings from my pocket, plucked several bills off, then stashed the wad in a flap I had made at the back of the bench seat on the passenger side.

Devyn hadn't spoken a word to me all day until now. And at this point, I didn't feel like answering his inquisition. I could tell he was still filled with anger. The muscles on each side of his jaw ticked. And he was squinting that squint. Like he was accusing me of something.

That was one thing about Devyn. He always wore his emotions on his sleeve. No poker face. Hope he never took up a gambling habit. *Cha-ching.*

At one point, on the truck ride home last night, he was so pissed, I thought he'd pull over to strangle me as I pretended to sleep. Then, when we got back to town, Devyn uncharacteristically dumped me at the County Boys' Home. I had tumbled from the truck in shock. Which reminded me.

"You seen my sack?" I asked as I climbed onto the truck's wheel to search over the bed's sidewall. "I left it back here."

We used to bunk in his garage too late on Sunday nights. Devyn and me.

He'd drink himself into a stupor, and I'd wander among the bull riding equipment feeling some strange nostalgic connection to his collection. I'd finally wrap up in a sleeping bag and collapse among the strewn mattresses under the practice barrel. When dawn came, we'd struggle to get to school.

Just as well he dropped me at the County Boys' Home. Sheriff Taylor had been fuming last night also. I didn't want Devyn involved.

I'm glad Luce wasn't there.

I probably wouldn't get to see her too soon since I went against the sheriff. But once I got her out of foster care, no one would keep us apart. Family sticks together.

Sheriff Taylor didn't express his fury at the rodeo grounds because the doctor lady was on his arm. They'd been seeing of lot of each other lately. I figured he was due to come looking for me when he was done with his date.

Luckily, he never showed.

Michael was the only one who had found the happy in the entire messed-up situation. He hooted enthusiastically from the stands and hollered to beat the band. He was so ecstatic by my win that he could have wet himself. He had wiggled around and waved while running at me after my win. His spindly arms had clutched me in a hug.

There will be consequences. The threat resounded in my head.

I hadn't seen Michael before school this morning.

Devyn and I walked most of the way to the school's practice arena in silence. Finally, he said, "Your stuff's at my house. My mother said she'd wash it."

Shoot.

He stopped short. "Hey, I saw Sheriff Taylor acting real friendly to you last night."

Before I could explain, Laney leaped onto the scene. She draped over Devyn's shoulders, intending to walk with us. Laney smiled in a conspiratorial way then said to me, "Thank you for the carnation. Devyn said it was from you."

My mouth gawped. Luckily, it was too cold for flies or I'd have been catching a lot them. I looked to Devyn. He continued stomping forward. I eventually stammered, "Yeah, well, you're welcome and all."

The three of us walked in silence the rest of the way. We only split up behind the chutes. Devyn mumbled something about coaching the junior varsity riders. Of which there was no such thing. All of us rode or we didn't.

Devyn followed Laney to where she climbed onto one of the platforms.

Brr. I closed the top button of my shirt against Devyn's chill, then fished out my rope, glove, and rosin.

"There you are, Chris." The vice principal walked over with Scuzz-cut at his side. "Sheriff Taylor thought it would help the boy's rehabilitation if he participated in a sport." He beamed a smile at Scuzz-cut and patted him on the shoulder. "As a personal favor to the sheriff, I guaranteed he would be coached by his classmates and could follow the team to the competitions."

Yeah, to keep an eye on me. And to make sure I understand his threat.

"Sheriff Taylor sees some promise in him. With the sheriff's background, he ought to be able to discern a champion." He winked. *The high school vice principal winked. True story.*

He continued. "Chris, since you're in a similar situation, why don't you two pair up."

"No, thanks. I'd rather not." I went back to working rosin along my rope.

"Chris?" The vice principal's plastered smile collapsed.

"We're not in a similar situation. We're no more similar than a rat's fart and a summer breeze."

"Now, Chris, I think it would show maturity and responsibility if you mentored your fellow student." He spread his feet apart and settled his weight onto his heels before crossing his arms over his chest. "The sheriff asked for you, specifically. And the sheriff has been a big supporter of this team. He's given equipment and money to nurture the best high school bull riders who compete. As a Taylor, you should understand that."

"Well, I'm not one of *his* Taylors."

Devyn sidled over with three other guys. They took up bored poses in a semicircle between me and the vice principal.

Scuzz-cut played it quiet, calm, *and demure*. He acted like a girl hoping to be invited to a tea party. And he looked like an altar boy headed to church on Sunday. He had worn a pair of starched and ironed Wrangler jeans with a pressed button-down shirt. I don't know where he got the clothes. Gangster grunge or prison orange were his usual styles. And he was cleanshaven.

But his appearance had a shiny, plastic look like a thickset Ken doll that Luce might pose next to her Barbie in the tree house mansion.

Barbie has everything. And everything is perfect in Barbie's world.

I wanted to punch Scuzz-cut in the nose just to watch his facade crack.

Laney jumped down from the chute's platform and walked over.

No one spoke. They just stared.

Mostly, they stared at me. As if I was some evil spawn of Satan.

"He knows nothing about riding bulls," I said to break the tense silence.

The vice principal cleared his throat. He opened and closed his mouth in succession. Finally, he sighed.

Devyn stepped in. "Neither did you once. Neither did I." Devyn turned from me to face Scuzz-cut and the vice principal. "He can learn like we all did. And he has a right to attempt to better himself. He has a right to use bull riding to set his sights on getting out of this town. Maybe go to college."

"He's not trying to better himself," I said to the back of Devyn's head. "And he's certainly not going to any college. I doubt he'll go anywhere except to prison one day. The sheriff—"

Devyn swung around to face me. He smacked both of his palms into my chest.

I reeled from the hit. The sting of his hands was nothing to the mark his viciousness left inside me. *I thought we were friends.*

Laney pushed between us. "You ride for a team." She was helping out as a flank man at practice today. She was always helping out. Not like the other girls who only rode their pretty ponies around the arena for forty minutes, then went home to check their hair and nails.

"If the team says he practices," Laney said, "he practices."

High school bull riders lined up behind Laney to take her side. Guys always took her side. And they rode better, to impress her, when she was on the platform.

I'd line up behind her if it didn't mean I had to be all chummy with Scuzz-cut. I loved the fire in Laney's eyes. I didn't even care that her furnace blasted its ferocity at me. She was beautiful nonetheless. Maybe she'd understand reason? "Can't you see what he's doing?" I asked her.

She stared at me. Her lips pressured into a thin line. She stared and said nothing.

I faced Scuzz-cut. "Have you ever even been on a bull?" I asked.

"I rode a pony at the state fair once. How hard can it be?" He rolled up his sleeve and flexed his bicep. "I'm plenty strong. Not a problem."

I deliberately rolled my eyes. "Not going to work." I shook my head.

Devyn grabbed my arm and jerked me off to the side. "What are you doing? He's got a right to take a chance on the bulls to get out of podunkville."

Devyn was always so angry about being trapped in small town nowhere that escape was all he thought of. Even if it was someone else's escape.

"I'm telling you, he's not trying to get out," I said. I yanked my arm from his grip and walked away.

I was walking away a lot lately.

I took down my bull rope while chewing on the inside of my cheek until it bled. I went over to the chutes. *On second thought...* "Give him my ride. If he'll take it."

"I think we'll put him on the muley first," Devyn said.

"Suit yourself." I stood on the platform shoulder to shoulder with my teammates who were working as a chute crew.

I stood next to Laney. She didn't even look my way.

The practice bulls were old pros. My daddy used to say that these seasoned bulls could be my greatest teachers. If I let them. I draped my rope past the bull, then got it wrapped around his heart girth.

Devyn and Scuzz-cut hopped onto the platform.

Devyn gave a running monologue to Scuzz-cut. "That's how you'll set your rope. But we'll help with that part. Then once you're out, your back pockets should never hit the bull. It's like standing on your tiptoes. Never sit down. You get a little bend in your knees, then put all that weight in your thighs."

I tuned Devyn out.

Winky to the pinky. Slide and ride. I slid up onto my hand and nodded.

Little Red Fred was like the village bicycle. Everyone's had a ride. But that's how you learn. Getting thrown in two seconds only teaches a cowboy how to eat dirt.

My daddy always said to be thankful for the easier rides, because you're there longer, with a chance at an education. Those rides let you practice a solid foundation. *When the crap hits the fan we all go back to our foundation. What you're made of. What's inside you. It all comes out in your ride.*

Little Red Fred was swapping ends under me. It was too late for him to unseat me when he eventually settled into a spin. The buzzer sounded, but I set my spur on the inside and went around a bit longer. I felt it all come together—my foundation. I was made from the right stuff. I was from good stock.

I pulled the tail of my rope and let fly. Stuck the landing too. Little Red Fred had been as smooth as the rocking horse I had when I was four. Or was it three? By four I was probably mutton busting.

I dug my rope from the arena dirt where the bull had tap-danced on it. The bells clanked with their peculiar sound.

"Chris. Chris."

"Luce." I leaped to the top rail of the panels and climbed down the outside.

She hugged onto my waist. Rupert held his hand out in a manly greeting. We shook. He nodded then backed away.

"I've got something for you." Luce handed me a photograph of herself on the first day of school. In it, she was holding a dumb sign. *1994.* I ran my fingertips over the glossy picture. *She was so pretty. When had she gotten so big?* I lingered on the empty space next to her where I would have stood when Daddy was alive to take our picture.

Tears burned as they strained to emerge. I swallowed hard.

"It's so you'll remember me," she said.

What? It feels like she's pulling away. Letting go. Moving on. What?

"I could never forget you for a second, monkey girl." I drew some folded bills from my back pocket. "For us. You hold on to it. When I earn enough, we can be together. Maybe we'll leave here. You and me."

Her eyes seem mesmerized by the cash in my hands, but she didn't take it. "Chris, I don't want to go with you." Her lower lip quivered.

She was lying. I could always tell when she lied. Her feet shuffled, not standing their ground. And she couldn't look me in the eyes.

"I like Mrs. Margaret and Mr. Rupert. They want to adopt me."

That was the truth. Her eyes had stared into mine for the seconds it took to say it. Then her lids lowered but she didn't shuffle when she next said, "The sheriff said I need a loving family who doesn't forget about me for a better offer, like chasing the rodeos. Like Daddy always did." She swiped at her nose with the back of her hand. "You don't spend any time with me, Chris. Not like you used to."

I was dumbfounded. *How could I? I've had no time to spend time with her. I'm doing all of this for her. For us.*

She sniffled, bowed her head, and turned her back on me. "You have your life to live without needing to take care of me. That's what Sheriff Taylor said. You're better off without me."

She ran. Before I could blink back a tear, Luce ran to Rupert. "He's wrong," I said in her wake.

She grabbed Rupert's hand and intertwined their fingers.

"Never…" I said. She couldn't have heard me. "I'd never be better off without you," I spit through gritted teeth. "I'd never forget you."

My tears threatened to gush. I choked on a sob and swallowed in succession. It felt like air couldn't reach my lungs for the short gasps I was taking.

Rupert walked my half sister…my sister…my only family back to me. "Say good-bye, Luce."

"Chris, hang tough," Luce said. She lunged into my arms. I lifted her in a squeeze. Her warm tears flowed over her cheeks to kiss my neck with their wet trail.

"Be dangerous," I whispered into her strawberry-blond hair. She smelled of apple shampoo and sunshine. "I love you. Always."

"I love you, Chris." She slid from my grasp and scampered to Rupert's truck.

"Son, we don't intend to keep you from seeing her. You're welcome to visit. Just give her time to adjust first."

I slumped against the rails of an arena panel and watched them leave. Rupert drove slow through the parking lot. I hoped my monkey would look back. I raised my hand, ready to wave. The truck drove from sight. Her little head never turned.

Mullet-head and the Sergeant sidled up to me. The Sergeant leaned on the panels as Scuzz-cut made his debut on a muley that played girly hopscotch, then headed toward the out gate.

The muley stopped dead and waited for the gate to open. Scuzz-cut got in a tear and walloped the bull with both spurs. The rowels jammed in the muley's hide. The muley launched Scuzz-cut.

Bulls don't get hurt in their training. They're pampered athletes, raised on trust. Never get mad at them.

My brain was on fire with too many thoughts coming too fast.
Raised on trust…
I never meant to hurt her or disappoint her, Daddy.

Devyn patted Scuzz-cut on the back as he climbed from the dirt. They laughed and hooted.

Jealous. Am I jealous?

Friendships…relationships never happened that easily for me. I felt my face tighten. It seemed I couldn't hold on to friends. Or family. *I can't hold on to anyone.*

My molars ground against each other. I smothered a sniffle into my sleeve. *I don't need anyone.*

"Now that boy is like the son I never had," the Sergeant said. His eyes twinkled as he stared with pride at Scuzz-cut out in the arena. "Grab your gear. Bus is leaving," he said to me.

The Sergeant spun around too fast and unsteady. He knocked into Mullet-head, who had stood behind him like a puppy on a string. "Outa my way." With a swing of his fat arm, he drove Mullet-head into the panels.

The look in Mullet-head's eyes made me feel sorry for him. Maybe we both wanted the same thing in life. Maybe we wanted someone to be proud of us. We wanted family. I'm sure neither one of us wanted to feel so alone.

"You heard him," Mullet-head snapped at me. "Bus is leaving."

Why am I here? Why am I going back to a cell in the County Boys' Home if there is no point? And there is no point. Not with Luce gone.

I sat in the front of the bus, apart from Scuzz-cut's gaggle of gossiping girlies. He had commandeered the back of the bus and was surrounded by his sycophants. Thankfully, the ride to the County Boys' Home was quick.

At dinner, Scuzz-cut continued to hold court. "Check it out," Scuzz-cut demanded as he got up from the table. "I think I got road rash when I hit the dirt." He rolled up his sleeve and flexed his muscle. That was his real objective. "Stayed on for eight seconds, but there's only ever one way to come off."

Scuzz-cut pointed to a tiny raspberry mark on his bicep that he probably scratched in himself. "See? Right there. I hit the dirt hard after I gave the bull what-for."

There were obligatory oohs and ahs heard from around the table. Scuzz-cut took these as a cue to keep his story rolling.

It's bullshit. All of it. Bullshit.

Mind your business. Mind your business.

Michael sat next to me with his head down and picked at his meal. He tortured his mashed potatoes around the plate in silence.

I'd heard enough from Scuzz-cut.

My chair scraped the floor.

Michael stabbed his fork into a hunk of Salisbury steak. "Chris, don't," he pleaded. He grabbed my hand with his own, then let go as if the touch scalded. Michael reached for my arm instead.

I jerked from his light grip.

"It's no big shit to make the buzzer on a muley that my little sister could ride all day long. A muley's not even a genetic bucking bull. It's a beef herd bull. He gets put out with the cows most of his life. He lollygags in the sun swishing at flies."

Scuzz-cut began slowly rolling his sleeve down. He buttoned the cuff methodically, like he had to concentrate to get the little button through the tiny hole.

"Jeezuz. Get over yourself." I knocked my chair backwards and left the dining room.

"Chris. Chris." Michael scurried after me. "Chris, don't taunt him. Chris. Listen to me."

Scuzz-cut's bellow snuffed out whatever it was Michael had to say next. "That's a pretty mouth." He covered the distance between us like a charging bull. "Keep it closed or I'll fill it." Scuzz-cut shook his fists in the air.

The Sergeant loomed in the hallway. He put his hand on Scuzz-cut's shoulder. "Back away, son."

Scuzz-cut shrugged the Sergeant off and stormed down the hall. He punched Michael in the gut on his way by. Michael buckled to the floor.

"Michael." I tried to go around the Sergeant, but he blocked my way.

The Sergeant slapped his meaty hand to my chest and shoved me into my cell. He grasped the door to yank it closed. I wrestled with it for a moment. When I let go, the door slammed shut. Keys rattled in the lock. *Click.*

"Michael?" I pounded my fists against the solid wood. "Michael, are you okay? Talk to me." I pressed my ear to the door but heard nothing. "Say something."

The house fell silent. It was like I got sucked into a vacuum. I heard nothing. But maybe there was nothing to hear.

I slumped to the floor and thought to peek under the door. But there was nothing I would see.

I crept to my bed. The springs sagged. My pillow was thin. The blanket was threadbare.

I curled up. I wanted to sleep. I tried to will myself to sleep. Count sheep. Sing a song in my head. Bore myself to death by reciting the periodic table. Nothing worked.

If I drifted off, busy brain woke me. My thoughts ran out of control. Worries kept me awake. My mind was ablaze.

The social worker wasn't ever going to get me out of here. She was under the sheriff's spell. The doctor lady was dating the sheriff. Did she tell him? She told Laney. Devyn knew. Devyn was mad at me. Seemed a lot of people were mad at me. *Luce.*

My little sister, Lucine. She had been the apple of Daddy's eye. She was only nine years old. Couldn't blame her for wanting a life. What could I give her? *I've got nothing. I'll probably get killed bull riding one of these days.* Lane Frost died in the arena at Cheyenne Frontier Days on July 30, 1989. A bull named Takin Care of Business struck him in the back when he landed in the dirt on an eighty-five-point ride. The bull's horn broke several of his ribs and severed an artery.

I stood on the cot to look out the window. The night was a murky bleakness. The stars refused to break through the mire. I slid the window open. The old wood squealed in complaint. Fresh air rushed onto my face. I breathed deeply.

I could climb out like so many times before. I could leave.

There was nowhere to go. And how long had I stood here already? Dawn was beginning to lighten the sky even though morning in the County Boys' Home wouldn't start for hours.

Click.

Michael? I heard a thud in the hall, followed by a yelp. *Michael.*

I jammed the window down, then jumped from my cot before my door opened. Scuzz-cut held Michael by the neck. He shoved him through the open door, then slammed it shut behind him.

The lock clicked.

Michael's face was pasted in red lipstick.

Red eyebrows were painted in arches on his forehead, like the McDonald's logo. Garish circles plastered his cheeks. His swollen lips were drawn even larger with the red. And red smeared downward from each corner of his mouth.

He looked like a clown from a horror film.

"Michael?" His name came out with my intake of breath. It was barely a whisper. "I'll kill them," I uttered.

He shook his head. "Chris, don't."

Chapter Eleven

Michael slumped onto my cot and pulled off his shirt to scrub at his face.

There were old cigarette burns dotting his shoulders. A gnarly scarred slash ran across his upper arm. And hash marks made long ago plagued his back.

I tried not to stare.

Michael knew what I saw. "The Sergeant," he said. His shoulders rounded, hollowing his chest. "He's my father." Michael balled the T-shirt and tossed it to the mattress. "Bio donor really. I can't call him a father. He doesn't rate." He folded his hands in his lap and waited.

His father?

I sat on the bed next to Michael. The mattress slouched more in my direction. Michael was too thin. Frail really. Light as a bird. I wondered how he had survived each assault, every time, year after year.

"I'm not like him," he said when I hadn't filled the still air. "I'll never be like him. At least I can change that."

A handprint glowed around his neck. The red-purple of a new bruise shined over his sunken cheek. He sniffled and ran his hand under his nose. It came away bloody.

And they had held his wrists.

"I'm so sorry," I said in a whisper. "I never meant for you to get hurt." I felt tears well behind my eyes. I thought I felt my face burn. I knew I was ashamed.

I hate myself for letting him get hurt. I hate myself more than I hate them. I hurt everyone around me with my selfishness.

Michael had always extended himself in friendship. Even though being my friend got him hurt. He didn't have much, and still, he never thought of himself first.

"I'm sorry," I said. I wished there was more I could have said. Sorry wasn't enough. I wished there was something I could do.

"No big. I'm used to it." He gingerly touched his swollen lips with the very tips of his fingers.

His face was hideous from the assault.

I stared down at my thighs. Stains marred the blue of my jeans. I wished I could have scrubbed the stains out to make them bright blue again. But all of the marks were permanent now. No amount of scrubbing would make the stains disappear.

Michael hiked a hip. A loud groan escaped his lips. He fished around in his pocket, then drew out a fist-sized lump of cash. "For you and your little sister," he said.

Bills fell loose from the crumpled mass. Some landed on the mattress. A few hit the floor. Michael laid the bulk of them in my lap.

"Where did you get this?" I poked at the treasure like it hid a scorpion inside.

"I bet on you." Michael laid his hand on my thigh. His fingers were long and thin. They stretched to cover the grimy stains on my jeans. "I'll always bet on you." He squeezed my leg.

I hugged him. It was a girly thing to do, but I threw my arms around him like he was my little brother. Like he was family. Like he was a lifeline. Like he was a tether to a better world.

"I don't deserve you," I said. I gave his back a couple of slaps to make it a man-hug before releasing him.

"Look," I said, "this is your money. I can't take it. You keep it." I scooped up handfuls of loose bills, then shoved them toward him.

He shook his head. "Nah, keeping it would be worse for me if the Sergeant ever found out."

"Michael—"

"It's not like he notices me. But, you know, if he did notice." Michael picked up fallen bills and smoothed them out. A stack of crinkled cash grew taller and taller from his ministrations. He absentmindedly began plucking money from my hands to smooth and stack also.

To break the uncomfortable moment, I said, "My daddy never paid much notice of me unless I rode bulls. It's all we had together." I placed the cash on the mattress and scooted to the foot of the bed. "I became an excellent bull rider under his instruction. But he was a better father to Luce, my little sister." I fidgeted my empty hands.

"I think my daddy was always disappointed that I'd never compete professionally. Only men can compete in professional bull riding." I paused. I felt my throat claw at a lump of saliva I was having trouble swallowing.

I knew what I was going to tell Michael. He deserved to know. I wanted to tell him. I owed him that much. Knowing and owing didn't make it any easier.

"Truth is, my daddy was always disappointed that I wasn't born a boy."

I held my breath for Michael to interrupt. For him to be surprised. To get angry with me. To leap from the cot. Give me a look of disgust. Or just move away and put as much distance between us as he could.

When he didn't react, I breathed out. "Bull riding with Daddy at our ranch was the only time I didn't feel his disappointment. It was the only time I felt he could love me."

Michael sat too still. He didn't fidget with his fingers. He didn't pick at the loose threads on his baggy shorts. I barely heard him breathe.

"Michael, I was born a girl."

"It doesn't matter," he said. His slight shoulders shrugged. "Not to me. I don't care what parts you have or don't have. I can see who you are."

He held his hand out to me.

I grasped it.

We shook.

"Brothers," he said.

"Brothers."

"Hang tough," Michael mumbled.

"What?"

"Isn't that what you say?"

I nodded. "Be dangerous," I whispered in reply.

Michael lay down on my cot. In minutes, his breathing eased. He seemed at peace.

I planted my back against the wall and listened as his breaths grew long and deep.

When the door clicked open in the morning, and the County Boys' Home came alive, Michael continued to sleep curled around my thin pillow. I dragged the blanket over him, pulled it to his ear, and tucked it under his chin.

His face was a blotchy mess of red lipstick and cuts and contusions. Underneath that, his cheeks were flushed with warmth. His muscles had slackened and smoothed, which made him appear to be at peace with the world. And I wished it were so.

He had suffered for every wrong move that I made of late. He had suffered because he was easy to hurt. Michael was sensitive and different. And gay. But it was me who had exposed him from hiding in the shadows. It was me they wanted to hurt. My fault Michael took the brunt of Scuzz-cut's abuse.

It had to stop. I had to be the one to stop it.

How? I was tired. I was dead tired.

If you get tired. Rest. Don't quit.

I gimped from my cell as boys filed past. I had slept crunched in a small ball at the foot of my bed. Every injury I'd ever had was infuriated. My body hurt just to breathe. It was a minor miracle that I hauled myself up the stairs of the short bus and plunked down on the first bench seat.

In the clamor of boys, I dozed.

I went to my locker by rote. I moved from one class to the next in a trance. School was school. It was easy to get A's with my eyes closed, but that would bring attention to myself. I tried not to make it look too easy. Besides, teachers might expect more of me. I didn't have time for that.

My focus was on the bulls. Settling onto a bull tended to make anyone focus. I knew my head would clear at rodeo practice.

At the end of the day, I dropped my books in my locker, went out to retrieve my gear from the back of the truck, then headed to the arena.

Clink, clank. That was the sound of my particular peculiar bells.

But my bull rope and bells were still nestled inside their gear bag. I knew there were two sets of these hand-hammered riveted bells made by the good friend of my daddy who had gifted him this set. Until now, I had never heard the other sound off.

Clink, clank.

The noise brought a mixed wave of love and loss and longing. *Daddy?*

Dead men didn't emerge like risen zombies or vampires. And if they did, because I wouldn't count anything out at this point, they didn't show up to high five with a howdy hey or an attaboy.

I rummaged in the bag and grasped on to my own bells as if to stifle them by placing a hand over their mouths.

Two men were talking below a chute platform. The low rumble of one voice sounded somewhat familiar. The other voice, I was sure, belonged to Sheriff Taylor.

I crept closer.

"You're targeting him for what? Your family's ranch? That run-down old place? It rightfully belongs to him when he's eighteen."

"It's mine. And no snot nose kid will take it from me," the sheriff said. "I never let my brother run me off of it. I won't let his kid. It's mine."

I peeked around the panels. Red was the one arguing with Sheriff Taylor.

"His daddy got that ranch out of trouble. Your trouble." Red poked a pointer finger to the sheriff's chest. "Paid off second and third mortgages which you put on it. Bought the place out of bankruptcy." He stuffed his fists to his hips and leaned in. "Paid the back taxes that *you* neglected to pay on for years. Years."

"Yeah, well, I had debts of my own to pay off." Sheriff Taylor mirrored Red by stuffing his own fists to his hips. His tongue darted out to wet his cracked lips.

"My brother left me," Sheriff Taylor said. "He left me with hateful parents. My father's cruelty knew no bounds. Who did my brother think our old pappy would turn on when he left?"

Sheriff Taylor's hands opened and slid to his gun belt. "My big brother left me to take that old man's abuse." The sheriff's face glowed red. He reached to pick at the sores on his neck. "I was only a kid. A kid shouldn't have to shoulder that kind of burden."

"That was your deal, Bubba Taylor. He wanted to take you. You wouldn't leave. Had something of your own to prove. You resented him from day one. Jealous that he was making it at riding bulls. It makes no sense that he should have stuck around just to save you any abuse."

Red stepped back and relaxed his stance. I could almost feel sympathy softening him. In a quieter tone he said, "You soured yourself. Got into gambling and who knows what else." The sheriff crossed his arms in front of him.

"Don't you be making that the kid's deal," Red said. "Don't you be making that any of these kids' deals any longer." He smoothed his palms down his thighs. "And you're going to cut that Devyn boy loose. He doesn't need to be doing your dirty work."

Devyn? Devyn's in with the sheriff?

I'd heard enough. My best friend was conspiring with my worst enemy. *My ex best friend.*

I stormed from the arena. I don't know where I had a mind to go, but it wasn't here. I tucked my chin to my chest, gritted my teeth, and stomped from the chutes.

Devyn bumped into me. Or I bumped into him. But that detail didn't matter. My hat flew off. I dropped my gear.

"Sorry," he mumbled, "wasn't paying attention."

"You're working for the sheriff," I accused him. I was outraged. I was hurt. "All this time."

I took a swing at him. Missing. I knocked him in the ear. "I thought you were sorry that you were some victim of the sheriff's games. And here you are instead, working for him. Is that how you get all of your equipment? You're on the sheriff's payroll? Is that how you make entry fees? Sell out your *friends*? You always seem to have spending money."

Devyn stumbled backwards. More so from the shock of my words than the impact of my punch.

His lips tightened into a straight line. "What do you know about any of it? I've lived here all my life and I don't belong here. All I've ever wanted was to get out. But I'm trapped. And all I've got is bull riding. Only that can pay for college. I almost made it out too. Until you." Devyn socked me in the eye.

We lunged at each other.

I flailed at him. None of my swings connected.

Devyn slugged me in the gut. "You don't appreciate anything. You don't work hard for anything."

I doubled over with the wind knocked out of me. My diaphragm seized. My brain panicked for breath. I flung my arms around Devyn in a grisly hug.

He tried to shrug me off.

I held on.

"You were your daddy's little girl until what? You wanted to play at being a boy? Here's what boys play at." Devyn punched me in the kidney.

I buckled from him and flailed for balance.

When I staggered near to upright, I wrapped one arm protectively across my belly. My brain was on fire. My body filled with pain. I struggled to suck air. Little gasps tortured my gut to greater spasms. My lungs screamed with their need to fill. And all I could do was clutch at myself and wheeze.

"I hate you," Devyn spit through his clenched jaw. He kicked my legs from under me.

I plummeted to the ground. My back hit the dirt flat. That drove out of my lungs what little air I had.

I tried to sit up. I couldn't rise. I coughed. The metallic tang of blood coated my tongue. My throat burned with rising bile.

I tried to roll to my side. Devyn dropped onto me and straddled my chest. "I hate you."

He twisted my shirt collar in his hand. His knuckles pressed into the side of my neck. Devyn pulled his free arm back like loading a shotgun. His fist poised to smash my face.

His eyes flickered from anger to sorrow and back again. The muscles on either side of his jaw twitched with rigidity.

I lay still. He was bigger and stronger than me. His weight on my chest was crushing.

There wasn't anything I could do. But if his fist came crashing down, I'd kill him.

I clawed at the dirt, searching for purchase. I searched for anything I could use against him. There was nothing. I found nothing.

And what did I mean to do? Bash him with a rock? I couldn't. I wouldn't. Or could I? *Would I?*

Seconds turned into an eternity.

Devyn's eyebrows squared off against one another. His forehead strained in furrows. His eyes changed color, from their bright blue to steel gray.

Sweat ran cold under my binding. Breath began to seep into my lungs regularly with my short, struggling inhales.

"I hate you," Devyn shouted at me again. "Everything was fine until you got here."

He pressed his knuckles harder into my neck. I felt my pulse throbbing like the beat of a bass drum.

"Sheriff Taylor was helping to get me out of here. I was going to go to college. Until you showed up." Tears ran from his eyes. They pooled at his chin until they dripped onto my cheek. "I thought I had it all. I thought I had everything. Until I wanted you."

He rolled onto his back pockets. "When I thought I knew you."

My stomach took his weight.

"You don't even know who you are," he said.

Maybe it was the pressure on my belly? Or the blood supply being cut off at my neck? My own tears blurred my vision.

"Hey, man. Get off of him."

Devyn's weight was torn from me.

Mullet-head appeared above. The sun formed a halo around his Aqua Net hairdo.

With relief, air whooshed into my body on my full inhale. I panted like I had just run a marathon. I rolled to my side and spit blood from my mouth.

Mullet-head? Was this a trick? Some sort of joke? I nodded thanks at Mullet-head, even though I waited for him to call in his bully buddies for a shark feeding frenzy.

"Yeah, well, just this once," Mullet-head said. He scurried away as if he hadn't wanted to get caught helping me.

Devyn gained his feet. Tears poured from his eyes. He stared down at me for a moment, in silence, then picked up his fallen hat and left.

I sat up, brought my knees to my chest, and hugged them. I don't know how long I'd stayed there rocking before the doctor lady interrupted me.

She squatted beside me and lifted my chin.

"That's going to swell. You'll have a shiner for sure. But you'll live."

"That's because I'm dangerous," I said.

"Maybe you should quit your charade? You can't run with the big boys."

"I've been doing all right so far." *Hang tough.*

She pressed a chemical ice pack from her jump bag to my face.

"Better than all right," I said. "I'm the best bull rider this town's ever had."

"Not the best." Her hands slid down to palpate my ribs. "No new damage." She stood. "Your daddy was the best."

"Well, he isn't here now. Is he?" It was time to let him go. It was time to live my own life. *Stop hoping he'd approve. Stop searching for validation from my dear old dead daddy. It's never going to happen. Wasn't happening when he was alive. Wouldn't happen now.*

"Ohmygod. Chris? What's the other guy look like?"

I squinted up at Laney. "You mean your beloved Devyn?" The question came out in a sneer.

I wished she could like me. I wished she would look at me with half of the love and devotion her eyes had always shown for Devyn. But sure enough, Laney's eyes immediately scanned the distance for him.

Stop denying it. Get a room already.

I turned to the doctor lady. "And for the record, *she* approached me."

"What do you mean by that?" Laney turned her head back toward us and asked.

"We don't even like each other," I said to the doctor lady. "I mean, yeah, no, not any more. If we ever really did."

I rolled to my knees, then climbed to my feet like I was eighty years old. My body felt about eighty. I stifled a groan from escaping my lips.

"She's not my type," I said to the doctor lady. *No. Not at all. I totally hate drop-dead gorgeous girls. Too much trouble.*

"Chris, what are you talking about?" Laney asked.

"Don't worry about it. I won't be around much longer."

Chapter Twelve

"Need a lift?"

It was too early in the morning. Laney must have been waiting at the end of the County Boys' Home driveway through half the night. It looked like she hadn't slept. I climbed into the passenger side. It beat hitchhiking.

"You're wrong about him, ya know." Laney shoved an open thermos at me as I settled against the door. I sniffed at the rising steam. The moist heat got trapped under the brim of my hat. I closed my eyes to its soothing sensation across my forehead.

Laney crammed the gear shift into drive. "Devyn's always walked a sharp edge between that sheriff and getting forward. If you were from around here, you'd know it's not black and white, right and wrong, good and bad. Those aren't always clear-cut choices." Laney shifted in her seat. I watched her from beneath my hat's brim. Her lips puckered liked she'd sucked a lemon.

I couldn't be concerned with "Taylor Town" drama. I had my own ills to worry about. Foremost, my body ached all over. I now had much greater sympathy for those punching bags in boxing gyms.

Water under the bridge. I'd heal.

I needed to scare up a bull rope and whatnot when I got to the rodeo grounds. I still had my own plans for my own future that didn't involve sticking around "Taylor Town." I scooted lower on the seat and concentrated on the warm steam of the potent coffee.

"Look, I had it out with my sister," Laney said. "She told me that she warned you to stay away from me."

Warned me? More like threatened. Blackmailed.

"She doesn't think it's right. What you're doing. You. I mean, who you are. She doesn't get it is all."

Get it?

I sipped the hot coffee with a loud slurping sound like I'd been raised on the wrong side of the tracks. I didn't feel like conversing. Laney took the hint. It was an hour or so of peace and quiet. I could have dozed. I didn't.

The truck slowed at the rodeo grounds. We trundled through the gates behind a line of trailers.

Laney turned off the heat and fiddled with every knob and dial on the dash. The radio blasted. She turned it down, then turned it off. Her lights worked. High beams struck the horse trailer we sat behind. The windshield was washed. Windows moved down then up. Mirrors adjusted. "It's not her decision whether I see you or not," Laney blurted. "Whether I like you or not."

She could ruin my life.

We crept forward. I stared out the passenger side window and wondered who would loan me a bull rope. I'd need some rosin—

"I'm going to see you," she said.

I swung my head to look at her.

She wrung the steering wheel in a fierce grip like she was twisting water from a washcloth. "I told her as much," Laney said. "And I told her there would be no consequences to you from her." Laney stopped the truck to wait for the horse trailer in front of us to back into a parking spot.

"You should ask me out at this point," she said.

I spit coffee onto the dash.

She stared at me with a wide-eyed look of frustration that instantly turned into something like horror.

I swiped at the dash with my shirt sleeve.

Laney slowly drove forward again. "You don't have to," she said in a quiet voice. "I just thought…maybe…" Laney drove to the back of the competitors parking lot.

"You don't have to," she said. She pulled in next to the three-quarter-ton and jammed her gear shift into park.

"Laney, I—"

My door jolted open. "'Bout time," Devyn said. He seemed genuinely happy to see me.

It felt weird.

"Nice shiner," he said. "I do throw a mean right hook." He held his hand out to shake. "I'm willing to forgive you for hurting my knuckles."

I switched the thermos into my left and put my right forward. I didn't grab hold. I think I was waiting for the other shoe to drop. *Why the change of heart?*

"Sorry, man," I said to Devyn.

He took hold of my hand with a firm grip.

When he didn't let go immediately, I said, "Yeah. I made a bad assumption. I mean, I should apologize."

"Yeah. You should." He hauled me from Laney's truck. "Your gear's in the front of your truck."

"Laney," I said while swinging around to look at her. She was gone.

"Here," Devyn said, "change into this." His blue logo shirt hung free of wrinkles from a wire hanger.

I fingered the sleeve. "Starched and ironed?"

"Mom."

"Well, this one's yours," I said.

"I won't be needing it," Devyn said.

"Aren't you riding?"

He hung the coat hanger on my outstretched hand. "I'm not entered. I missed the books." Devyn reached over the sidewall of the three-quarter-ton's bed. He flipped open a cooler and liberated a bottle of beer from the ice. *Glass bottles? That's new. High-end now?*

I felt my top lip curl in disgust as I eyed the bottle. "They'd let you ride," I said.

"Nope. Sittin' this one out." Devyn twisted off the cap. "I think I'll head up into the stands and enjoy the bull riding as a spectator." He tipped the bottle to his mouth. "You'd better change into that shirt."

My eyes must have darted around like wild horses trapped in a canyon.

Devyn said, "I won't look. I'm a gentleman after all." He jounced his beer bottle in a salute.

I didn't make a move.

"Oh, c'mon. It's not like I don't know." He smiled. "It's not like I haven't seen a girl before. Not that you're a girl. I mean, the body you were born into."

Uncomfortable.

Devyn squirmed in his boots. "I've been with a naked girl in the bathtub." He took another swallow of beer. "Laney. I've taken lots of baths with Laney."

Okay. That's funny. "Like when you were three?"

"Probably all the way up through four. Jealous?" He swigged from the bottle and turned around to stare in the opposite direction. "Put your shirt on." He turned away to fuss in the three-quarter-ton's cab.

I switched shirts, then tucked the tails. Devyn tossed the yellow-shafted boots over his shoulder. They landed at my feet. The spurs chinked when they hit the dirt.

"You can turn around," I said. "I'm worried about what you'll throw next. And your aim."

He dropped my gear bag to the ground as he faced me. "Ima gonna head. I'll be the one cheering for you from the stands." He slammed the truck door then chucked me on the arm. "The only one." Devyn flicked his eyebrows up and down. "I crack myself up," he said. "Hang tough."

"Be dangerous," I retorted.

Devyn sauntered off in the direction of the main arena.

My exhale was long. I sank onto the running board of the three-quarter-ton truck. I sank down to change my boots. To be truthful, I think my body was already there before I had a mind to change the boots. My back slumped against the door. It took me a moment before I got to strapping the yellow boots on.

I need to win. I need the money. I stood and stamped my feet.

"Here's how this weekend's going to go." Scuzz-cut stepped in front of the two trucks and blocked my passage from between them. He hauled Michael in front of him.

Michael.

Scuzz-cut gripped the back of his neck. Michael's knees began to buckle as Scuzz-cut squeezed. His nails dug into Michael's neck. Blood welled around each one.

"Leave him alone," I said.

"Only after we get it straight," Scuzz-cut said.

"What do you want?"

Scuzz-cut must have eased off because Michael straightened his stance. He shook his head ever so slightly at me.

What?

"Like I said," Scuzz-cut began again, "here's how this weekend's going to go."

Michael lurched from Scuzz-cut's loosened hold. All of a sudden, he cackled like a maniac gone wild. Tears began streaming from his eyes. Not from pain. Not from sorrow.

Laughter.

I'd swear he'd about wet himself with laughter.

"It won't work," Michael said. He grabbed his stomach and doubled over. Snorts emanated from him. "Last night I told Chris I'm gay." He struggled between breathing, snorting, and laughing. "Think he wants anything to do with me now?"

Michael collapsed to the ground still clutching his stomach. "Not Chris. He's not like you, *Scuzz-cut.* He's not into little boys."

I felt my eyes strain, widening as wide as they could get. My mind raced. *What's Michael doing taunting Scuzz-cut? What's he thinking? Scuzz-cut will kill him.*

Scuzz-cut kicked Michael as he rolled around on the ground. His boot's contact resounded with a sickening thud.

Michael laughed and wrapped his arms around himself.

Michael. Stop. Hear me, Michael. What do you want me to do? What should I do?

I stepped forward.

Michael pointedly stared into my eyes and shook his head no.

I can't, Michael. I can't stand here and watch this. I shook my head back at him. I again stepped toward Scuzz-cut.

Michael perched onto his knees. He clutched on to Scuzz-cut's jeans, practically pulling them down. Tears ran from his eyes. His face contorted in a miserable grin. "Don't you see, you big dumb oaf?" He looked up at Scuzz-cut. "You can't use me against him anymore. He doesn't care. He doesn't care what you do to me. No one does."

I do. It's not true. I do.

Michael batted his eyes and stared up at Scuzz-cut like a little boy clinging to his daddy's thigh in waiting for his daddy to lift him up. He beamed a broad smile while continuing to grip on to Scuzz-cut's pants.

Scuzz-cut seized Michael's hair. He wrenched his head backwards.

He raised a fist in the air.

"You gonna punch the kid? Now?" I hoisted my gear bag. "While he's on the ground?" I walked toward them.

Scuzz-cut still blocked my way. Indecision plagued his eyes.

"You're a big man, Scuzz-cut. A big man." I slammed into him with my shouldered bag. It knocked him from my path. He let go of Michael.

I grinned in his face. *Take that, Scuzz-cut.* I hoped Michael knew I wouldn't leave him. *He did, didn't he? He's the one who started this performance.*

Or did he want me to stick up for him? Did he want me to deny that I'd abandon him?

I walked past them.

I hoped Michael knew what he was doing.

"Punk," I heard Scuzz-cut say.

And I didn't know if he meant me or Michael.

I bit the inside of my cheek until blood seeped onto my tongue. I kept walking.

Behind me, Michael laughed. His cackle was akin to the wail of a wounded hyena.

The thick air carried the report of thumps and thwacks. Michael went silent.

I wanted to look back. I wanted to run back. I'd punch Scuzz-cut in the head. I'd kill him.

And I'd pick Michael off the ground and hug him close to me.

Instead, I hefted my slipping gear bag farther onto my shoulder and held my resolve. I continued walking toward the arena.

Michael.

I dropped my gear bag and hung my rope. But I wasn't into it.

If the head game was half the battle, I was going to lose.

My feet had me wandering through the penned bulls. I didn't know what I was looking for until I got there. "Hey, Thunder."

Thundering Bunny stood calm and commanding like a general in front of his troops. I leaned on the rails of his pen. He lumbered over, bobbed his head, then blew snot. His small eyes were bright with intelligence. Thundering Bunny had a calm, cool, confident demeanor like he owned his world around him.

He stuck his nose to the ground and blew a determined breath that disturbed the dirt. When he pawed, dirt flew up and over his head in an arc back at me.

"Hey, now." I brushed clods from my arms. "Some of us don't live in a barn."

He approached. His big, wet nose reached toward me. His raspy tongue snagged my sleeve.

"I'm supposed to stay clean. Look decent for my ride. You're not helping."

Thundering Bunny sidled up to the panel.

I reached through the rails and gave his shoulder a rub.

He lowered his head and twisted his nose toward the inside of his pen. When he started bobbing up and down, I dug my nails in harder. Thundering Bunny rocked back and forth like my hand was a scratching post.

I smiled. I think it was the first occasion in a long while that I'd had something to smile about. They really were like people. The bulls. They each had their own personalities. They had likes and dislikes. They had opinions. And when the time came, they were all business.

Which reminded me. I had a rope to rosin and a bull to tie down on.

Music blared over the loudspeakers. Bulls were loaded into chutes.

I set my rope on a black brindle named Blue Suede Shoes, then stepped out to wait.

I hated the waiting. This was the time when my daddy would recite his mantra. Only he'd never called it that. Game plan? Pep talk? I needed my own self pep talk.

Anyone who says they aren't scared when they climb on isn't telling the whole truth. Fear is healthy if kept in check. Fear gives that edge. Managing fear is key, though.

Keep your posture. Keep your feet. Keep your hands. Follow him jump for jump.

It was time. Blue Suede Shoes lurched in the chute as I lowered myself onto him. But that was mild compared to what I'd seen this bull do. I took a wrap, punched my knuckles, shifted, wiggled, punched again, winky to the pinky, then nodded.

The gate opened.

Game on.

Instantly, I found the sweet spot. My body took over.

That's when it got real quiet in my head. Man, I loved that. I was in a zone. I could do no wrong. Jump for jump. Me against Blue Suede Shoes.

Blue Suede Shoes threw everything at me but the kitchen sink and still I got him rode.

I tugged the tail of my rope, let loose, and hit the ground running. The crowd was on their feet before the score was even announced.

Red's voice screamed over the loudspeakers. "Eighty-eight points."

Bullfighters slapped the back of my vest. Devyn jumped into the arena. I slammed him in a hug. Someone shoved my fallen rope at me.

And I don't remember the rest.

Laney was there. Behind the chutes, she took hold of my hand.

My insides shuddered at her touch. "What about your sister?" I asked.

She shook her head. "She was trying to protect me. It's what family does. I told her, not from you."

The only thing I wanted to remember about the entire night was Laney by my side. She clung to my hand like we'd been together forever. She was akin to a cool glass of water for a man wandering weeks in the Sahara Desert.

When Laney flipped my hand over and ran her fingertip along the callouses, I nearly melted into a puddle at her feet.

"Wondered where you two got to," Devyn said.

Sadly, we arrived at the trucks before I knew my feet had traveled.

Devyn belched. "I got pizza, but I already ate half of it."

"I'm starved." Laney let go of my hand and jumped at the box balancing on the sidewall of the truck bed. "You better take him home," she said around a mouthful of cheese and pepperoni. "Pick you up early tomorrow?"

I nodded like a bobble-headed doll. "At Devyn's."

Devyn was already smeared on the truck seat. The window held him upright. His cheek was plastered against it. And he slept. How he was comfortable was beyond my understanding.

The armrest had been chewed by a cattle dog years ago. I knew the vinyl and hard plastic shards were relentless with their stabbing torture. And still, Devyn slept.

The truck's lights flooded Devyn's garage. The door had been left open. The practice barrel, perched on its steel spring, looked like a humped buffalo calf. The drop barrel appeared as a mountain lion crouched to pounce. Odd reflections from the horizontal bars of the panel on the side wall ran to the back wall. They pointed the way to Devyn's vast closeted collection.

Hanging vests topped by shelved hats looked like an army of stout soldiers standing at attention behind the bench seat.

When I opened the passenger side door, a sleeping Devyn practically fell into my arms. He woke suddenly. I shoved him upright.

"Are we there yet?" Devyn asked.

"You're home."

He stumbled from the truck, staggered into the garage, and tumbled onto the bench seat.

A glass bottle crashed to the floor.

I winced and touched my fingertips to the scar marring my cheek.

"I don't have to babysit her anymore," I said to myself. My stepmama was in a coma. "I don't have to watch her. Or clean up her messes." I breathed in through my nose and out through my mouth. I slowed the intake on my next breath to make sure my lungs filled to straining.

The night that my face was cut flooded my mind just like the truck lights were flooding the garage.

My stepmama walked out of our decrepit trailer house before dinner. I watched her go. The straps on her high heels hung loose. Her ankle twisted as she staggered with the shakes. The heel of a shoe broke off. She kept walking.

"Where's Mama?" Luce asked.

"She's running an errand." I smoothed the hair from her face. "Hey, how about raviolis for supper? I think there's a can above the stove."

We ate. We waited. I paced. Luce sobbed quietly into her favorite blanket.

"She doesn't love us anymore, does she?" Luce asked.

"Sure she does, monkey. She just got lost is all. She loves you very much. More than anything." I hugged Luce to me, wishing it were true.

"I'm nine. I'm not stupid." Luce pushed away from me and ran to her mattress on the floor of the back room.

I followed, then bundled her into my arms. She was so light. She felt frail.

I wrapped Luce in her blanket and stuffed her on the seat of my truck. She pretended to sleep as I searched each bar and back alley in town. My stepmama was there, somewhere. She had to be.

I wanted desperately to find my stepmama, for Luce's sake. I wanted Luce to stop crying. I'd have given anything to see my monkey girl smile again.

But I dreaded finding my stepmama for all of the continued heartache she was causing. In fact, I never wanted to see her again. More than anything, I wished she was dead.

When I found her at two a.m., slumped on a bar, two men fighting over who would haul her carcass out with them, I wanted to walk away.

I couldn't. I didn't.

I shook my stepmama by the shoulders. She didn't rouse. I tried to lift her. It was like holding water in my hands. No matter how hard I tried, she dribbled out of my grasp.

I remembered the sound of breaking glass. A blur slashed across my face. There was so much blood. Too much blood. It gushed down my face and into my shirt collar. And my stepmama just lay there as I went down.

It's okay. It's over. It's done. She's in a coma.

I breathed the chilled night air in through my nose, then out through my pursed lips. In through my nose, then out through my lips. Long, lung-filling breaths calmed my racing heart. Enough to get the truck shut off.

Moonlight lit the garage. I left the door up. It was comforting somehow. The stars twinkled like billions of diamonds spilled over black velvet.

"I want you to have my stuff," Devyn said.

"Okay. Sure." I walked to him. Broken glass crunched beneath my feet.

"No. Really. I want you to have it. I'm giving it all to you. Take anything you want."

"Okay." I lifted an old sleeping bag to cover him against the night's chill. "We'll talk about it tomorrow."

Devyn rolled onto his side to face the back of the bench seat.

I scooped broken glass from the floor.

When Devyn snored low and deep, I wandered among the training equipment. It was soothing. All of it. The place. The dark. The rhythmic snoring. The equipment, so exact to what I'd practiced on as a kid. It was the closest thing I'd felt to a home since Daddy's death.

I ran my fingertips along the bucking barrel. Trails disturbed the layer of dust. I walked to the back wall to admire Devyn's collection of vests and shirts and hats—Daddy had had a closet full—

He's gone.

I'm here now. This is my time.

I looked back at Devyn sleeping soundly. *Our time. Me and Devyn.*

Content, I sat on the floor and leaned my back against an older gear bag. No sooner had I drifted toward sleep than I felt the familiar nightmare take over. I wanted to wake, but the rich clarity this time drew me in.

Instead of vague splashes, I saw vivid details.

It was the sheriff. I saw his face illuminated by the flashing blue lights. It was him. Sheriff Bubba Taylor. He was grinning. But that didn't seem right.

The sheriff smacks his hands together and swipes dirt from his pants. He throws something to the side of the road. It's swallowed by the brush.

Red and blue lights flash in the dark. Sirens wail. Flames from the flipped truck lick the night sky. Dual back wheels rotate slowly in the smoke-filled air. Daddy's lifeless body is covered by a sheet.

I let the night terror run its course. Per usual, it ran amok with surreal visions. I swore my body jerked in response.

Bright daylight stings my eyes.

I run to my three-quarter-ton truck.

The dented door groans in complaint as I wrench it open. A lifeless body sits behind the steering wheel. The sun washes over his pale face. I yank him by the sleeve. He falls into my arms.

I jolted awake.

CHAPTER THIRTEEN

"Don't wake him," Laney said as she walked into the garage.

I stuffed my hat over my wet hair. *Ew.* "Well, he slept all day Sunday. I found him in almost that exact same position last night. Except there were more bottles on the floor."

"Let him sleep," Laney said. "He's been out of sorts lately." She smoothed Devyn's hair from his face. "He won't talk about it."

"Yeah. Devyn's mom said the same thing."

"Aunt Mary?" Laney asked.

"She got up when she heard me in the shower," I said.

"It's the middle of the night for her."

I shrugged. "Maybe she went back to bed."

"We're going to be late," Laney whispered. She walked to her truck and coaxed the door open.

The mood on the ride to school was somber. I wanted to be elated. I was with Laney. Not just in her truck. I was *with* her. I reached to take her hand.

"Is this all right?" I asked.

She laced her fingers through mine and squeezed.

I slid over to sit in the middle of the bench seat. My thigh rested against hers. Her warmth permeated my jeans. A sigh escaped my lips. I clamped them tight in reaction. *Hope she didn't hear that.*

I stared at her fingers threaded through mine. My stomach somersaulted. I wanted to kiss each knuckle. Press my lips against her skin to feel its softness. At that thought my body surged with energy and lightness. I felt like I'd float. I felt giddy, like I'd snorted laughing gas at the dentist's.

I marveled that her hand fit so perfectly in mine though they were opposites. One rough with callouses. The other silky smooth. I was sure they were made for each other.

At the thought, my heart pounded so hard that if Laney spoke, I wouldn't have heard a word she said. I looked to her lips so as not to miss a thing.

Worry etched across her face. As we pulled into the school parking lot, I let her hand go and moved to the passenger side door. It was okay if she didn't want anyone to know.

"Later?" I asked.

She nodded. A strain tightened her forehead and crept into her eyes.

I didn't see her at all through morning classes. At lunch, I passed the office. Laney was talking to the school's counselor.

"Move along," the vice principal said. "Move along."

I sat alone in the lunchroom. Laney didn't show. Devyn hadn't either.

At the end of the day, I hung out at Laney's truck to meet up with her. *Maybe I shouldn't be here. Maybe she changed her mind about me. About us.*

"Chris. Get in." Laney climbed behind the wheel and tore out of the school's parking lot. We headed toward Devyn's.

The bucking barrel had been dragged from the garage. Marks in the dirt told of its eviction. A limp chain still choked the spring propping its middle. Mattresses were heaped in a pile. The garage doors were down. Fumes festered along the bottom like a low-lying fog.

The muffled sound of the three-quarter-ton's engine alerted me to its whereabouts.

Panic pounded through me.

Bile rose in my throat.

I thrust the garage door up. The fog engulfed me in its rush to escape. I waved my arms.

"Devyn! Devyn!" I yelled.

"Devyn! Devyn!" Laney's shrill scream echoed mine.

When the fumes dissipated, sunlight bathed the truck's cab.

A lifeless body sat behind the steering wheel.

I bolted to the driver's side. The dented door groaned in complaint as I wrenched it open. "Devyn." The sun washed over his pale face.

I yanked him by the sleeve. He fell limp into my arms.

"Devyn!" I held him tight.

"Devyn," Laney cried. "No, no, no, no." She climbed over us and twisted the key from the truck. The engine died.

Laney felt for a pulse then shook her head. Fright filled her eyes. Her mouth opened in an *O*.

Devyn's legs flopped to the cement floor as I pulled him the rest of the way from the truck. "Call for help! Call for help!" I lowered him to lie flat.

Laney ran to the house.

I pinched Devyn's nose and blew a breath into him. I blew again, and again. I watched his chest rise each time like an inflating balloon.

Devyn's skin was cold. His lips were blue. I tasted exhaust from his lack of breath.

Laney?

Laney was gone too long.

Devyn had no pulse. I couldn't find a pulse. And where was Laney? "C'mon, Devyn," I shouted into his face. "C'mon."

Help me, Laney.

I put my hands to his chest as we'd been taught in health class years ago. I pumped to a count. "C'mon, Devyn."

Laney. Help me, Laney.

"C'mon, Devyn. C'mon." I pumped his heart. I gave him mouth-to-mouth. "Devyn!"

Tears flooded my cheeks. "Devyn!" *It's no use. It's no use. Laney. C'mon, Laney.*

I dragged Devyn's body toward Laney's truck. His heels jumped and skittered over the dirt driveway. He slipped from my grasp.

"Laney!"

I heard the screen door of the house slam. Her boots slapped the driveway in rapid succession.

"Laney. Grab his feet."

She jerked the tailgate down. We hoisted him into her truck bed.

"Go. Go. Go," I hollered and climbed in the back with Devyn.

The truck roared to life. Laney gunned the gas and sped from the driveway. The wheels spit pebbles in their wake.

We bombed down the road. My hat flew from my head with the blast of wind. It rolled around inside the truck bed. I pumped at Devyn's chest and gave him mouth-to-mouth.

I swore his cheeks pinked. I thought he drew a shallow breath. I continued.

Laney took the corner into town too fast. I was thrown to the sidewall. Devyn careened onto his face.

She slalomed through the few cars sauntering down Main Street. I was tossed from one side to the other in the truck bed.

I managed to wrestle Devyn's body over as the brakes squealed and the wheels screeched.

The truck plunged to a stop outside the emergency room.

A team of medical personnel engulfed Devyn.

A handheld respirator covered his mouth and nose. Needles were thrust into his arm. The doctor lady mounted the gurney to kneel over Devyn's chest as she manually pumped his heart.

Then, everyone was gone. In a blink of an eye. Gone.

I drooped to the asphalt beneath the open tailgate. I didn't know how long I was there. Eventually, I grabbed my hat and wandered into the waiting area.

Before I could sit, the doctor lady came out. Laney rushed to her and collapsed in her arms.

I caught the doctor lady's eye.

She shook her head.

Laney ran through the double doors into the heart of the hospital.

"He's on life support until his mother arrives," the doctor lady said as she walked over to me. "If you'd like to say good-bye…"

No. No, I wouldn't like to say good-bye because he's not gone. He's not dead. We have a lot to do. Too much to do. Me and Devyn. We're going to chase the pro circuit.

And I knew we never would.

I slammed through the double doors. *Devyn.*

Laney was sitting in a chair next to him. She gripped his hand in hers. He looked like he was sleeping. Just like I'd seen many times before. *Except for the apparatus protruding from his mouth and shushing in a slow rhythm. And except for those wires attached to his chest, and that sound of monitors beeping instead of the low rumble of his snoring.*

I stood rigid in the doorway. My feet wouldn't move any farther. I couldn't make them inch closer. I blocked half the door in my petrified state. If there were low-flying pigeons around, they would have perched on me, mistaking me for a statue.

Laney sobbed at Devyn's side. She laid her forehead to her clutching hand and threw her arm over his ribs.

I swear, what little there was left of my heart broke.

My heart broke for Devyn. It broke for Laney. But I wouldn't let it break for me. No, I didn't let it break for me.

I had no right to hurt. I hadn't seen his pain. He was more than my friend. He was my brother. And I didn't see his pain. I had no right to let my heart break for me. What was my loss? What was my sadness? If I had been a better friend...

And it wasn't about me. It was about him. About all of the things in life he'd miss because he wouldn't be here. My heart broke for him. My heart broke for Devyn.

For Laney.

Most of all for Laney, because they were two halves of a whole. They were like twins who could feel *of* each other, their friendship was so keen. They grew up together. They grew into one another. Like trees too close, their roots were entangled. To love one was to love the other. And I hadn't understood any of that until now.

I had been jealous of them. Now, I felt ashamed of that. I had assumed the worst about Devyn at one point. That was shameful. I hadn't listened to more than his words. I didn't see his pain. I wasn't there to help him when he needed someone. *What kind of selfish monster am I? Shameful.*

Mary Langdon brushed past me to rush to her son's side.

The few times I had gotten a glimpse of her, it struck me how she didn't look at all like her son. She wasn't anything like Devyn.

He was broad-shouldered and wound tight. His hair lay in one length of blond strands, which had looked like a parted mushroom cap on his head. Mary Langdon was, in all appearances, opposite.

And she was nothing like I had envisioned a night owl barkeep to have been. No cigarette hanging precariously from her lower lip. She wasn't tipping the Visine bottle into bloodshot eyes every few minutes. No visible tattoos. To be fair, I had only ever seen her in a long, pink, fuzzy robe or a serious jacket. So I couldn't attest to a total lack of tats.

Mary Langdon sort of reminded me of my daddy. It was her short, wavy brown hair tousled carelessly on top of her head. It was also in the way she moved—kind of relaxed, loose, and lanky. She had that easy confidence my daddy had. Like *get on board or get out of my way, cuz I'm already there.* That was my daddy.

And none of that was neither here nor there at this moment.

I shuffled backwards to leave them to their grief. I hadn't felt right in interrupting with my own. I'd only known Devyn a few short months. Not even. Six or seven weeks. It wasn't like we'd had a lifetime together.

Nor would we.

That made me angry.

I went to find my stepmama's room. Why not? She had been the one who initiated me into this hate-filled town where not even the law could be trusted, and where great evil was awarded greater power. A town where good people were tormented. The town where the best of them died.

Don't be so dramatic. Suck it up.

I was tired of sucking it up.

C'mon, stepmama. Where're you hiding?

The "coma" wing of the hospital was quiet. Too quiet. My bootfalls echoed all around me. And still it was too quiet. It could have been a morgue. No one moved. No doctors stood at the ends of beds scrutinizing charts. No nurses fussed over their patients' IV drips. For a moment, I thought I was in the wrong place. Then I recognized her blond hair spread over her pillow like the translucent wings of a fairy.

The air in her room was a scorching breath of antiseptic. The walls were the color of surgical scrubs. The tile floor was glossy white. And the silent stillness was deafening.

Creepy.

More creepy because my stepmama was still alive. She looked dead. She should be dead. Nope. Still alive. And she had it just how she liked it—waited on, hand and foot.

I sidled up to the bed and peered down at her face. She looked like a wax figure from Madame Tussaud's famous museum.

Monitors jumped in slow, jagged lines. The rise and fall of her chest was barely a whisper under the thick hospital blanket.

I absolutely hated that she looked entirely clean and healthy.

"We had it all. *You* had it all."

Her monitors blipped with a steady pulse. I didn't understand why they bothered to monitor her. Her heart beat, or it didn't. She breathed, or she didn't. What did it matter?

"You had it all. But you were always a spoiled, rich witch. You didn't appreciate anything. You never worked for anything. You never even cared for your own baby daughter."

My stepmama still had an IV drip in her arm. Of what, I wasn't sure. I *was* sure she didn't need it. Or the high-test oxygen going up her nose. She wasn't worthy. Both were wasted on her. Awake, she'd never have appreciated either. The social worker said she had a stomach tube put in. Why feed her? She didn't bother about getting Luce fed.

"You shipped us kids off to boarding school so you wouldn't have to deal with us. Spent my daddy's money on shopping sprees and spas. You lived a perpetual vacation."

I wanted to rip the leads off of her. Jerk her IV out. Clamp the oxygen tube in half.

"When he died? You blew through it all. No one to stop you. Did you think the Autry Academy would keep us kids for free? Just because you didn't want the work of raising us. Just because you didn't want to mother Luce? What the hell?"

I wanted to slap her. *Wake up. Listen to me.*

No, I really didn't want her to wake.

I took a step back.

"Now look at us." I held my arms out and scanned my own

appearance. "Look at me. Look what you've done. I'm a vagrant, living in a halfway house with criminals." I shook my fist in her face. She didn't flinch. Why would she?

What a self-centered bitch. Lying there like you're tanning at the beach.

"Luce doesn't love you anymore. Luce doesn't want you. She wants to be adopted by real parents who will love her and care for her the likes she's never gotten from you. Do you hear me? She doesn't want you. You're no good. You never were. Selfish rich bitch."

I felt my face grow hot. My teeth were clenched. I now understood that saying, *spitting mad.*

"The sheriff's trying to get you locked away. It's where you belong. Never to be seen or heard from again."

Her monitors were steady. They hadn't registered any upset. Nothing unusual there. She never cared.

"Why don't you do us all a favor and die—"

The door slammed open. It thudded against the rubber knob stopper on the wall.

"Chris. Chris." Michael rushed to my side. "Chris. I overheard the sheriff's radio. He was at the County Boys' Home. He was talking to the Sergeant." Michael grabbed my arm and gently tugged. "You have to come with me. Now. The sheriff will be here any minute."

"What does it matter?"

"He's going to arrest you for murder. He told the Sergeant."

"It doesn't matter," I said.

"It does to me." Michael tugged at my arm once again. "It does to Luce." He let go of me when I didn't budge. "I don't think Devyn would want to see you in prison. Not for him. And what about Laney? I think you love her. I think she loves you. What about her?"

Laney.

I followed Michael back through the hospital.

"Wait." I stopped him in the hallway before an exit. "How did you get here?"

He puffed his chest and plucked a set of keys from his baggy shorts. "I stole the bus." The key ring dangled from his pointer finger. He flipped the keys into his palm then closed his hand around them. "They'll have noticed it's missing by now. They'll search for it. C'mon."

I let him lead me through the parking lot behind the hospital. The blue short bus hid stashed among the dumpsters. Sadly, it fit, like a hen gathering her chicks.

Michael shoved at the accordion door, then bounded up the steps. He had the key in the ignition, and the engine turned over like he'd been driving all of his fourteen years.

I hauled myself in by the handrail. I was tired. Too tired.

Michael backed the bus out of close confines. He tagged one of the dumpsters. It yielded. But not before the bus's plastic light cover crunched under the pressure. There was scraping of metal on metal. *That's gonna leave a mark.* And the front tire rolled up over something that tossed us in the air like the swell of an ocean wave.

He ambled down Main Street as if he had all day, so as not to attract attention. Out on the highway, Michael crammed the accelerator to the floor.

The engine was quick to respond with a groan. But its speed remained constant.

Constantly slow.

That's when I began to worry.

I questioned Michael's sanity. *How could he help me after all he's been through? What possessed him to steal the short bus? What was he thinking? Why did he get involved? What would happen when he gets caught?*

He would get caught.

"Stop the bus," I said.

"What? We're almost there."

"Stop the bus."

He lifted his foot from the accelerator and jammed the brake down hard.

I'd never seen a bus skid like it could do donuts in the middle of the road. I'd never heard of a short bus taken for a joy ride.

As we careened onto the gravel shoulder, I was afraid it would roll over.

It stayed upright. We crunched in the gravel to a stop.

"I'll walk from here." I held my hand out to him. "Thanks."

We shook.

"Any time, man. Now go to your truck. Get in. Drive away. And never look back." His face was scrunched with pain or fear. "Don't look back. Never, never come back. You can't." With a sniffle, Michael threw his arms around me. "Not for anything. Not for anyone."

I returned his hug. I didn't want to let go of him.

"I'll draw them off," he said. "They're probably looking for the bus by now."

I levered the door open and leaped down the stairs.

The bus strolled away like it had all day. Like it had all the time in the world and not a care to think of.

I waved. It was stupid. But I waved.

The three-quarter-ton truck was exactly how I had left it mere hours ago. Its dented driver's side door hung open. The keys lay in the middle of the bench seat. I thought I'd see some hint of Devyn. I thought it would all look different somehow. But there was nothing amiss. It was like nothing had happened.

I climbed behind the wheel and stuffed the key into the ignition. But I couldn't turn the engine over. *The muffled rumble. The engulfing fog. The choking exhaust.* It all came rushing back to me.

I pressed my forehead to the steering wheel and clenched my eyes shut.

His face was there. Devyn's face with its gray skin and blue lips.

Devyn's face.

Daddy's face.

Devyn.

Daddy.

Devyn.

I lifted my head and opened my eyes. Devyn's image remained. "You've got this," he seemed to say. "You've got this. Just ride." His image began to fade. "Hang tough," he said.

"Be dangerous," I whispered.

Before I could leave, there was something I had to do. I got out of the truck.

I wanted Devyn's mom to have my winnings.

On the passenger side, I lifted the vinyl at the back of the bench seat. My growing stack of cash was nestled against the springs and stuffing. Now, there was one other thing lying there too. A neatly folded white piece of paper lay on top.

I was afraid to touch it.

I was afraid of what it might say.

I was afraid of what it wouldn't say.

It wouldn't tell me that Devyn was alive and well.

It could only confirm that he wasn't.

I didn't want it.

In the driveway, gravel crunched beneath the tires of a slow moving vehicle. Someone was coming.

CHAPTER FOURTEEN

The radio in the patrol car squelched.

I smoothed the vinyl down over my stash of cash with shaking fingers. Slowly...gently...without any noise...I closed the truck's door and crouched low to the floor.

At that same time, Sheriff Bubba Taylor stepped from the patrol car. He opened its back door. Scuzz-cut and Mullet-head tumbled from the rear like clowns at a circus.

It was obvious they were here for me.

A shiver ran the length of my spine. My legs felt shaky and weak. There was no way I was going back to the County Boys' Home. There was no way Sheriff Taylor would get me in custody. No way I'd let him arrest me for murdering my best friend.

But there was no way I could leave town either. Not without Luce. And she was content to stay.

"Don't damage anything. Don't disrupt anything. Just find him if he's here." The sheriff slapped a pair of work gloves against his leg for emphasis. Scuzz-cut's face cracked in a sly grin. Mullet-head snapped to attention and saluted. In the next moment, Mullet-head buckled over from Scuzz-cut's halfhearted slug to his belly.

"Quit your kidding around." The sheriff grew impatient. "I don't want anyone to know we came here looking for him. You hear me? No one's to know we were here."

"Yessir," Mullet-head said.

"I'm going to drive the highway. If you get him, you hold him. Nothing else. He's mine." His face glowed red beneath the brim of his hat.

Scuzz-cut faked a yawn. Mullet-head nodded like an eager child.

The sheriff got into the patrol car and sped off. The tires sprayed dirt and gravel in their wake.

Devyn's garage, which I'd once marveled at as the Disney World of bull riding, had suddenly become very very small. I saw nowhere to hide. My heart struggled to beat, like a ton of bricks was sitting on my chest.

"Where should we look?" Mullet-head asked.

"Well, duh, Devyn's garage. He told me it was his hangout. Was gonna show it to me. Let me practice on his equipment."

I was trapped.

"But Chris ain't here. He'd have to be stupid to come back," Scuzz-cut replied.

I crouched lower and watched them contemplate the distance from in front of the house, where the sheriff left them off, to the garage.

Mullet-head started this way.

"Hey." Scuzz-cut grabbed his arm. "If we find him, he's mine. Not the sheriff's. You hear?"

Mullet-head stared at Scuzz-cut without acknowledging.

"Do you hear?"

Scuzz-cut's grip must have gotten fierce because Mullet-head winced.

I lay on the cement floor to roll under the truck. The hiding place was too obvious. I'd be found in a second. My pulse raced. It drummed throughout my body. My binding felt too tight. It grew clammy with the sticky wetness of cold sweat.

Mullet-head started in my direction again.

My breath hitched. The truck wouldn't hide me for long. And then what?

Would they haul me out by my feet? Would I get a chance to stand before Scuzz-cut started pummeling me? Or would he kick me where I lay?

I needed a plan. My brain surged with what-ifs, but it didn't focus. I couldn't focus.

If I could hold out until the sheriff returned… Would he be any safer than Scuzz-cut and Mullet-head? Or would he use them to hurt me?

Did he want to control me?

Or did he mean to kill me?

Scuzz-cut turned and went toward the house.

"Where're you going? You said the garage." Mullet-head followed Scuzz-cut for a few steps.

I breathed out. My sigh could have been heard in the next county. I bit onto my lower lip and mentally chastised myself. My head began to throb.

"You go ahead. I just wanna have a look to see if the house is unlocked." Scuzz-cut yanked the screen door. It screeched in protest.

"We're not supposed to wreck anything. No one's supposed to know we were here."

"No one's gonna know we were here." Scuzz-cut let go of the screen door. It smacked shut. "Besides, what if he's hiding in the house?"

I shimmied from under the truck and rolled to a crouch on the other side. Maybe I could escape the garage. If I did, the wide-open space was rugged enough to hide me. There were hillocks and brush—

Scuzz-cut opened the screen door again. As ever, it squealed in complaint.

I waited for Mullet-head to follow. When he did, I'd make a break for it.

If I could get around the back of the garage unseen, I could drop into the brush.

Mullet-head stood his ground in the driveway. "I'll wait here. It's not a good idea to go that house."

Go with him, Mullet-head. Go with him.

"Great. You wait. More for me. Door's unlocked." Scuzz-cut grinned at Mullet-head then thrust the door wide.

Go on. Go on. Follow him. Follow him in.

"It's not a good idea," Mullet-head repeated under his breath. It was only that the breeze had brought his words to me rather than Scuzz-cut that he was still standing. He winced. Realizing his mistake, I was sure.

Mullet-head leaned toward following Scuzz-cut. He took a step in Scuzz-cut's direction. Then he stiffened his spine and his resolve. "That's breaking and entering. It's a felony." Mullet-head planted his feet.

"What? I didn't break anything. I'm only entering. It's only half a felony." Scuzz-cut laughed. "What are you? A pussy?" He let the screen slam shut. "Besides, the sheriff told us to."

"He didn't tell us to go inside the house."

Scuzz-cut surged toward Mullet-head with a speed I didn't think his thick frame possessed. He wrung Mullet-head's sweatshirt at the neckline and stuffed a fist to his nose. "Shut up. You wanna be a pussy, stay here. But shut up."

I could have used that moment to make my move. I should have escaped my confines. I didn't. Instead, I stared.

It was like watching a train wreck. As anyone could get caught up in. *Human nature.* I wanted to see what happened because it might get epic. But I didn't want to see, because there wasn't enough bleach in the entire world to wash it from my brain afterward. My feet lodged. My mouth opened. My mind was captivated.

He had helped me once. Mullet-head. He had pulled Devyn from me when we fought. I wondered if he'd help me again. I didn't think so. "Just this once," he'd said.

I wondered if I should help him.

I know I should have run while they argued.

Scuzz-cut released Mullet-head. "C'mon. We'll check the garage first." He smoothed Mullet-head's sweatshirt over his shoulders to right any wrinkles he caused. "But then I'm going into that house. You'll stand watch for me. Let me know if anyone comes up the driveway."

I scurried to the back wall like a trapped rat. I wrapped my fingers around the full-length curtain that closed off the wall-length closet. I fussed with its folds to find the opening.

"Check this out. Devyn's truck." Scuzz-cut pounded on the hood. "The dude was totally sorry with this hunk of junk."

My hat. It's on the floor in plain sight. Right where I got down to hide under the truck.

I drew the curtains in front of my nose.

Their bootfalls slapped the cement. They had come into the garage. Past the truck. One of them set the drop barrel to rocking. It squeaked on its hinge.

My heart pounded in my chest. I thought it would explode. At the very least, I thought they'd hear it.

Their steps came closer.

My palms were wet with sweat. My mouth went dry.

I shrunk against the wall, behind the protective vests. The hanging vests shifted with my movement. The coat hangers scraped the rod.

The sound—the sound echoed in my head and amplified tenfold.

"Hey, what's behind the huge curtain?" Mullet-head asked.

A set of footsteps scuffed the floor right in front of me. They stopped.

I could hear their rapid breathing just beyond the thin veil.

I held my own breath.

In the middle of the garage, a glass bottle skittered. It rolled over the cement until it crashed into a nest of other strewn bottles.

I winced. I touched the scar on my cheek in a knee-jerk reaction.

"The Devyn kid drank some serious beer," Scuzz-cut said. "Wonder if he's got any more laying around here?"

I almost breathed a sigh of relief. I could envision them popping tops off beer bottles and guzzling brew down. I wished they'd cop a squat on the bench seat to get totally wasted. I hoped—

I gripped on to the rod that held the vests. I slowly drew my knees to my chest.

The curtain was pulled open but it caught before exposing me.

I squeezed my eyes shut and tried to make myself as small as I could.

I clung to the rod and kept my feet from the ground.

"Check it out. Devyn's got like a warehouse of bull riding fashion. The guy was a maven." Mullet-head trailed his fingertips over the shoulders of the hanging vests. They moved in front of me.

I held tighter to the rod, kept my knees to my chest, and mashed myself against the end wall.

"Where'd you learn a word like that?" Scuzz-cut asked. "Maven. Maaaaven." He laughed.

"Sometimes I pay attention in school."

"What for?"

A vest, two away from my nose, moved from his touch. Mullet-head plucked one of the protective vests from its hanger. The empty hanger swung.

"What for?" He slipped his arms into the vest. "So I don't have to ride bulls to better myself." He shrugged his shoulders into its bulk then zipped it up.

"Found it," Scuzz-cut said. "Devyn's stash."

"What do you think?" Mullet-head turned from the closet. Arms out, he pivoted in a full circle.

"I think it's time to drink." A bottle top popped. Beer splashed the floor.

Slurping, sucking sounds assaulted my hearing.

I dared to peek over the rod.

Scuzz-cut flopped onto the bench seat. Mullet-head joined him and twisted off a bottle cap also.

Before they got too deep in beer, gravel crunched beneath car tires out in the driveway.

Mullet-head jumped up to strip off the vest. Scuzz-cut stored bottles of beer in his waistband at the small of his back. He tugged his sweatshirt over them and walked to the door.

The patrol car's radio squelched.

"All clear, boss," Scuzz-cut reported.

I didn't dare breathe a sigh of relief. I didn't dare let my feet touch the floor. Not yet. Not just yet.

I don't know how long I hung there.

Late afternoon turned into evening. The sun was going down. A chill wind came up.

My stomach muscles burned. My arms cramped. My legs were permanently folded to my chest. The tips of my toes tired of clutching at the wall for purchase.

Still, I refused to let go of the rod.

When the gray haze of dusk bathed the driveway in obscurity, I finally dropped and ran.

My first steps faltered. I stumbled through the garage. Fell to my knees. Clawed my way to the door. And ran.

I ran through the chilled evening air. I dodged brush and sent rocks fleeing as I ran to the highway.

On the road's edge, I stuck my thumb out as an old Subaru Brat zipped toward me. *The rest of the world doesn't know of Devyn's death. The rest of the world isn't looking for me.* The car pulled to a stop on the shoulder.

It was driven by a man in his mid-thirties. His wife, or girlfriend, or sister for all I knew, sat in the passenger seat next to him. She was heavily pregnant. A girl about Luce's age was strapped in one of the jump seats out back.

"Need a lift?"

"I sure do, sir." I schooled my breath so he wouldn't become alarmed.

"Where ya going?" His face was friendly. His smile seemed genuine.

"Nearer to town. Farther down the road will do." I purposefully flashed a disarming grin at him.

"And that's just about where I'm headed. Farther down the road." He laughed. "But I'm not going as far as town." He looked over at the woman and placed his hand on her leg. "Not yet anyways."

She smiled an envious smile at him.

"Hop in if ya have a mind to," he said.

"Thank you, sir." I jumped into the Brat's bed. The little girl giggled. The Subaru Brat ripped onto the highway.

When the Brat left me, I stayed well off the side of the road, in the scrub brush. Laney's was just over the next rise.

Cattle dotted the horizon. They were black splotches on a gray background. I made my way toward them.

As I approached, I heard them lowing. I got close enough to hear the soft suckle of a calf on her dam's teat. I heard their soothing rhythmic cud chewing. I smelled the fermentation on their breath. Any other time, in any other place, I'd have lingered, to lose myself in their tranquility.

I scurried past the cattle to the barn. No, I didn't have a plan. Laney's was the only friendly face I thought of with the sheriff hunting me.

Her truck isn't here.

Of course not. She's at the hospital.

I hunkered near the barn. A yellow bulb flickered overhead. It had plenty of power to illuminate the opening and then some. Light stretched into the yard. Inside, the barn was well lit also.

I listened. There was no noise.

A car was driving up. Followed by the heavier sound of a truck engine.

I dodged into the barn.

The barn aisle ran straight through to an opening at the other end. Horse stalls lined one side. Hay was stacked in bays along the other. The packed bales left nowhere to hide. I didn't have time to climb to the top. Someone might come in at any moment.

I listened for voices. Heard none. Three of the car's doors slammed in succession. One heavier door slammed after. *Laney?*

I was exposed in the aisle. All anyone needed to do was glance this way.

I grabbed the nearest latch and rolled its stall door open a crack. I slipped in, then reached through the bars to relatch the door.

When I turned around, Gold Rush met me. She fussed at my arm. I showed her my empty hands. "I haven't got anything, girl," I whispered. Her ears flickered back and forth. I stroked her neck. She pressed her forehead to my chest.

Two sets of footfalls entered the barn.

I crawled under the hanging corner grain bucket where it was impossible to see me.

Breathe. Breathe. Slow. In through your nose. Out through your mouth. Like blowing over the top of a thermos of hot coffee. My heart rate slowed. I rocked in place, hunched over my folded legs.

"You didn't have to take off from work." Laney's voice was strained. As if she might cry at any moment. "I told you I was all right."

"I heard you," the doctor lady said. "But I wanted to make sure." A bale of hay thunked to the floor. "I'm here for you, Laney. Really. I don't want anything to happen to you."

Gold Rush nuzzled my knees. She blew a warm breath in my face that smelled of alfalfa and sunshine and happiness. I placed my hand on her forehead.

I bit into my cheek. Blood oozed onto my tongue. Tears slipped from my eyes.

Grain rattled in the tub above me as Gold Rush's dinner was poured in.

Gold Rush lipped at the tears on my face, then licked her lips. She put her head in the air to curl her upper lip in a flehmen reaction.

"Rush? What's wrong?" Laney asked.

The latch slid open with a bang and the door rolled away.

Laney gasped.

"What is it?" the doctor lady asked. Her footsteps slapped along the barn aisle.

I placed a finger to my lips. "Shh."

"No. Nothing. It's nothing. Gold Rush is acting finicky is all. I think I'll groom her for a bit while she eats. It'll soothe her."

"Are you sure it's nothing? Should I call the vet?"

"She's fine. I just want time alone. With Rush." Laney stepped into the stall and shut the door. "I'll be up to the house in a little while." Laney hugged Gold Rush.

"Okay then," the doctor lady said. I heard her footsteps retreat.

"She's gone," Laney whispered.

I stood.

"Where'd you go?" Laney continued to whisper.

"I had to leave." I swallowed. "The sheriff—"

She clasped my face between her hands. Her fingers were hot against my ears. Laney's eyes searched my own.

I sniffled.

I was embarrassed by the wetness she'd feel on my cheeks. Embarrassed that my face must be red and my eyes puffy. I wasn't prone to crying. I mean, not in front of anyone. Not in front of a girl. A girl I liked.

I hiccupped on a sob and couldn't speak.

She drew my face toward her, ever so gently.

We stared into each other's eyes.

There was too much pain clouding Laney's eyes. Too much sorrow.

She moved her face to mine. Our noses brushed. Laney kissed me. Her lips were a soft caress. I almost didn't believe it, their touch was so light.

My heart thumped against my ribs. My stomach somersaulted. Laney had kissed me.

Her lips had softly trespassed over mine, like a whisper on a breeze.

I hugged my arms around her and twisted the back of her sweatshirt in my fists.

She released my face. Her hands roamed my neck. They were sticky with wet. She raised up on her toes. And pressed her body to me.

Our lips collided hard and fast. *Fireworks!* All of the stars in heaven exploded inside my head to create fireworks. Her kiss was all that I'd ever dreamed of and more. I clung to her. She clawed at my neck. We danced like two feral cats.

Our tongues tested then tasted then wrestled. As if—as if the world would end at any second and we would be torn apart for all of eternity.

"Laney," the doctor lady shrieked. The stall door slammed open.

I ran. I ran past the doctor lady. I ran from the stall. From the barn.

I ran because the doctor lady had dated Sheriff Taylor. I ran because she had ratted me out before and could easily rat me out again. I ran because she wanted to protect her sister from the likes of me. I ran because she didn't like who I was. What I was. How I was.

I ran because bigoted people were dangerous hopped up on their self-righteous indignation.

I ran.

Darkness had descended in full. The clouds moved across to cover the moon. The stars couldn't pierce the shroud. And still, I ran.

Out on the highway it was nothing to get picked up. A boy. Alone. Late at night.

I didn't scrutinize. I took the first ride that slowed down. What did it matter anyway?

Luce. It wasn't fair for me to become a statistic and leave my sister alone with grief.

Laney. She didn't deserve any more pain in her life. Not after Devyn. She didn't deserve my selfish risk-taking.

Michael. Michael needed a friend. I was his only friend. I couldn't let him down.

"Let me off here, please."

The car continued to speed along the road. The man held a lighter to the tip of a cigarette that hung from his lips. The momentary flare lit his gaunt face. He was in need of a shave.

"Let me out."

The man puffed the cigarette to glowing. "Boy, there's nothing out here. Town is miles in the other direction."

"Stop. Now."

"Okay, okay. Keep your shirt on." He slowed to a stop.

I bolted.

The chill wind whipped through my shirt, making me shiver. Brush snagged my pants, causing me to slow. I stumbled and fell. I had to carefully pick a path over the rubble-strewn ground in the darkest of dark.

At first, I didn't know where I was headed.

When I looked up, I knew I shouldn't have gone back.

It wasn't home. But Devyn's garage was the only place that had felt like home this past year. Since my daddy died.

I knew it wasn't my home. And the only thing that had made it feel like home—the only one who had made it feel like home—was dead.

I dropped to my knees in front of the garage. I dropped to my knees and sobbed.

A keening escaped my lips.

Lights flickered on in the house.

Spooked, I skittered into the garage in the dark.

The front door of the house opened. The screen door squealed. "Who's out there?"

I sat statue still.

She finally went inside. The lights went out, except for a struggling bulb in the kitchen.

I didn't move. Maybe it was twenty minutes. Maybe it was an hour. I was afraid to move. Afraid to be found out.

When I was sure all was quiet, I crab-walked to the three-quarter-ton and opened the passenger side door. Of all the times for the cab light to work and the buzzer to sound off. I couldn't believe it. Those had faltered years ago. But now the buzzer sounded in alarm. And that light lit the entire garage.

Which wasn't true. Not the entire garage. But that's what it felt like.

I closed the door to squelch the alarm and its unforgiving floodlight. It was too late. I had been found out.

The house was ablaze with lights.

I rolled beneath the truck to come out on the other side.

Déjà vu.

I was getting tired of running. Tired of hiding.

She cautiously approached.

My brain screamed run.

Instead, I stepped out from hiding and waited.

Devyn's mom stopped in front of me. She was wearing her nightgown and pink, fuzzy robe. A double-barreled shotgun was in her hands. Her thumb caressed its hammers.

"Chris. You can't be here." She looked conflicted between chasing me off and hugging me tight. "You can't."

"I know," I said. I wondered if I should put my hands up.

"No. You don't. They're looking for you."

"I'm not going to cause you any trouble," I said. "Um, Mrs. Langdon, could you point the gun down?"

"Oh. I'm sorry, dear." She lowered the shotgun. "Just for the night."

"Ma'am?"

"You can stay for the night. We'll figure something out in the morning." She sniffled back a sob and wiped her nose on her fuzzy sleeve. Her face was a bloated mess. "Do you want to come into the house?"

"No. If you don't mind, I'd like to be in the garage."

She looked worried. Her forehead wrinkled in concern like Devyn's had. Her eyes squinted in concentration, like Devyn's had.

"Just for the night," I added.

Mary Langdon pulled the garage door closed.

I felt trapped.

I know I wasn't. I could leave any time. I could take the truck and drive from here. But I had nowhere to go. And what about Luce? I'd never leave Luce.

Why, Devyn? Why?

I thought of the letter. I needed to read it. Maybe then all of this would make sense. I had to read Devyn's letter. But I didn't want to.

I opened the truck door, sat down, and got the letter out. I placed it on the floor beside me and smoothed it flat.

The truck's cab light flooded over it.

Chris,

I found my father. He and my mother were high school sweethearts. He wasn't aware of my existence. They had separated when he could no longer deny that he was gay.

My mother came back to her hometown pregnant and had never mentioned me to him.

He never sent those gifts over the years.

Your father did. Buckshot Taylor.

My mother is your aunt. The older sister of Buck Taylor. Her name was Mary Lucine Taylor. She was called MaryLu. We are cousins, Chris. And we have an uncle far worse than imaginable. Bubba Taylor. He will be the death of his entire family. There's no escape.

He's coming for you.

CHAPTER FIFTEEN

He's coming for you.
    Why?
    I folded the letter, shoved it into my pocket, took a notebook from my locker, then slammed the door. School was a ghost town. Teachers' hushed whispers spoke of Devyn's memorial service on Friday. Much of the senior class hadn't come in. Many underclassmen that had grown up knowing Devyn hadn't shown either.
    If the sheriff wanted to find me, it wouldn't be difficult.
    "Faggot."
    I slowly turned around.
    "Devyn was a faggot," Scuzz-cut said. "You hung out with him all the time. Maybe you're a faggot too."
    "That's right," one of the football jocks said. I didn't know his name. I'd seen him around the halls, but we weren't acquainted.
    "You finally made some friends," I said to Scuzz-cut. They had me surrounded and outnumbered. "That's nice." I shifted my notebook to my right hand. "What'd you bribe them with? Devyn's beer?"
    Scuzz-cut's face flamed red. He clenched his jaw and pulled his lips into a slash.
    There was no way I would have known about the beer unless I was there when he stole it.
    It was almost painful to watch the strain on Scuzz-cut's face as he figured out what I was saying. *Lightbulb.*
    Duh, I was there.
    I waited for him to make the first move, knowing it wasn't his style if there was a chance he'd get caught.

"As long as Devyn didn't mess with anyone, and as long as he kept making a name for this school, we turned a blind eye," one of the jock kids said.

"Generous of you," I said without turning from Scuzz-cut. "And the invite to his parties? Being part of his *in* crowd?"

"You know nothing, Chris Taylor. You only just moved here."

"Tell me about it, stud."

I had my desired effect. The jock kid lunged at me.

"Break it up." The vice principal shoved through the crowd to haul the kid from me. But his buddies beat the vice principal to it.

"Move along," the vice principal said. "Move along."

Scuzz-cut mouthed, "You're dead." And I wondered if he knew of the sheriff's plans.

"Chris. I should have known. Trouble follows you everywhere." The vice principal placed his hands on his hips.

I glared at him. "Yessir."

"Don't you have somewhere to be?"

Okay. So that pretty much summed up my week. Wednesday was a repeat of Tuesday. Thursday was a repeat of Wednesday.

Friday, the school was closed for Devyn's memorial service. It was held at the high school's arena.

Devyn's urn was on the ground in a ring of flowers in front of the bucking chutes. He was normally larger than life, and I wondered how Devyn could be reduced to the size of a jelly jar stuffed in some fancy, oriental-looking crock.

I didn't literally question. I understand the process of cremation.

I stayed on the outskirts of the service. Funerals weirded me out. And I didn't know what to expect at a memorial.

No official words were spoken. No one blessed Devyn to keep him safe in his next journey.

A long, somber procession slowly passed in front of the bucking chutes where each person laid flowers or photos or trinkets of memories around Devyn's urn.

A mob gathered in the center of the arena, surrounding Mary Langdon, who clutched on to Laney. Laney's parents stood behind them, as silent and as white as ghosts. They shook hands with other mourners when offered. The doctor lady stroked Laney's dark hair from time to time.

I didn't really know any of them.

There were a few faces I recognized. Red. The vice principal. Some students. The owner of the grain store. And the sheriff. *Sheriff Bubba Taylor. My uncle.*

I didn't understand any of it. The procession. The mourners. Leaving a scant bit of memory in the dirt.

I didn't know how I felt. I knew how I should have felt, I guess. Maybe I didn't.

With Daddy, the hurt was gut-wrenchingly real. I couldn't escape the pain.

Devyn's death? It only made me angry.

And alone. Maybe I felt more alone for having had his friendship, then losing it. But that was selfish.

If I didn't understand, I wondered if many of them did.

It isn't fair to mourn a person's death if you didn't help them celebrate in life.

Michael's familiar pitter-patter approached me from behind. He had been down there. He had dropped a bauble for Devyn.

"What was it?" I asked without looking at him. I'm not sure if I resented him for knowing how to accept Devyn's death or envious because he could do so. Michael hadn't known Devyn. Not really. I mean, I shared all of my adventures with Michael. But he hadn't known him. Maybe that had made it easier.

"The bull. The one from my game board."

I nodded.

"I brought you something." He took a scrap of black T-shirt from his pocket. The patch had four tiny tails. Two hanging from either side. He pointed to his upper arm. "I was making them…for Devyn. It's all I could think to do."

Anger welled inside me. I could feel it creeping beneath my skin. "Why? You didn't know him." It came out like an accusation.

"You did. And I know you. It's something you do for those you care about."

He looked uncomfortable, like I'd put him on the spot.

I guess I had. I touched his arm and bit my lower lip. It was all the apology I could muster. *If I want to take someone's head off, that someone shouldn't be Michael.*

"Anyways," he said, "some of the guys at the County Home

saw me. A couple of them sat down at the table to help." He kicked his toe at the dirt. "'For Chris,' they said."

For Devyn. "Thank them for me."

I held out my arm when he pointed. A limp duffel bag slid from my shoulder. I let it drop to the ground.

The duffel bag contained near to every cent I owned. I picked it up after Michael tied the armband on me, then handed it to him. No hesitation. No second thought.

"I need you to place a bet," I said to Michael. "Put it all on my next ride. No matter what." I stared into the distance.

I heard Michael unzip the duffel. He whistled.

"I don't want to live another day waiting to get out," I said. "I don't want to live waiting for help. Help's not coming." Maybe I wasn't making much sense. "We're not children anymore. If we want to make a change, we have to help ourselves. He knew."

Devyn.

I could still see his blue eyes and disarming smile. He was ruggedly handsome. I still heard the low timbre of his voice in my head. I thought I smelled his aftershave on the stale arena air.

I had felt his excitement. I had known his hopes. His desires.

I should have listened.

I remembered him slumped on the bench seat of his garage, surrounded by beer bottles. I heard him slurp and belch. I smelled his stale, fermented breath.

I felt his angry punch. Sad eyes. Waning smile. Forced cheer.

I should have known.

"If anything happens to me, you take the money and get out. Make sure Luce gets some for college."

Michael didn't say anything. What was there to say? He quietly left.

I was alone again.

Evening descended. The crowd dissipated.

When there was no one in the arena, I meandered toward Devyn. *What remains of Devyn.*

A sob choked in my throat. I swallowed the lump. Flames on the candles danced on the slight breeze. I took my black felt hat from my head. "Devyn…" I played with the brim. "Devyn…I'm sorry." I held the hat over my heart. The turkey feather in the hat band scratched my chin. I slowly drew it out. "I'm supposed to say something, I guess. I don't know what to say." I twirled the turkey feather. "I don't know what to feel. I'm sad then angry then hurt then angry then sad. It always comes back to angry. I'm angry." I toed the dirt. Grit sprayed and snuffed out a candle.

"The world was a better place with you in it." I felt tears burn behind my eyes as I held them back. "Why?" A sob escaped me. I bit my tongue to squelch any others. "How could you be so much a part of me when we hadn't known each other for very long? I loved you, Devyn."

Cousins. We were cousins, though he had felt more like a brother. "I miss you already." I laid the feather at the base of his urn then walked away.

I'll do what you couldn't. I'll escape the sheriff. Or one of us will die in trying. Let's hope it's him.

"Who'd you draw?" Laney asked on Saturday afternoon.

She'd caught me by surprise. I hadn't expected her to come to the rodeo. Devyn's memorial was still planted in the arena. I had sat in the bleachers overnight to watch the sun rise from behind the chutes. The wind had blown all of the candles out and scattered many of the memories people left.

Would Laney be haunted with Devyn's memories? Being here? Watching the bull riding?

I was more than happy to see her. I missed her. I wanted more of us. But yeah, Devyn's absence was in our way forever now. It just was.

I remembered the first time I saw her. I mean really saw her. Devyn and I were hanging out on the bleachers. I'd almost swallowed my own tongue. The sun was shining. Her hair was as black and iridescent as a raven's wing. Big, beautiful brown eyes. Tall, thin, and beautiful. *Did I say beautiful twice?* Laney was gorgeous. She ruffled Devyn's bowl cut, and I'd wished it were me she touched.

What I'd give to have her fingers ruffle through my hair...

I released a sigh that originated from my booted toes. I wanted to hug her. To hold her. But it didn't feel right. Not now.

"Thundering Bunny." I answered her question. "I drew Thundering Bunny."

"It'd be easier to baptize a cat." Laney's face was lined with concern where grief hadn't already camped out. Her wrinkled blouse hung limp from her slumped shoulders. The black armband slipped to perch under her elbow. Her hair was hastily coiled into a bun. Dull wisps had escaped on each side of her face. She didn't have a hat. When did she ever go to a rodeo without a hat?

Laney was in some serious hurt.

"That bull's got his own fan club. You know who the crowd will be rooting for."

I nodded. "I wouldn't count me out, though. There's nothing I can't get ridden." What else could I say? *Sorry for your loss? My condolences?* I'm sure she'd heard those over and over again. Even to me, they sounded trite.

"I'd never count you out." She gave me a peck on the cheek and moved off. I swear she struggled to hold her composure. She was stiff. Her stride was clipped. "Luck on the Bunny," she said over her shoulder, just like Devyn had the first time I met him.

"Thundering Bunny. He's badass," I said under my breath.

I scraped at my rope with a wire brush, too hard. If I wasn't careful, I'd do more than take old rosin off. I'd take the life from the strands.

What did I care? How could I care? Like the saying goes, "Life is fleeting." Devyn's life was too short. Instead of being wrapped up in myself, I should have helped him live it. We should have left here. We could have chased the bull riding circuit. Like he had wanted to.

Red came up behind me. He placed his hand on my shoulder. I jumped at his touch.

He didn't speak right away. I watched his face for any clue as to what he'd say. His eyes were bloodshot. His cheeks were slack. His eyebrows lunged at each other as if squaring off for a fight, then retreated, then lunged again.

But it was in the way he stood, commanding yet soft. It was his firm, reassuring hold on my shoulder. The way I swear he knew all about me but would let me be who I was. He reminded me of—

My mother. I had studied photos of my mother. It was all I had had of her. I'd studied them until my mind made her walk and talk. Her poses were very telling. I felt her by the way she stood in those pictures. I knew her glances. Heard her inflections. I had thought I'd made it all up. What she'd say. How she'd sound.

But here she was, in Red. Her movements. Her mannerisms. He looked just the way I'd imagined her sad smile. The way she'd look at me full of concern and knowing.

I shook my head. I was just missing the things I didn't have. I was probably looking to find those in anyone. It was stupid. There was only me. There might still be me and Luce, though.

My monkey girl. I wanted her to have everything I didn't, and more. I wanted her to know she was loved. Daddy loved her. *To the moon and back.*

Last time I spoke to Daddy, we argued about me bull riding. We argued right before he died.

"Son, you can't help the yesterdays," Red said. "But you sure can do something about the tomorrows." He took his hand from my shoulder and stood to his full height. His black arm band had slipped too. He shoved it up. "Hang tough," he said as he walked away.

"Be dangerous," I replied. But he didn't look back.

Rank. That's how Thundering Bunny was best described. It was said he couldn't be ridden. Never knew what he was going to do. He had the kick, the drop, the blistering spin, and he never settled into a routine. He was rank. And clever. And talented. *A rising star.*

I dropped my bull rope along his side. He lazily flicked his head as if warning a fly.

I felt the crowd's collective intake of breath. I felt their waiting. I'd have to wait too.

Jump for jump. There's no reading him.

I missed Devyn. That time he smacked me on the boot and said, "Luck on the Bunny." I swallowed and choked.

Don't think on him now.

I planned a strategy to keep my mind busy.

That was all wrong. My daddy said never make a plan. The bulls won't stick to it. Nevertheless—

With my mind on sideways, I lowered myself back onto Thundering Bunny.

The rope puller held the tail of my rope taut. He wore a black armband.

I worked the rosin. The entire chute crew wore black armbands for Devyn. It was almost like Devyn was here, watching. Maybe. That might sound stupid. But I wanted it to be true.

When I asked, the rope puller hauled more slack out before I took a wrap.

I swear Thundering Bunny turned his head and rolled his eye as if to say, "No hard feelings. It's business."

The arena crowd sucked in one big, consolidated breath.

Right. Business. I tossed the tail over Thundering Bunny's hump and gave my gloved hand a last punch to tighten my grip.

Winky to the pinky. Slide and ride. I got up over Thundering Bunny and nodded.

The latch screeched. The chute flung open.

Thundering Bunny leaped straight in the air.

The crowd went into an uproar.

As soon as he came down, he turned back, *away* from my hand. He took a huge jump, belying his size. *Bam.* He landed on all fours. There was no shock absorption through his hocks. He had stiffened them like posts.

My ears slapped my shoulders. A crunching sound reverberated in my head.

A fog of dizzy nauseousness encroached. I felt my arm waver. My seat slid. I got behind.

I needed to be up over the bull. But I didn't have the raw strength to haul myself into position. *Sitting is quitting.*

If Thundering Bunny spun this second, I'd be thrown.

But Thundering Bunny sank to the ground in a crouch. He bucked backwards.

It threw me from my pockets onto my thighs. I got up over him again.

Then he spun.

With his short back, Thundering Bunny got around fast. I slipped toward the well. I tried to set my spur. It was like somebody had greased him. At one point, my free arm flailed too far across the front of me. My hips got wrong.

I worried on that. And playing catch-up wasn't the game to be in.

My brain got in my way. *Let it go. Breathe.*

I willed myself to stop thinking. Stop worrying about how everything wasn't going the way I wanted. Stop fighting the ride. Fighting myself. My fears. My anger. My loneliness. *Let it go.*

My mind quieted. Balance, flexibility, coordination, and quick reflexes flowed through me. *Meet him jump for jump.* Foundation.

My foundation was solid. I was made of good stuff.

Was it enough so late in the ride?

Yes.

I made it to the buzzer, jerked the rope's tail, and flew from Thundering Bunny.

When I landed, I was slow to get up. Cotton filled the space between my ears. I wasn't sure exactly where my head sat. Dizziness told me that the crunch I'd felt during the ride might have been something in my neck.

A hand grabbed my vest. The bullfighter lifted me to my feet. It was all a blur when he took a hit.

Thundering Bunny had doubled back from the out gate. He had slammed the bullfighter at a dead run.

I stumbled to keep my feet. I shook my head to rid it of the haze.

Thundering Bunny's mass bunched to a stop. He spun and lined that downed bullfighter up in both eyes.

The other two bullfighters scrambled to close in. But they'd be a split-second too late.

The downed bullfighter was barely to his knees. The next hit could destroy him.

Thundering Bunny's head bobbed. Arena dirt flew from his pawing.

His mass surged forward.

I was on my feet. I could take his hit. I was just as fearless in front of the bulls as on their backs. I knew how to do it.

Thundering Bunny lowered his head to slam the bullfighter. I jumped across and planted my rump on his poll.

He lifted his head from the bullfighter. It was enough. The bullfighter rolled away.

I wasn't so lucky.

Thundering Bunny threw me into the air like tossing the Mrs. Beasley doll Luce played with when she was four.

Coming down, I smashed against the panels. There were enough wits left in me to grasp the top rail. I draped from it like a bug splattered on a windshield.

The bullfighters closed in on Thundering Bunny to harry him out the gate.

Behind the chutes, I buckled to the dirt.

Michael rushed to my side. "Is it that bad, Chris?"

"It'll do till bad shows up." I unzipped my vest. "How's Thundering Bunny?" I asked with a smile. "Hope I wasn't too hard on him." I winked.

"He looks better than you. You're a little green around the gills."

"How'd you get here? Hitch again?" I asked Michael.

He waggled his thumb. "Mary Langdon picked me up. Ya know, she told me all about how she's never missed a rodeo. Sat in the crowd so Devyn couldn't see her. Had to chase him everywhere. Took a lot of time off work. Said she had to work all the wrong shifts just to watch her son ride."

"I didn't know."

"She said Devyn didn't want her at the rodeos. She has a canister of ticket stubs in her glove box."

I felt sweat sop my binding in the middle of my back. It's funny how you see people around and never really get to know them past a quick judgment and an even quicker dismissal.

I leaned my back against the panel. The bells on my rope clanked their peculiar sound, reminding me that I still choked their leash. "How'd we do?" I asked.

"You didn't hear the loudspeakers? You really must be hurt." He helped prop me against the panels. "Eighty-nine, brother. Eighty-nine. You've got this round. A few more riders to go. But no one's gonna touch that."

"Did you make the bet?"

"I put everything on you," Michael said. "I'll go collect when the event is over. Where we gonna meet?"

I gripped the rails and vomited. "Truck."

For old time's sake, I bought a soft serve ice cream. It would settle my stomach more than fried dough or those big sausages. My head was pounding. I pulled my hat brim low over my eyes. The gear bag on my shoulder weighed a ton. I lapped at the ice cream and forgot about my pains.

Sheriff Bubba Taylor was waiting for me in the parking lot.

Plop. My soft serve ice cream landed on the hard-packed dirt.

Uncle Bubba. His patrol car blocked the front of my truck. He leaned his buttocks on the hood and scratched at the sores below his ear. "You'll be coming with me," Sheriff Taylor said as he stood.

I walked past him to drop my gear bag into the truck. The passenger door opened with a groan and a squeak.

His hand flew to the grips of his gun. I heard him unsnap the restraining loop of his duty holster.

Okie dokie, Barney Fife. I showed him my empty palms. "I'd like to take my boots and spurs off. Put on my walking boots."

"Don't do anything stupid," he said.

I rolled my eyes, sat on the running board, and traded out my boots. *Stupid? Let's not go there again.*

When I slammed the door, Sheriff Taylor shucked out a pair of handcuffs.

CHAPTER SIXTEEN

The back of the patrol car smelled like puke.

It wasn't mine.

The sheriff slid behind the wheel, adjusted his rearview mirror, then stared.

He was twitchy. Worse, he was frenzied. His eyes darted everywhere and nowhere. His hands shook when he wasn't wiping them down the sides of his pants. He sniffled and wiggled his nose like it had a perpetual itch.

The radio in the car squelched. He slugged it off.

His handset squawked. He ripped that from his belt and threw it against the passenger side door.

The guy is unhinged.

"Why are you doing this to me?" I asked the sheriff. My head throbbed. The handcuffs were too tight. Complaining about them might thrill the sheriff. So, I didn't. He was the sort to delight in another's misery. "Why?"

"Shut up. Shut up. Shut up."

Does he mean me or is he talking to his radios?

I scooted to the middle of the seat.

"If I'm being arrested," I said, "I want a lawyer."

"Shut up." He wrenched his face into all sorts of contortions. "You're not under arrest. You were reported missing. I'm taking you home."

Reported? Home? Right. I glared at him. "Why the handcuffs?"

"So you don't hurt yourself." His face smoothed. He scratched at the sores on his neck. "In light of the recent suicide in town, I need to take extra precautions against you hurting yourself."

Touching. "I'm not going to kill myself."

He opened his mouth and moved his jaw around like he was having trouble chewing a hunk of meat. "Tell him. Tell him," he chirped like he'd acquired Tourette's syndrome.

I looked around to make sure we were alone. There was no one nearby that the sheriff could have been talking to.

Dude, paranoia will destroy ya.

Could I encourage his delusions? "So tell me, then."

"Shut up." Sheriff Taylor spun into my face. He spit like a rabid dog as he spoke. I was glad the steel cage separated us. He might have lunged on top of me and chewed off my head like a zombie in those movies.

"I need rid of you before your eighteenth birthday." Spray flew from his lips with every word. He huffed, then turned back to crank the key in the ignition. The patrol car roared to life.

"What are you talking about?" My voice squeaked in a higher pitch than an average boy my age.

"You'll never reach adulthood." He drove through the parking lot.

We left the rodeo grounds.

"This suicide's given me an idea," Sheriff Taylor said.

This suicide? Devyn. His name was Devyn. And you as much as killed him as anything else.

On the highway, the sheriff stood on the gas pedal.

The rush of speed would have been better with lights and sirens. But that was neither here nor there. I wondered at his screwy behavior. And the fact that the sheriff wouldn't have told me anything unless he was sure I could never repeat it to anyone.

"I'm not committing suicide." I sat back against the seat. My wrists shrieked in pain. The sun was going down. I wasn't exactly afraid of the dark. But I've always been afraid of monsters in the dark. "And when I turn eighteen, you'll never see me again." *I'm outta here. Creepville. I'm gone.*

"Well, let's make that dream come true *before* you turn eighteen." He steered down the long driveway to the County Boys' Home.

"What is it about my turning eighteen that you don't like?"

The sheriff stepped from the patrol car and jerked my door open.

Curbside service. Except there are no curbs.

"Get out," he snapped. His twitchiness had settled.

"I kept his room empty. He goes in there." The Sergeant pointed to my cell. His meaty fist wrapped around a ring of keys now attached to his belt with a retractable key chain. I'd be surprised if it could ever retract all the way, though. The Sergeant's once generous gut was slack. It flopped over the waistband of his pants and hid his leather belt completely.

The Sergeant was more slovenly than usual. That was saying a lot. He had never come close to fastidious. Now?

There was an odor coming from the Sergeant that would gag a maggot. And his breath reeked like rotten meat. When he moved, the smell of mildewed clothes hung in the air.

I coughed.

Weeping sores oozed from his ten-day stubble that might want to call itself a beard if it wasn't so thin and scraggly. Stains trailed down his shirt. I could tell what he'd eaten over the last few days as easy as reading a menu.

"Boots, boy," the Sergeant barked.

I sat on the steel cot. The springs drooped with my weight. The metal frame squeaked under negligible strain. I hauled my boots from my feet and tossed them at the door. They landed obediently at the Sergeant's feet.

"I don't want him marked. You hear me," Sheriff Taylor said as he opened the front door of the County Boys' Home to leave. "Not one mark." He slammed the door behind him. The lock clicked.

"Where's his stuff?" the Sergeant growled.

Michael held out a white trash sack. The tall, skinny kind that goes into a kitchen can receptacle.

It wasn't mine. I'd been given a green garbage sack a couple of months ago. August 27, 1994. The day Luce was taken from me. The day my stepmama ruined our lives. Back when the social worker made me and Luce gather some belongings "to stay in foster care until Mama got up from her coma."

Then Mary Langdon deemed that sack too holey. She put my

personal belongings into a duffel. That duffel went with the cash that I had handed to Michael.

So the duffel was gone. I hoped the cash wasn't.

"Only underwear and socks?" the Sergeant asked like I'd disappointed him somehow. He pawed through the white sack again. "And one shirt." He tossed the white sack onto the floor. "You can have those."

Michael nodded at me, making it look like he was lowering his head in deference.

I shook my head at Michael, attempting to indicate that I didn't understand what he meant. It reminded me of way back when he warned me not to fight the Sergeant.

"Now give me your pants. You won't go anywhere without pants." The Sergeant rubbed his knuckles. He practically jigged with happiness.

I jumped up. "I'm not giving you my pants." All of a sudden, my breathing came fast and furious. My chest swelled with the volumes of air I sucked in. The binding constricted. A flush of heat grew clammy beneath the wraps. My mouth went dry. Sahara Desert dry.

"Take 'em." The Sergeant waved as he moved out of the way.

My stomach roared. I thought I'd be sick.

I put my back against the wall.

Scuzz-cut entered my cell first. He leered and licked his lips. I figured Mullet-head would be quick on his heels. I was wrong. Mullet-head stepped behind the Sergeant allowing another kid to rush past.

Scuzz-cut grappled my lower jaw and peeled me from the wall. The other kid bundled my arms behind my back.

The Sergeant scruffed Michael. "Get in there." He tossed him into my cell. "I said take his pants."

Michael shrunk from me in an attempt to refuse. The Sergeant blocked his escape. "I said get in there." He slapped Michael upside the head. The wallop echoed off the walls of our close confinement.

When Michael turned toward me, his eyes pleaded for forgiveness.

For his sake, I didn't fight.

Michael unbuttoned the rivet to my Wranglers.

I was glad it was him and not one of the others. I was glad it was Michael. I hoped he could feign shock and disgust as the rest of them found me out.

I studied the ceiling. I had stared at it before. Counted all of the tiles—forty-eight.

He tugged at the gritty zipper. It gave him more trouble than I'd ever had with it.

There are forty-eight tiles. Some had cracked. Some would leak come spring. Water marks said they had already.

Scuzz-cut viciously shoved at my jaw. That crunch in my neck resounded again inside my head. A wave of dizziness followed. I sort of hoped I'd puke on them. But with my luck, I'd just choke on my own vomit and die. *The sheriff would love that.*

"Pull 'em down already or I'll do it myself," Scuzz-cut growled at Michael.

Michael jerked at my jeans. They caught on my hips.

"Jeezuz, I could have yanked them to his ankles twice by now and had my own zipper open to boot," Scuzz-cut said.

He tangled his fingers in Michael's hair and twisted. "Take them off him." Scuzz-cut drove Michael to his knees.

Michael slid my Wranglers to the floor. I let him lift each of my feet in getting them away.

The Sergeant's keys jangled. "That'll do. Leave him and get out." I heard the key chunk into my cell's door lock. "Get out," the Sergeant repeated.

The ugly kid behind me let go and followed Michael from my room.

Scuzz-cut squeezed my jaw harder. "Such a pretty face. Such a pretty mouth." He smiled at me and ran his fat tongue over his thick lips. "You're a pretty boy."

"Out. Now." The Sergeant's tone was cold enough to send the willies up my spine.

Scuzz-cut crammed my head against the wall. I had to step back so as not to lose my balance.

He released me.

I vomited.

It was a waste of the licks of soft serve ice cream I'd enjoyed… before the sheriff ruined that moment of pleasure.

"Clean that up." The Sergeant tossed Michael back into my room. He waved. A rolling bucket came down the hall and rounded my doorway. My door slammed. The lock clicked.

We were alone.

"How'd you know?" I asked Michael. "About the sack? And my stuff? How'd you know about the pants?"

"It's what he does. The Sergeant always plays the same games. He takes everything you own. Slowly. Eventually." Michael's eyes faded from the here and now. He was lost in another time. "Everything." His face contorted as if reliving painful memories. His eyes grew watery.

"There's only been one other who's more evil than the Sergeant that I've ever known. That's Sheriff Taylor. That one's smarter." Michael swabbed at the puke. "Chris, don't cross the Sergeant any more. He'll take your skivvies too. And when you're naked…"

"That's when you'd get those marks," I completed Michael's warning.

"Let me do that," I said. I crouched over my bare knees to wipe the mess off the floor. I felt a stale breeze from beneath the door waft over my boxer brief covered butt.

"What are you gonna do? About, you know." He pointed at my crotch. "That?"

"I still have a pair of your tighty-whities, right? And I've got a sock. Those under my boxer briefs should look convincing. Unless—"

"Unless your skivvies get taken too. Or Scuzz-cut—"

"Yeah. No worries, Michael. I've got this." I sounded convincing. I tried to sound confident.

Truth was, I was scared to death. I could have peed myself when my pants came down. It was a slight miracle that the tails of my button-down had obscured my crotch from view.

The door clicked open. "Out," the Sergeant growled. Michael scurried away with the rolling bucket. The door slammed shut. It locked.

In the morning, the sheriff returned. I heard his gravelly voice through my door. He argued with the Sergeant. The Sergeant wasn't bullied.

"Nothing more in it for me?" A dull thud hit my door. "For what I get, I'll keep him locked up but no more. You want more'n that, you can give me more product." The Sergeant stomped down the hall.

It was the sheriff's boots I heard scuffing the floor outside my door when everything else went quiet.

Monday afternoon, the lock clicked open. I shoved past the Sergeant and ran for the bathroom.

"Where're you going?"

It wasn't the Sergeant. I had dashed past Scuzz-cut. I was desperate to pee.

Boys loitered in the hallway. Their heads slightly bowed. Their eyes wouldn't meet mine. I slammed the bathroom door behind me with one hand and tore at my underwear with the other.

Bootfalls followed me down the hall.

My body was straining to hold back. My mind was arguing with it. I dug at my drawers. Michael's underwear was too small. They were too tight. They wouldn't come away easily.

"Get out of my way or you know how it'll go." Scuzz-cut grunted beyond my closed bathroom door. He stomped closer and closer.

I danced in place, struggling with the tighty-whities. A ripple rushed up my bladder, then back down. *It's coming It's coming. I'm gonna pee myself.*

My boxer briefs were a jumbled mess around my thighs.

Scuzz-cut was outside the door.

The tighty-whities finally pulled away. The balled sock was twisted inside them.

I collapsed onto the toilet seat.

In an instant, I was so relieved, tears sprang to my eyes. I didn't even care if Scuzz-cut barged in. I didn't care what he saw.

The balled sock hit the floor between my feet.

What am I thinking? I plucked the fallen sock from the ground and organized myself as I sat.

"Give him a minute." Michael must have stood in Scuzz-cut's way.

"What? Is he your boyfriend?" I heard flesh hit flesh.

Michael squeaked. Several thumps resounded off the door. There was heavy breathing. Footsteps scampered like rats evacuating a sinking ship.

The doorknob turned.

I yanked at my layers of underwear.

The door flew open.

I was ready.

Or so I thought.

Scuzz-cut clutched onto my jaw again. His fingers pressed into the bruises he'd already left.

He was holding an empty beer bottle. I recognized it. The beer had been Devyn's.

"Hold him," he commanded.

I punched. I kicked.

Resistance was futile.

The same bully locked my arms behind me.

Glass smashed against the porcelain sink.

I winced and struggled against the restraint.

The jagged edge of the broken bottle moved toward my eye.

I tried to turn away. Scuzz-cut held my face like a vise.

Shattered glass crunched beneath his boots. He licked his thick lips then clenched his tongue between his teeth. He studied my cheek for a second, before he pressed the sharp edge to my scar.

I've lived through it before.

This time, don't faint.

It doesn't hurt. It doesn't hurt. It doesn't hurt.

Don't let him see it hurts. He delights in causing pain.

Don't cry. Don't even wince.

Blood drooled down my cheek. It pooled on Scuzz-cut's hand that gripped my jaw.

His eyes smiled. His lips peeled back from his sharp teeth. His tongue wiggled in his bite.

Bzzz. Bzzz. The front door's buzzer interrupted Scuzz-cut.

"Chris...Can you tell Chris Taylor I'd like to see him?"

Laney.

Scuzz-cut moved his hand to clamp my mouth.

Blood smeared my face. Scuzz-cut's grip slipped with the ooze.

"Chris isn't here," Mullet-head said.

"We both know he is, James. It is James, right? Or do you prefer Jim? Or Jimmy?" Laney sighed loudly in a swoony way. She was putting it on a bit thick. Would it work?

"You look like a Jimmy." Her voice was low and husky like she'd just gotten out of bed in the morning. But it was late afternoon. School was over for the day.

"I've seen you around," Laney said. "My girlfriends have noticed you. Asked me if you were a friend of Chris's. Mm-hmm."

"Well, I…" Mullet-head stammered.

"I've brought Chris his homework. He must be sick. I didn't see him at school today."

"Well…yeah."

"I'm only going to hand these books to Chris. So you either let me in, or have Chris come to the door."

"You can't come in," Mullet-head said. "Like, no girls allowed. It's a boys home."

Really? Lame. I squirmed in a feeble attempt to break free.

"I'll wait, then," Laney replied.

"No. You have to go."

"What's Chris call you? Mullet-head? I can see why."

Even I heard the note of disgust in her voice. Mullet-head must have too. He wasn't *that* thick.

"Look, get Chris to this door now or you'll be ruined in school. No girl will ever look your way. The only friends you'll ever have are these degenerates. I'll destroy you. You'll have to move ten zip codes over to escape your new reputation."

Aaannd that's just how her sister would do it.

There was a moment of silence.

Scuzz-cut chuckled.

He flicked his head toward the doorway. He and his cohort moved me out of the bathroom and down the hall.

Behind the front door, Scuzz-cut slid his hand from my mouth. Blood smeared over my lips and chin. Its metallic tang slithered across my tongue. I swallowed.

Scuzz-cut's fingers dug into my throat. I'd have coughed on his choking if not for Laney.

The kid behind me wrenched my arms upward. The sudden jarring jolted tears to my eyes.

I knew what was expected. "Laney, give him the books," I said from behind the door's blockade. I didn't want anyone else hurt on my account. I didn't want Laney caught in my mess.

"Not until I see you."

"Get rid of her," Scuzz-cut snarled in my ear. "Or else."

Half of my face was shoved in front of the cracked opening.

"Chris. You're bleeding."

That's not the worst of it. I grunted from my arm getting hoisted again. "Cut myself shaving," I croaked.

"Let me in," she demanded.

"Laney, it's over between us." *It would never work anyway. She can't ever be with me. Not with her sister, the doctor lady, hovering. Not with the doctor lady dating the sheriff.*

"Look, Laney, I've been meaning to tell you. It's that, I like Marie Callander."

"Nice one." Scuzz-cut's stale breath blasted my cut cheek.

"I don't know her," Laney said in a breathy whisper. From the perplexed look on her face, Laney was searching her mind for any girl at West High with that name.

"She's scrumptious," I said.

"I'm—That's not true. It's not." Laney threw the books at the door, then stomped off.

Papers scattered on the growing wind. A storm was coming.

Mullet-head threw the door wide in her wake.

I was exposed. *They* were exposed. If Laney turned around now, she might see me. *In my underwear? With blood running down my face? Not an image I want her to remember me by.*

"I could love you," Mullet-head said to Laney's retreating back. "I could try," he mumbled. "I'm not really sure."

Everyone heard him.

The door swung closed enough to hide me.

Scuzz-cut laughed. "I could get her for you. But if I get her, I get first dibs. Then she's all yours." He flicked his tongue like a snake. "What's left of her," he added.

Mullet-head fled into the house.

Scuzz-cut smacked Michael for appearing at the doorway. "Clean up this mess," he grunted.

Michael dropped to his knees to collect the disheveled books and papers. I thought he stared wistfully after Laney.

I was taken to my cell. My door slammed shut. The lock clicked. I was alone.

Footsteps echoed in the empty hallway. When I could no longer hear them, I slid to the floor and pressed my hand against the door. *Michael?* I didn't dare call out.

It was after dark when I heard someone approach. I didn't know who was in the hall on the other side of my solid door at this time of night. I heard the footsteps stop. I shrank against the wall.

"Chris? Chris? I'm gonna get you out." It was Michael. "Laney came back. I saw her from the attic. She came back."

"Can you get the keys? No. I changed my mind. No. Don't get the keys. Get her to my window."

"We'll need the keys. I'm coming too."

"No. Michael. It's too dangerous." I grasped the doorknob and climbed from the floor. My head throbbed. I couldn't see well. Gingerly, I poked at the swelling on my cheek. The cut gaped like a canyon pass. Dried blood cracked under my light probing. "The keys. The Sergeant has them attached to his belt. It's too dangerous."

"I'll get them. And your books." Michael's footsteps pattered away.

"Michael?" I called through the door in a hoarse holler. "Michael? It's too dangerous." I clenched my hair in my fists and knocked my head to the door. Blood slithered down my ravaged face. "Michael, come back. Please."

Pleading was useless. He was long gone.

I stepped onto the cot and searched for Laney through the window. It was too dark to see anything through the glass. The wind howled against the pane. I lifted the window slowly, but it squeaked too loudly.

I stopped. I listened at the opening. Dry brush chattered. A night owl screeched. A snared rabbit screamed. The yowl of a feral cat was answered by another.

I clutched the sill and strained to catch sight of any of it. The night was too dark.

A wind blew across my face. My cut cheek throbbed like the booming of cannon fire. It had swelled to the size of a baseball. Blood gushed from the cut like a raging river of red. I touched my tongue to my dried, cracked lips.

When I heard determined footsteps out in the hall, I froze.

Is it Michael? Or could he have been caught?

The door's lock clicked.

I couldn't take any more of this. I wouldn't take any more.

I crammed the window up higher. It squealed like a stuck pig.

I swung my naked legs outside and jumped.

I thumped to the ground.

A flashlight beamed in my eyes.

"Oh my God. Your face."

I wrapped my arms onto Laney and hung from her. I choked on a sob and buried my face in her neck. She smelled like sunshine and horses and everything good in life. "I'm sorry. I'm so sorry." I cried.

Her embrace said it all. I was forgiven.

The window slammed wide with a clatter. Michael's contorted face stared out. "Don't forget this." His lips twisted in a sneer. Michael held Devyn's letter out the window. It flapped on the wind. His T-shirt was ghostly white against the black background. It made him look like an apparition. An angry apparition.

"That's my letter. That's my personal business," I snapped. "Did you read my letter? It's personal." I snatched at the page but only managed to knock it from his hand.

It took flight on the wind.

"You did, didn't you?" My tone accused him when I should have explained.

Laney dodged after the fluttering letter.

Let him think what he wanted. There wasn't time for this.

"He's your family," Michael spit. Fear plastered his face. It replaced his anger.

Michael was afraid of me? Me? That hurt.

His face changed again. This time, his expression said that I had betrayed him. And that hurt me even more.

He wouldn't have known that I'd gotten the letter only after Devyn's passing. He wouldn't have listened that I'd only just found out.

Well, that's his problem.

Or was it? "Michael?" I implored. With that one word, I'd begged. *If he came with me, I could explain.*

"When were you going to tell me?"

He didn't climb from the window.

"I only just found out."

He dropped my books to the ground with a resounding thwack. I winced.

Laney grasped my arm. "Come on. You two are yelling. Someone will find us any second now."

"Michael?" I pleaded.

Thunder crashed. Lightning flashed.

Michael bit onto his lower lip. He looked like he'd cry.

Laney tugged my arm.

A deluge plunged down. It sopped us instantly.

Water ran from my shirttails onto my bare legs. From there, streams gushed the length of my legs to my slouched socks.

"Michael, come on," I half yelled and half whispered.

Runoff rippled over my feet. I shivered.

"Chris," Laney hissed.

"Michael."

Chapter Seventeen

Laney half dragged, half guided me to her truck. She hauled the driver's door open. The cab's light reached out to us. Laney nudged me in. "We've got to go. Fast," she said.

"My truck is at the rodeo grounds," I said as I slid across the vinyl bench seat to the other side. "That's where I left it."

Tuesday morning was still just a thought on the horizon. Rain drummed on the windshield as Laney sped down the road. The wipers slapped at it.

A deer bounded across the beams of the headlights. Laney jammed on the brakes.

The wheels skidded.

The back of the truck fishtailed.

The deer leaped clear.

We both sighed in relief.

Laney's fingers clutched at the steering wheel. I thought, by the light of the dash, I'd see white knuckles. But her fingers were blue. That's when I noticed her teeth chattered.

"Cold?" I blasted the heater. The rushing air was still cool. No help. I wished I had a dry coat to offer her. I didn't even have pants. Not that I'd offer her my pants...well, I would if she needed them.

Goose flesh rose on my legs. My toes tingled inside the wet socks. Water dripped from my earlobes and chin. "I have a sleeping bag in my truck. And dry clothes."

Laney nodded with great effort. Her jaw was clenched tight, probably to try to keep her chattering to a dull roar.

The windshield wipers slapped in a rhythm. The tires sloshed over the drowning road. The engine droned.

"Do you have that paper?" I asked.

"The one that flew? Yeah. I went after it. I've got it here." Laney squirmed her hand into her front pocket and pulled the crumpled paper out. It was damp. I carefully smoothed it. The writing hadn't smeared. *Phew.*

"What is it?" Laney asked.

"Nothing." And that wasn't true. It was so much more than nothing. It was proof I had family. No, not the sheriff. Mary Langdon. Devyn's mom. *I'd had a cousin.*

I folded the paper. Mary Langdon must have known about me. She was my father's sister, for crying out loud. My father sent Devyn equipment every year. They would have talked. They would have passed a letter…a note.

I'm sure she had her reasons for not saying anything. To Devyn. To me.

"Seems like something. You're gripping it awfully tight."

I breathed deeply in through my nose. "It's a personal letter." Laney deserved more than that. I sighed my breath out. "Like a snapshot to hold on to." It was proof I belonged somewhere. I belonged to someone. Even if my family wasn't all peaches and cream, I had family.

Sometimes just knowing was enough.

"Do you want to talk about it?" she asked.

No. I didn't want to talk about any of it. I didn't answer her.

I was missing that sense of security I hadn't had since Daddy died. Life was structured then. My life was entirely mapped out. I knew who I was supposed to be. *For him.* How I fit.

Sure, I'd been confused. In the past, I'd wanted to fight against Daddy's expectations. They felt claustrophobic. He never understood me. He never knew me. I'd wanted to break away…To do my things my way. Discover me. But I didn't. It was easier not to.

I lived mostly at a prep school where I was told what to wear, how to eat, and when to sleep. My days were filled with studies. Holidays and summers were less rigid but totally directed. My life was planned to the minute. It was easy to just go along. It all made sense.

And feeling different? Feeling out of place even in my own

body? Well, that would all go away if I just conformed to the expectations surrounding me. Right?

It didn't. It doesn't.

"I know why those snooty girls don't like you," I said in changing the subject. The heat finally filled the cab. Laney's shoulders slouched in relief. She looked exhausted.

"Why would I care about them?" she asked.

"I don't know. But I know you do care." My face was beginning to throb like the beating of a bass drum. I licked my cracked lips. "You care," I said, then chewed on the inside of my cheek.

She squirmed in her seat. The vinyl squawked.

I stared at her as she drove. I couldn't stop looking at her. Watching her. I wanted to memorize every last detail in case—

"Why, then?" she asked.

I slid the folded letter into my chest pocket. "They're jealous." The shirt was soaked but the letter was wet too. At least this way, it would be out of sight. And as the saying goes, out of sight, out of mind. I hoped it was true.

Her eyes flicked from the road. They had caught my movement. They saw me secrete the letter away.

"Jealous?" Laney laughed.

"Jealous," I repeated. "Cuz they're struggling to learn their makeup so they can hide all the ugly. And you just walk right by, fresh and clean-faced, making à-la-natural look oh so desirable. You make it look easy."

The rain broke. Even the last bit of drizzle stopped.

Laney smiled at me.

A gray smear of dawn fought the lingering clouds as she turned into the rodeo grounds.

Water ran over the hard ground in rivers. Red Solo cups bobbed on the currents while dodging abandoned paper plates and ricocheting off overfilled trash barrels.

A stray dog ran along the outskirts sniffing at floating garbage. In places, the water swirled to the dog's knees. Under a light post, its short coat shined slick with wet.

Laney hadn't said anything, so I pointed to the obvious. "My truck's over there."

I hopped out before she shifted into park.

The door of the three-quarter-ton groaned as I yanked on it. My gear bag slouched on the seat. My clothes were spilled in the foot well where I'd left them. I had a sleeping bag behind the bench seat. I dug it out.

A chill ran through me. I climbed onto the running board and stripped off my sopping socks. I was pretty much half-naked. Soaked socks weren't doing much for me.

Laney stared. When I caught her eye, she looked away.

In that moment, I shed my briefs, the crotch sock, and soaking tighty-whities. The tails of my button-down still hid the private parts from sight. But I was quick to drag on dry boxer briefs regardless. Jeans were next. Socks. Boots. I unbuckled my spurs from the yellow-topped bull riding boots before shoving my feet into them.

"You must be freezing," I said to Laney. I handed my starched and ironed black logo shirt to her. "I won't look if you won't."

She nodded. "But close the door," she said as she pointed up at the blaring cab light.

Done.

My three-quarter-ton's door was still open and the cab light illuminated more than I'd wanted to share. If I shut the door it would plunge me into the dim gray of early morning. I couldn't bear the feeling of darkness at the moment. *Lonely. Foreboding.*

I peeked under my arm at Laney's truck. Light gleamed off of the wet metal, but the inside of the cab was pitch-black.

I hesitated before shucking my drenched shirt. *She knows. What am I worried about?*

Laney might have known I was born a girl, but that wasn't the me I wanted her to see. Of late, *I* didn't want to see that me. It didn't match who I was. *I am Chris. Masculine. Rugged. Bull rider extraordinaire. Yeah. Okay. A little over-the-top with that last one. But I am Chris. I am all boy.*

A cold wind pierced my wet shirt. It chilled through my binding. I shuddered. But waiting wasn't warming me up any. Slowly, I pealed the soaked shirt from my body. I was quick to shove my arms into the dry one. Only then did I unwrap the Ace bandage from my chest.

My skin was red and wrinkled. I would have liked to towel it dry. I would have liked to let the air at my chest—

"Chris?"

No time. "Almost finished." I wrapped up and buttoned up. All dry.

"I'll follow you home," I said. "To make sure you get there safe." It was the least I could do.

The road was one long stretch of empty. I chased the taillights of Laney's truck. My mind wandered.

What would I do about the sheriff? What *could* I do about the sheriff?

I'd stay out of his way. *Mind your business.*

I wanted my high school diploma. And I wanted my sister.

He wants me dead.

What was he going to do? Take out his gun and shoot me in public?

My brain stopped its ceaseless flurry when Laney turned into her driveway. I pulled behind her and shut the three-quarter-ton off.

"I can't go in," Laney said as I quietly opened her truck's door. "No one knows I was gone. I snuck out."

"What do you want to do?" I asked.

"The barn," she said. "We could take the sleeping bag."

The outside barn light reached into the aisle. I threw a few bales into the loose straw of an empty stall. We'd bunk in there to wait for a sane hour of dawn.

When I rolled the stall door shut behind us, it snuffed out much of the light. Neither one of us moved.

Laney clung to my sleeping bag like it was a life preserver in a flood.

I wiped my sweaty palms on the outsides of my thighs and toed the loose straw bedding.

The upper half of the stall wall was made of iron bars. Dim light shined through to mark their shadows on the opposite wall.

"Well," I said.

"Yeah," Laney replied.

I offered my hand to help her to the floor.

She handed me the sleeping bag, then plopped herself down.

We leaned our backs against the bales. I covered Laney with the sleeping bag. I was plenty warm enough.

I wrapped my arms around myself against the chilly early morning and shivered.

"There's enough room under here for two," Laney said. She held the edge of the bag open. I shimmied next to her. I tried not to sit too close. I tried not to press against her.

She curled into my side. "Is this okay?"

I nodded, which was probably lost on her in the dark.

A swallow struggled down my throat. My heart beat thunderously against my chest. I wondered if she heard it. *Did she feel it?*

Her hand lay lightly on my belly. My muscles tensed from the tickling touch. I wanted to squirm away from her. I wanted to squirm into her.

I squirmed in place.

Finally, the warmth beneath the sleeping bag made both of us drowsy. I put my arm around Laney's shoulders as she dozed off. I wanted to kiss her head. I wanted to press my lips to her.

I knew I wouldn't sleep. I couldn't sleep. If I closed my eyes, I'd miss this moment. I couldn't. I wouldn't.

Laney snored softly. Her head rumbled on my chest. My breathing slowed to match hers. Her face was slack and calm, like she didn't have a care in the world. And I wished that were so.

A strand of her hair slid onto her cheek. I held myself from brushing it back. She'd wake. I didn't want to risk her waking. It would break this quiet moment.

I don't know how long we lay there. Perhaps it was an eternity, but it wasn't nearly long enough.

When a rooster crowed in the distance, Laney stirred. Her eyes fluttered open like birds straining against a down draft.

"Good morning," she mumbled, then smiled.

I brushed the pad of my thumb over her bottom lip. "Good morning."

She reached for me and drew my mouth to hers.

"Oh, hell no!" The stall door rolled back. It crashed to a halt. Daylight poured over us.

Laney held her arm up to shield her eyes.

The doctor lady rushed in. She squatted at Laney's side. "Are you okay? What has he done to you?" She rolled Laney toward her. Away from me.

"Let me look at you," the doctor lady said as she cradled Laney's face between her palms.

"I'm fine." Laney pushed at her sister. "It's Chris that's been hurt."

I pressed my fingertips to the gaping cut on my face. It had become hot and angry. Just the feather-light touch sent screaming pain through me.

The doctor lady climbed between us and pinched my jaw with her thumb and forefinger. I felt every bruise come alive to sting me as if I were trapped in a hornet's nest.

"Serves you right," she said to me. "You're playing a dangerous game." The doctor lady dragged a pen light from her pocket and shined it in my eyes.

"I'm not playing anything. This is me."

"What's you? What? Not a girl. Not a girl playing a boy. What? A thing? It?" She clicked the light off, stuffed it in her pocket, then released my face. "The wound is infected." The doctor lady climbed from the straw-strewn floor.

She addressed Laney from the doorway. "Have you asked yourself what he had to do with Devyn's death? Devyn was fine until he showed up."

"That's not true," I said. He drank all the time. He drank until he passed out. How was that fine?

"What part?" She moved her head like a venomous snake attempting to find an opening. "You know he was arrested," she said to Laney. Her eyes never left me.

"No, I wasn't." I jumped up. My side of the sleeping bag doubled over Laney.

"That's not what Sheriff Taylor said." She looked back at Laney. "He's lying. Look at his wrists." She pointed. "Handcuffs made those marks. He tried to escape once before. Before he used you to help him run."

Laney rolled to her knees, then stood. The sleeping bag lay abandoned in the straw.

I felt heat rise to my face. It made the carving on my cheek throb to a wicked beat. "It's not true," I said through my grinding molars. "Laney, I wouldn't. I didn't."

"Laney, you were fine too. Before Chris got to town. But now you question yourself—who you are. Who you'd have to be for Chris. For her. For him. For it." The doctor lady wrapped herself on to Laney's arm. "It's not about questioning yourself. Question Chris. His mother is a junkie lying in a coma. His sister's in foster care. His father is dead. Who is he? What's he hiding?"

Laney's face changed. It was like a dark cloud moved over it. Lines furrowed her forehead. Her cheeks pulled taut. Her eyes tensed into slits.

She folded her arms over her chest. Her sister continued to cling on to her.

"What's on the paper, Chris?" Laney asked.

I looked at my feet. I couldn't tell her. Especially not with her sister here. Not with the sheriff hunting me. He wanted to kill me. How could I tell her that?

"The paper?" She spread her legs into a wider stance as if she were ready for battle. "That letter?"

"It's personal," I said.

"What was your friend at the County Boys' Home angry about? Who's your family?"

"It's personal," I said again.

"If you can't confide in me, in us, then I can't help you."

You couldn't help me any way. You wouldn't, if you knew.

"Okay then. Good-bye, Chris." Laney walked from the stall. She walked from the barn. She walked from my life.

I followed them at a distance.

My feet dragged. My boots felt full of lead.

The doctor lady stopped near the three-quarter-ton while Laney continued toward the house.

I thrust the door of the truck wide. The doctor lady backed off.

The spring on the screen door of the house screeched at being jerked. Seconds after, the door slapped closed.

Laney.

I turned the three-quarter-ton's engine over.

"I get it," the doctor lady said. "I get it. I get your whole masquerade." She folded her arms across her chest like Laney had just done. "If I was that good, I'd do anything to ride too. But chasing girls is going too far." She thrust her head forward. "Going out with Laney?" She pressed her fists to her hips and leaned her body in. Her eyes squinted. Her lips pursed. "Not with my sister. You hear me, freak? Not with my sister."

I jammed the three-quarter-ton in reverse.

"You come clean with your games or I'll tell the world all about your little secret."

I gently pressed the gas pedal. Was I hoping Laney would change her mind? The truck slowly rolled backwards. Was I thinking she'd burst from that screen door at the last second and we'd be fine? Us. Together.

"You have until Monday," the doctor lady howled. "That should give you plenty of time to sort out your crap."

I drove away. *Where could I go?*

West High's parking lot was crowded.

"You have until Monday." It was Tuesday morning. The doctor lady had given me a week before she ruined my life. *Generous.*

I read a lot of psych books back at the Autry Academy. I took their classes in psychology. Growing pains. Self-exploration. Rebellion. There was always an innocent, one-word explanation as to how I felt. Those had always brought me back to heel. Brought me back to being a good girl.

Until my survival was threatened.

Nothing prepared me for needing to survive. Nothing prepared me for any of this. No family at my side. No friends in my corner. Nowhere I belong.

My best friend killed himself. My girlfriend ditched me. The doctor lady hates on me. The sheriff wants me dead. He also happens to be my uncle. And Luce doesn't need me. She has a new family now.

But if I ran from here, now, I'd be giving up my future. I needed to graduate high school. I needed that diploma to get anywhere in life. Then college, maybe. But how could I think on that at the moment?

I took the letter from my chest pocket.

Devyn. Why?

The page crackled as I unfolded it.

I missed him. I missed Devyn's easy swagger. His lighthearted kidding. I missed his seriousness too. *Why hadn't I seen his pain?*

I laid the page next to me on the bench seat and smoothed it flat.

I had wanted to be like him.

He's coming for you. Those were the only words that jumped from the page.

I muddled through the week of school. Aced my tests because it was too much effort not to. Studied every waking moment so my mind wouldn't think on other things. Handed in all of my homework assignments. And when the last bell rang on Friday afternoon, I panicked.

Now what?

Laney was waiting for me as I stepped from the school into the waning afternoon sunshine.

"Laney?" When I walked toward her, she backed up.

She clutched her books to her chest in protection, like a shield. "She's right, you know," Laney said. "My sister. She's right. It won't work." Her face was red and puffy. She'd been crying. She was holding back tears now.

My heart ached at her upset.

I was her upset. I didn't want to be the cause of her pain. But I didn't want to lose her. "Laney—"

"You don't get it," she snapped at me. "I'm going to college or I'm going pro. I'm not going to sling hash at the local diner until I'm eighty years old and decrepit."

"Laney, I—"

"No, Chris. No."

Chapter Eighteen

After school, I wandered along the desolate highway toward the next rodeo. Truckers were the only ones to frequent this lonely patch of interstate. And only to pass through podunkville. Never to stop.

Halfway to the rodeo grounds, I pulled off on a dirt road leading nowhere and slept. It wasn't until I could no longer ignore the glaring strobe of headlights from passing big rigs that I sat up and cranked the engine on.

I'd chase the rodeo circuit. If not for me, for Devyn. For Luce.

Luce might be happy with her new family, but she was going to need college money at some point. And if I wasn't going to college, I'd make damn sure Luce could.

"And let's face it," I said aloud, "my life is over in podunkville."

I drove into the rodeo grounds. The arena lights were on in the dead of night.

That was odd.

The bulls had already been settled in during the week for this weekend's rodeo. There was no reason to light the entire arena overnight.

I drove around to the back. The blue short bus sat askew in front of the huge arena opening. The sheriff's patrol car was cocked in the opposite direction. I swear the tiny hairs on the back of my neck bristled like a dog's hackles.

I parked well away from both, then got out to investigate.

The accordion door to the bus squeaked as I pushed on it. A muffled struggle emanated from within. The thumping got the short bus rocking. I poked my head in, but I'd have to commit if I wanted to really see anything.

How badly did I want that?

I shoved my toe onto the first step but didn't commit. The bus kneeled toward me. The noises increased as if a flurry of large squirrels wrestled over a nut.

The darkened interior was too dark. *Nope. Nuh-uh.* I didn't need to go any farther.

Whatever was in there wasn't any of my business. I wanted nothing to do with the County Boys' Home. Nothing to do with the Sergeant. Nothing.

Michael? I never wanted to hurt Michael. He's like a little brother. He should know that you can't choose your relatives.

I stepped down and backed away.

"Help," a garbled voice pleaded.

I leaped onto the bus.

Michael lay splayed in the aisle, bound and gagged. His eyes were huge with fright. They softened when he recognized me.

I shucked a bloody gag from his mouth. It drooped around his neck. The neckline of his T-shirt was stretched and hanging to the middle of his chest.

"The bulls," he said. Michael jerked against a set of handcuffs that trapped him. "They're hurting the bulls. I tried to stop them. I tried."

Blood from his scraped wrists trickled to his fingertips. He had fought to free himself.

Michael kicked and thrashed in a renewed fit. "The bulls," he said.

The handcuffs were secured around the rusted metal leg of a bench seat.

I squatted to the floor. His wrists looked like raw hamburger. I took hold of his forearms to still his thrashing. "Stop. You're hurting yourself."

"They've got hot shots." He twisted from my hold. "Cattle prods," he said. "To make the bulls angry." He fought against the restraints again. The links of chain slapped at the metal bench leg over and over.

"Michael—"

Chute gates slammed and crashed inside the arena. Bulls bellowed.

"They're zapping the bulls with cattle prods." His eyes filled with tears. His face scrunched. Saliva drooled from his bottom lip. "So the bulls will kill you tomorrow." He jerked harder against the secure cuffs.

"It's no use," I said. The leg of the school bus's seat was rusted, but it wasn't breaking loose for all of his yanking.

"I felt it move." His voice was thick with desperation.

The bulls howled. Their cries of pain carried over the chill night air.

"Go," Michael spit in anger. "You have to help them."

I stood up.

"Wait," he said. "The sheriff wants you dead. He can't hurt you himself. He can't touch you. You've done nothing wrong. And too many people know." Michael's hands were slick with blood. He concentrated on them. "If something happens to you, all fingers point to him. So it's got to look like an accident." Michael folded his palm inward and rotated his wrist within the handcuff's grasp. "They can't hurt you," he said very quietly.

They?

"But they can hurt everything you love."

The bulls hollered. Their bawling roared over the grounds.

"You'll have to fight them eventually. The Sergeant. The sheriff." Michael collapsed forward. His shoulders slumped. His legs fell flat to the floor. "And when you do? You'll lose. One way or the other."

He pushed himself slightly upright. "I'm sorry. I'm so sorry."

"Shh." I ran my fingers through his hair. He was still just a boy. A boy who had been forced to grow beyond his years, too fast.

"Why?" I asked. "Why are they doing this?"

"Because of who you are—"

Bellowing like howls from the bowels of hell tore the empty night air. The sounds were frightening—sickening.

I glanced over my shoulder at the arena. *Thundering Bunny.*

Michael looked me in the eyes. "Go. Stop them."

I jumped the steps of the bus. My feet were already running when they hit the ground.

Inside the arena the Sergeant leaned on the main gate of the alleyway to the pens. His back was to me. A three-foot-long cattle prod slumped in his fist.

I crouched behind a garbage barrel.

The Sergeant's body bobbed and bounced in delight. He was chuckling. He drew a new packet of C batteries from his pants pocket.

Scuzz-cut scurried atop the rails, harrying bulls toward the bucking chutes. He leaned over and reached with his prod. Zzt. Zzt. Zap. Crack.

A bull roared. Metal crashed. The rails shook.

Scuzz-cut jumped down to work the gates as he harassed the bulls.

Zzt. Zap. Crack.

"That's it, son," the Sergeant cheered.

Bulls bashed the pen rails. They smashed at the panels with their polls. Horns hooked. Hooves pawed the ground. Dirt flew.

The Sergeant laughed.

I hated him. I hated him ten times over. There was only one other I hated more.

I can't turn the other cheek, Daddy. A man's got to stand for something. Even if it kills him. Or how could he ever be called a man?

I stood to reach inside the barrel. I fished through the trash while I kept my eyes focused on the Sergeant. Something squished under my touch. I hoped it was ketchup. *Ick. Please be ketchup.*

I leaned in to search deeper. I needed something more solid than dirty paper plates, napkins, or empty chip bags. I needed a weapon. I only had one chance.

The papers in the garbage barrel rustled at my intrusion.

I winced at their noise.

Near the bottom of the barrel, I wrapped my hand around a glass bottle. I had never hit anybody with an object before.

I'd have to get close. *Arm's length.* I didn't know if I could. I wasn't that brave.

I eased the bottle from the barrel. My hand grew sweaty. What if the bottle slipped from my grasp?

If it did, it would clatter on the bottom of the bin. It would alert the Sergeant.

Heaviness infused my veins as if my blood congealed. My heart thumped against my chest. Thump. Thump. Thump. Thump. Its relentless pounding jarred all the way down my arm. My grip became unsteady.

My binding grew clammy.

My head wanted to succumb to wooziness. How could I blame it?

No. I stared at my fist wrapped around the bottle's neck and willed it to hold on. *I can do this.*

C batteries dumped to the ground at the Sergeant's feet. Packaging fluttered to the tops of his unlaced work boots. He kicked at the dead batteries.

I can't do this. I shook my head. *No, no, no, no.*

I held the glass bottle with both hands.

I'm scared.

I had read somewhere that I should give my emotions credence. Call them out. Make them known. That was the way to grow past them.

I—am—scared.

Didn't work. My belly soured. My bowels threatened.

What am I thinking? I should have made a plan.

Like the bulls, I doubted the Sergeant would stick to any plan that I came up with. I'd have to trust my instincts. But how? I didn't have any instincts to bash a man over the head.

I gripped the neck of the bottle and moved toward the Sergeant's back. *I have to do this.*

The Sergeant stood from leaning on the rails. Sounds of crackling and jostling told me he was fiddling batteries into the cattle prod.

If he turned around, I'd never get close enough.

A chill ran up my spine as if somebody walked over my grave. *I have do this. I can do this.*

My feet rooted.

I don't want to kill him. I'm not a killer.

I don't want to tickle him either. He has to go down.

I rolled the bottle in my hand.

I'd never felt more alone than I did right now. Not since that first night in the County Boys' Home. At least then, thoughts of getting Luce back kept me company. I missed my little sister. *My monkey girl.*

She has a new family now. We've grown apart.

I felt so tired. Exhausted. I wanted to sit on my back pockets in the dirt. I wanted the world to pass me by.

I didn't have the strength to fight. Not all of them. *One, maybe. Not all. Not the sheriff.*

I had to stand tall.

Sitting is quitting.

I was no quitter.

I squeezed the neck of the glass bottle until my knuckles turned white.

I took another step forward.

One. Then another. *I've got this.*

A piece of paper crunched in the gravel beneath my foot.

I winced as if I were struck.

The sound alerted the Sergeant.

I stood frozen.

The Sergeant slowly turned.

He wasn't surprised to see me.

In fact, he seemed delighted that I finally showed.

"We've tried to provoke you, boy," the Sergeant said. "Time and time again." He farted. Sulfur stench wafted over the short distance left between us. "We needed an excuse for your disappearance."

Confusion must have shown clearly across my face because the Sergeant answered my expression with a laugh.

"You don't even know who you are? Do you?" He snorted then wiped his nose on his sleeve. "You're the prince of *Taylor Town*, boy. You're your father's heir." He yanked the waistband of his pants higher. "You stand to inherit the ranch. The ranch that built this town." He fidgeted and scratched and farted. "For that, Bubba Taylor wants you dead," the Sergeant said. "I'm tired of baiting you. I'm tired of waiting for you to decide when we're going to kill you." He stuffed the last battery into the handle of the cattle prod. "You ought to be as easy to get rid of as the rest of them. The only trick is to make it look like an accident."

I stepped to the side. Could I get out of the reach of that cattle prod? I needed time. I needed a plan.

"Is that what you did to Devyn?" I growled. "Got rid of him? Made his death look like a suicide?"

"Don't be stupid. That was pure tragedy." He snorted, then spit the loogie.

I searched the rails for Scuzz-cut. Where did he get to? Would he come up behind me?

"Bubba Taylor liked that boy," the Sergeant said. "Earned a lot of money off him. Nope. No. It's your family Bubba Taylor's after." The Sergeant shut the cap over the batteries and twisted the lock nut.

"*His* family," the Sergeant sneered. He tapped the end of the prod on the ground. When he touched it to the steel rails, sparks flew.

His intent was clear.

The Sergeant lunged. He wielded the cattle prod as if it was a sword.

I smacked the prod away with the bottle. The glass cracked. Hairline fractures appeared like a spider's web. I felt my eyes grow wide at my mistake. *What did I think would happen? It's glass.*

And that was the problem. I hadn't thought.

I jumped to the side of the Sergeant.

I'd have to stay out of his reach. But then how could I get close enough to knock him out?

The Sergeant was fat and cumbersome. Maybe I could outmaneuver him. I hopped sideways again.

He proved surprisingly agile.

He lunged. *Zap.* Contact.

Ouch. Crap. The cattle prod didn't hold enough charge to kill me. But I sure wanted to roll around on the ground and sulk on its sting.

Zap. The Sergeant struck again.

I swear my thigh went numb after the shocking jolt ripped through me. I tried to put more distance between us. I looked for an opening.

The Sergeant laughed. The leer slitting his face said he intended to play with me like a cat plays with a mouse.

"You can't treat me like this. You can't treat others like this." This time, when he lunged, I grabbed the rod behind its pronged head and hung on.

The Sergeant wasn't deterred. He jerked the cattle prod.

I flung toward him.

I raised the bottle. *Whack.* It struck the Sergeant over the head. Glass shards rained down.

He let go of me. I danced out of his reach.

The Sergeant staggered but remained upright. He put a filthy palm to his slimy scalp. His hand came away bloody.

He laughed. He raised the cattle prod and waved it in my face.

I backed a step. A broken-off bottle neck was all that was left in my grip. There was nothing left to use now. I had had my one shot.

The Sergeant waggled the prod at me. He was savoring this moment.

He swiped the stream of blood from his eyes with his filthy sleeve. "Perhaps I'll tenderize you a bit more first." The prod pointed at my cut cheek. "Fresh batteries," he said with delight.

I took a step backwards. The pen rails stopped me as solid as any prison wall.

I pressed my back to them. I was trapped.

I wanted to close my eyes, but I wouldn't give the Sergeant the satisfaction. I ground my molars and braced for his next zapping blow.

The Sergeant lifted his foot to advance on me. His foul stench assaulted me first. I flinched. But it was more than a flinch. I swear my head tried to crawl into my shoulders.

I fought myself from turning away. I struggled to stare him in the eyes. I wasn't going to make this easy on him.

He stumbled.

His foot was in the air, and the next thing I knew, he was falling.

I watched him topple to the ground like a stiff board. Dust kicked into the cold air as he hit the dirt. It was the way he hit, face-first, that told me he wasn't going to get right up.

I was too stunned to run.

When I looked up from the inert body, Michael was standing

there. A splintered two-by-four was gripped in his hand. Blood-slicked handcuffs dangled from one wrist.

His face was as white as a ghost. His wobbling knees gave out.

Michael disintegrated to the dirt at the Sergeant's feet. "He's still my father," he said as he placed his hand over the Sergeant's boot. Michael fiddled with a loose lace. He rocked back and forth.

Bulls bellowed. Metal crashed and clanked.

"Go," he said.

In the pens, the bulls were crazed. They bobbed their massive heads and slammed at the rails. Their horns clanged. They thrashed.

They didn't understand cruelty. It had never played a role in their lives. They were bred to buck. Raised as star athletes. Trained with care and consistency. Reliant on trust.

Mistreated. Distrusting. Enraged. These animals had the power to kill.

I hoped none of them got loose.

At the bucking chutes, Scuzz-cut tied down onto one of those pissed-off pot roasts.

Not a good idea.

Sheriff Bubba Taylor stood inside the arena, manning the gate latch.

I couldn't believe what I was seeing.

"Let's have us a rodeo," the sheriff yelled.

Scuzz-cut nodded.

The latch squealed. The gate flung open.

Game on.

The bewildered bull leaped into the arena. Pink snot blew from his nose. Red froth covered his muzzle.

Wild with pain and fear, Grits Ona Griddle ran.

I watched, helpless, as he uncharacteristically charged the length of the arena.

He should've bucked. Bucking bulls loved to buck.

Grits Ona Griddle wasn't an aggressive bull. He was laid-back most days. I had heard he delighted in a sneak snack of buttermilk biscuits. Grits Ona Griddle had his place on the circuit because he had speed and agility. He was quick to get around.

Tonight, he ran.

There were no outriders on horseback. No bullfighters working.

Grits Ona Griddle blasted the length of the arena unchecked.

Scuzz-cut hung on. He stopped swinging his free arm. He tucked both his hands on to the rope.

Sheriff Taylor hooted and hollered from the bucking chutes.

Grits Ona Griddle, faced with the end of the arena, spun back.

Scuzz-cut should have pulled the tail of his rope. He should have let go. He should have dropped off.

He held on.

His face was white with fright. His arms were locked against his sides. He clutched at the bull rope as if it would save his life.

Wrong answers.

From beneath the bull, the bells clanked a murderous ruckus. Grits Ona Griddle open-mouth bellowed with a horror I would never cleanse from my mind.

Scuzz-cut rooted onto his back pockets, then grabbed with his heals.

Wrong answers.

The sheriff threw his hat in the air. "Ride him. Ride him."

Grits Ona Griddle thundered toward the closed out gate.

There was nowhere to go. Grits Ona Griddle bucked.

The bull was enraged with fear and pain. He tucked into a tight circle and whirled.

"The tail of your rope," I shouted. "Pull the tail."

My words were swallowed by the vast, empty arena.

It was no more than a second, Scuzz-cut got sucked into the well. His seat slipped to the inside, and down, down, down he went.

The bull spun harder. Grits Ona Griddle's hind end twisted to kick out with each revolution. Scuzz-cut draped limply along the bull's heart girth. Grits Ona Griddle bashed at his body.

Sheriff Taylor was in the arena. Surely he would save Scuzz-cut from getting mauled?

When he made no move to do so, I launched in as fast as I dared. The problem wasn't in getting in. Would I come back out? A half-insane, rampaging bull? A rider hanging limp from his rope? The sheriff standing around like a spectator?

I probably shouldn't have rushed in. I was doomed to get injured. Maybe killed.

For what? To aid a criminal? To aid an enemy? A bully? Scuzz-cut?

Wouldn't the world be better off without him?

What of the bull? Grits Ona Griddle? He didn't deserve this fate.

I ran as hard as I could. The harder I ran, the farther away they seemed to get. Time slowed, like it had when I tried to make an eight-second ride. Seconds took hours.

The temperature had dropped. I could see my breath on the air. *Is it my imagination?* It wasn't my imagination. I struggled to suck in volumes with each breath. And each breath stung with iciness.

Scuzz-cut slapped against the bull's side. His shoulder rotated in an unnatural position. He flopped like a Raggedy Ann doll.

Sheriff Taylor gawped. He clutched his hands together and licked his lips. His intrigue for the wreck was evident. I could almost see him salivating.

He disgusted me. There was no way I was truly related to the likes of Sheriff Bubba Taylor.

As I ran forward, I gnawed on the inside of my cheek.

When I reached the spinning bull, I didn't think. My mind went blank. I no longer had any worries. No cares. The world was miles away. I had only one thing I needed to do. And it didn't take thought.

I jumped at the bull to yank the rope's tail.

Scuzz-cut dropped.

I was tossed clear.

But it wasn't over. Scuzz-cut lumped in the dirt. He showed no signs of movement. And that made him a sitting duck.

What should I care? Really. *What. Should. I. Care?*

Therein lay the difference between me and the sheriff and all of his evil henchmen.

I cared. I couldn't help but care. It did me no good to do so. Still, I cared.

I think I hated myself in that moment.

But I was a good person.

The instinct of a good person is to help. They don't stand around debating how much help another individual deserves—or if he deserves to be helped at all. A good person jumps in to help.

I was a good person. I might be a dead person shortly.

I ran at the charging bull. In geometry, that would have been called bisecting as I shot the gap between him and Scuzz-cut to offer Grits Ona Griddle an easier target. The bull zeroed in on me.

Out of the corner of my eye, the sheriff sauntered toward the gates.

"The out gate," I hollered as Grits Ona Griddle twisted after me. I spun from the tip of his horn as he attempted to skewer my leg. "Throw open the out gate."

Sheriff Taylor threw a leg over the top rail and sat down instead. I glimpsed a can of Skoal in his hands before I got back to concentrating on staying one step ahead of the bull.

Grits Ona Griddle dropped his massive head for a killing blow.

It would do no good to run.

A split second before impact, I sat on his poll.

When he lifted, I was catapulted into the air.

The out gate swung wide. But Sheriff Taylor was nowhere in sight.

I hit the dirt hard.

Grits Ona Griddle made his escape.

Mullet-head rushed into the arena. He hauled on Scuzz-cut.

I rolled to my feet, recovered, and ran over to grab on to Scuzz-cut's vest.

The two of us dragged him into the open bucking chute.

"Get off me," Scuzz-cut barked as his senses returned. He jerked from my grasp.

Mullet-head kept hold of his arm. His eyes squinted. His mouth tightened so that his lips were nearly nonexistent. "We just saved your life," Mullet-head snapped.

Scuzz-cut backhanded Mullet-head. "You made me look weak."

I rolled my eyes and stepped from the bucking chute into the arena. Short breaths came fast and furious. I leaned against a solid panel, then slid to the dirt. Not enough air filled my lungs. My heart hammered in my chest. My hands shook.

Their bickering continued. Mullet-head and Scuzz-cut. They argued like twin girls who were annoyed at each other since the womb. I blanked them out. Eventually, they climbed from the chute.

Minutes later, the out gate banged closed.

It was over.

I grabbed on to the panel and gained my feet. My legs felt like rubber. I didn't know if they'd hold me. I smacked my dry lips together and ran my tongue over the ragged flesh inside my cheek.

It's over. The bulls are safe.

The cold night air seeped through my sweaty clothes. I swear I could feel its chill all the way to my bones. I shivered.

It's over.

On shaky legs, I moved to exit the arena.

Sheriff Bubba Taylor stepped out to block my way.

"The Prodigal Son," he said.

CHAPTER NINETEEN

October 21, 1994

I didn't know what he meant. *Prodigal Son? The parable?* The sheriff had it all wrong. It wasn't about a favored son returning so much as it was about family and forgiveness. It was about humility, and what it really took to be a man.

"I'm sure you've guessed by now." The sheriff unsnapped the restraining loop over the hammer of his gun. "I killed them all." He spit a glob of brown goo. "All of them. Starting with the grandparents you never knew." Shards of Skoal peppered his lips. He didn't bother wiping them off.

"The ranch was supposed to be mine. But I was cheated out of my inheritance." Sheriff Taylor scratched at the sores on his neck. "My parents left the family ranch to your father, Buck Taylor." Spittle ejected from his lips. "My big brother," he snarled. "Upon his death, it was left to you, at the age of majority. *If* you reached that age." He sniffed and scratched.

"Every one of them cut me out of my inheritance. Now you're to own everything? Ha." The whites of his eyes glowed red with spidery lines.

"Your daddy thought he had you bubble wrapped by lawyers. But your death, before your eighteenth birthday, would free me from you."

He waved his hand as if flapping at flies.

I scanned the arena. No one was in sight. I knew there were others around. Unfortunately, I didn't think any of them could, or would, help me against Sheriff Taylor.

"You know, your stepmama was the easy part. She'd follow a lick of drink or drugs anywhere, any time. I didn't need to kill her to get to you." He chuckled. "You probably never knew it, but I dated her. Yes, right after your daddy died. I dated your stepmama to get her hooked on drugs." He tipped his hat off his eyebrows. "A lot of druggies overdose. I could have killed her fast and been done with it. But it was more fun to watch her lose everything your daddy bought with his big winnings. To watch her lose your daddy's beloved bulls. His horses. I watched her lose his ranch."

I clenched my hands into fists at my side. *I hate him.*

"See? There's the old Taylor temper coming out." The sheriff pointed a finger at my nose.

I smacked it from my face.

"Careful, boy. I am still a sheriff."

Zzt, zzt crack. A bull roared behind the chutes. Metal clanged.

"Where was I?" The sheriff paced in front of me like a caged tiger. "Yes. Bonus. When she lost everything to her addictions, she came looking for me. She was a pretty thing. I almost imagined marrying her to control you." He stopped to grin at me. "Can you imagine? Your father's wife marrying his brother? You could have called me Uncle Daddy." He slapped his leg with his hand and burst into laughter.

I didn't know what my next move should be. Could I rush past him? I wasn't liking the crazed look in his eyes. And the fact that he carried a gun. But he couldn't shoot me. Could he?

"Your stepmama slipped into a coma before I got around to marrying her. But that still left your fate to me. The hitch was, you were in the spotlight from your debut in bull riding. That had everyone's eyes on you."

I stuffed my hands in my pockets. "You're my uncle," I said more to myself than to him. I hated how small my voice sounded. I hated that it came out with a yearning—in a whine—like a little girl—I mean, I knew he was my uncle from Devyn's letter. But to hear him say it…

"Uncle? Family? I could tell you a few things about family. My sister, MaryLu, abandoned me. She left because of something my father did. He was an evil man. I can only imagine what finally drove her away. I told her I'd kill him for her. We could have been happy without him. She could have stayed. But she chose to leave me when I was just a small boy."

I jerked my hands from my pockets. If I timed it right, he'd pace one way, I'd dash the other.

"She left me," he repeated. "I was only eight years old when she ran off with some boy from school." He spun on his heel to pace back the other way.

Now. I tried to sprint for the gate.

He lunged into my path and knocked me backwards. I fell on my butt.

"Just like your daddy. Running out on me." He snorted a laugh. "But you I can stop." He swiped his sleeve across his mouth. "Where was I?"

Oh, for chrissakes, at least my attempt to escape could have shut him up.

"Your spoiled daddy was born to bull ride. He never had to work at it. Never had to earn it. Bull riding came too easy to my brother. Everything came easy to my brother."

"That's not true," I shouted. I climbed from the dirt.

"It is. There was nothing he couldn't ride. No one that didn't adore him. A real town hero. Golden boy Taylor. God, it was exhausting living in his goody-two-shoes shadow."

As I made a big show of dusting off, I checked my surroundings again. We were closer to the gate. If I could push him farther, I could try to run again.

"I worked hard. Scraped for entry fees," Sheriff Taylor said. "Struggled to make the eight each time. Had my elbow broken when a hoof came down on it. Eighteen years old. Shattered." His eyes glazed. His mind seemed to travel far away. "Couldn't ride after that." The sheriff looked at his arm. He hinged it up and down.

I made another break for the gate.

He snapped back to the present and clothes-lined me without a hitch in his tirade.

"You think your daddy could remember his kid brother? No. He just kept making his rides and getting all famous, leaving his baby brother in the hands of a cruel father."

I got up from the dirt again.

"But I showed him," the sheriff said. "I showed *Buckshot*

Taylor. And he never suspected a thing." The sheriff smiled at me. A few of his sores burst from the tension of that repulsive grin. "His big ol' truck flipped like a flapjack on a Sunday morning griddle when I ran into it head-on with the patrol car." He shrugged. "He wasn't even driving fast. I was." He laughed. "Speed kills."

"You threw the headlight into the brush," I recalled aloud.

"That's right." He said it as if he were thrilled I'd remembered.

I shook my head hoping to shake off the memory. *Flashing blue and red lights. His flashing lights.*

"I killed my parents and my brother. Would kill my sister too if I ever find her. But tonight, it's all you." He pulled on his duty belt then hooked his thumb behind its buckle.

"You're gonna ride one last time. Cuz the story's simple. You thought you'd sneak in some practice on the rodeo bulls." Sheriff Bubba Taylor, my uncle, licked his lips like he was staring at a sizzling steak. His face flushed a raging red. He stuffed his nose a hand's width from mine.

I could count every sore that oozed with pus on his jawline. I could smell the stale tobacco on his fetid breath.

Zzt. Zzt. Zap. Crack. Zap. Crack.

Bellowing the likes of spooks in a haunted house blasted from the chutes.

"Sounds like it's time to ride. Let's have us a rodeo."

Zzt. Zzt. Crack.

Metal crashed. The panels around the arena shook.

"I won't ride. Not on one of them. I've seen what you've done to them. What you've turned them into. I won't ride." If I refused, I could wait him out until the stock contractor came to feed the bulls.

The sheriff couldn't make me ride if I didn't want to.

"Oh, you will. On him." Sheriff Taylor pointed.

Thundering Bunny was barely contained in chute two.

The bull slammed inside the tight confinement. His eyes were wild and unfocused. His body dripped with sweat from fear—or fury.

If he gets loose, there will be no stopping him.

"I won't get on him." I crossed my arms over my chest. It wasn't like the sheriff could haul me up there and tie me down. Not if I were conscious and unwilling. He'd be in for the fight of his life.

"You will." Sheriff Taylor put two fingers in his mouth and whistled. "Or he will." Sheriff Bubba Taylor pointed to the platform behind the bucking chute.

Scuzz-cut held Michael by the back of his neck.

Michael was a mere shadow of himself. He was gray and gaunt. Vomit smeared the front of his T-shirt. "Don't do it," he said to me in a monotone, as if it were rote. His head hung in resignation.

I shrugged at the sheriff. "Seriously? That threat only worked for so long. After a while? It got old."

"No matter. You're going to die here tonight regardless of how it plays out." He popped his gun loose in its holster as if he were a bad hombre preparing for a gun fight. "The only question is, how many die with you?"

I rolled my eyes. "What are you gonna do? Shoot me? Shoot Michael?" My shoulders shrugged again. Of their own volition. It wasn't on purpose that time. But it was fitting. "There's no way to hide our cold-blooded murders. Not with a bullet hole in each of us."

"No. I wasn't thinking on shooting you boys." He plucked his revolver out.

I thought it was over. I thought he'd shoot us regardless of what he just said. I thought calling his bluff might have sent him over the edge.

The sheriff eyed down the short barrel. It aimed straight at me. He rotated the cylinder one click at a time. Each chamber was loaded.

He's going to shoot.

"I've got enough rounds to put that bull down. What's his name? Thundering Bunny." He swung the revolver from pointing at me to Thundering Bunny. "Friend of yours?" He grinned like he had said something clever.

Mullet-head walked into the arena. He dropped my gear bag at my feet. We eyed each other. His head bobbed a slight nod.

"Where've you been?" the sheriff asked him. "And what does he need that for?" Sheriff Taylor jammed his revolver back in its holster.

Mullet-head stared the sheriff in the eyes with a courage I hadn't seen him possess before. "How's it gonna look like an accident if he's not geared up?" He toed the gear bag.

It was almost imperceptible, but he nodded again. "No one would believe Chris'd get on a bull without his equipment."

"I'll ride," I said quickly. "With my equipment, I'll ride." I didn't know why he would help me, but it seemed Mullet-head had a plan. Then again, maybe I was wrong.

Maybe I just signed my death warrant.

"No, Chris," Michael shouted. He had come out of his stupor.

"On one condition," I said to the sheriff. "No one else gets hurt." I chewed at the inside of my cheek until blood seeped through the ragged mess. It was a habit I'd need to break if I lived through the night.

I didn't want to die here. But I didn't want anyone else to either.

The sheriff took too long to consider my proposal. He scooped the Skoal from his lip, then spit. He eyed me to discern any tricks.

I had none.

"Let Michael go," I said to press the issue. The metallic tang of my own blood flooded over my tongue.

"Let him go," the sheriff said to Scuzz-cut.

I picked up my gear bag. I'd stall.

Sheriff Taylor escorted me from the arena to behind the chutes.

When I took my bull rope from the bag, the hand-hammered bells clanked their peculiar sound. *Maybe Daddy is with me. I hope he's watching. I hope he's proud of me. I hope he sees the kind of man I am.*

I reached to hang my rope on the rails. I could make a long process of scraping old rosin from it with a wire brush.

"Nuh-uh," the sheriff said.

So I slowly zipped into my vest instead.

Sheriff Taylor huffed with impatience.

When I donned my glove, he'd had enough of my antics. It was no use attempting to tape it tight. I climbed onto the platform.

"Pull my rope, Michael?" I asked.

He nodded.

"I'll get the flank," Mullet-head said.

Scuzz-cut knocked him out of the way. "I'll get the flank."

The sheriff hopped back into the arena.

I could run. Right now. I could run.

But that isn't fair to Michael. It isn't fair to abandon the bulls.

Thundering Bunny.

In minutes, I settled onto Thundering Bunny's back. He was oddly calm.

Now would be a good time for a cavalry to rush in.

Well, hell, the sheriff is already here.

"Let's rodeo," Sheriff Taylor shouted.

I took a *truck and trailer* wrap through my palm.

Mullet-head wouldn't look me in the eyes. Maybe I had only imagined he might have somehow tried to help me. No matter, I was the best bull rider in these parts since my daddy. Better than Daddy.

But how long could I stall on an eight-second ride?

"No harm to any of them," I repeated to the sheriff.

"I only do what I have to," Sheriff Taylor said. He aligned himself to jerk the latch of the chute gate open. "With you dead, I wouldn't need to do any more."

I suddenly have a plan.

I know. I know. But this time, I have a really good plan.

I tucked my chin. Drove my winky to my pinky. And nodded.

The latch squealed. The gate flew wide. My bells clink-clanked.

Thundering Bunny made his giant leap to escape confinement. He came down like a pile driver on all fours. *Nothing can prepare a rider for that jaw-jarring jolt.* When he came up, I set my spur and marked him out.

He spun.

That's what I'd wanted.

I sat on my back pockets, opened my hand, and slingshotted off. *Gotta love inertia.*

It was a beautiful thing. I landed on my feet.

Thundering Bunny turned. He lowered his lopsided head and lined me up.

I froze.

Thundering Bunny charged. His hooves pounded over the dirt. Drool dripped from his gaping mouth as he hollered like a desperate foghorn.

I dodged sideways. Thundering Bunny tracked me.

The sheriff never saw the wreck coming. Well...he had. He just never imagined it was gonna happen that way. He had no time to move.

I hurled myself into Sheriff Taylor, twisted his shirt in my fists, and hugged him close.

When Thundering Bunny hit, he bashed the two of us.

The sheriff slipped from my grip. Thundering Bunny stomped over the top of me. I was smeared into the arena dirt like a squashed bug. His hind hoof slapped me in the head on the way by. My ears rang. I couldn't get up.

Pain roared in my brain. Blood leaked from my mouth onto my lips. Grit stuck to my teeth.

I curled into the fetal position.

The sheriff was luckier. He had rolled to his feet and ran.

I didn't regret it. I'd have made the same decision again and again to save my friends. To save the bulls. How could I have any regrets? Even if I died here and now, I had few regrets.

I had lived.

I found me. I had lived me. The me I was born to be. *I am Chris.*

My brain was rattled. Lightning-like strikes blasted through my entire being. Movement had to be forced, as if I waded through poured cement.

Thundering Bunny?

He whirled back.

I got as small as I could and waited for Thundering Bunny's killing blow. *No regrets.*

But Thundering Bunny stormed past me.

He powered after Sheriff Taylor. The sheriff plucked his revolver from its holster.

Thundering Bunny's lopsided head smacked the sheriff.

A shot fired.

The sheriff fell beneath the bull's churning hooves.

Thundering Bunny? The bells stopped clanking.

My head felt stuffed with cotton. I could no longer see the bull. Or the sheriff. I couldn't see anything. I couldn't move.

I lay too still in a mess of pain and confusion. Visions taunted my sight. *Daddy in his Sunday best at the altar. My stepmama dressed in white. Daddy covered by a white sheet. My stepmama ripping a broken shoe from her foot while wobbling toward—Bubba Taylor.*

The muted screech of a gate latch dragged my focus back to the arena. Back to pain. Back to struggling. Back to uncertainty. And cruelty.

Back to reality.

Metal slammed. Voices—Shouting—*Red? Laney?*

"He's concussed." Fingers prodded my scalp. A sharp pain stabbed my brain. The gritty zipper of my vest was pulled down. Cold air penetrated my sweaty shirt. The binding—

"Stay with me, Chris."

Laney?

I'm not going anywhere, Laney. Not now. Not while you're here.

I couldn't speak. I wanted to tell her…

I don't know.

I wanted to say…

I couldn't remember. I couldn't think.

"Jimmy called me," Laney said.

Jimmy?

"He said it was bad."

I heard panic in her quivering voice. *Don't cry, Laney. Don't cry.*

A thin, cold hand touched my cheek. *Michael?* "He'll be all right? Won't he?"

"Oh, Chris, stay with me," Laney pleaded. "Don't you dare leave me, Chris Taylor. Help is on the way. The ambulance is coming."

I felt her tug at me. I think my body shifted onto her lap.

Consciousness evaded me. It was there. Then it wasn't. I couldn't grab hold.

I attempted to swim through a thick fog toward her voice.

"I love you, Chris Taylor."

I swear my body floated over the ground. As if hovering. There were a few ruts and bumps along the way. But I thought it must be love that carried me.

A wailing siren broke my euphoria.

Then nothing.

I couldn't remember anything else when I woke up.

Red was sitting in a chair next to my hospital bed. Monitors beeped a steady rhythm. A nurse lingered over my chart. A doctor came and went. An intercom chirped every now and again.

I lifted my arm to touch my head. "What happened?"

Red gently pushed my arm back to the bed. "Leave it alone," he said. "You took a wallop."

"Thundering Bunny?" I slowly sat upright. Monitors frenzied to tattle. "Thundering Bunny? Is he okay? Did the sheriff shoot him?"

"Settle. Thundering Bunny is fine." Red scooted his chair closer and leaned on the side of my bed. "I was almost too late. Thundering Bunny would have killed him."

"Killed him?" I groaned. "The sheriff?" My mouth was dry. I smacked my lips. "And that's a bad thing how?"

Red offered me a sip of water. He held the straw to my lips. The water was cool and refreshing as it drowned my dry throat. I coughed. The ragged sores in my mouth came alive. I prodded at them with my tongue.

"A killer bull wouldn't be allowed to buck again on the circuit. Maybe nowhere. Maybe he'd have to be put down."

No one would put Thundering Bunny down. "Thundering Bunny lives for the sport. He thrives on it. He's an athlete." I tried to shift my legs off the bed. I felt weak. I grew dizzy.

Red grabbed hold of my arm. Nurses rushed in. He shook his head at them.

"Settle. You're not going anywhere, even if you could." Red's bushy eyebrows moved like spiky caterpillars mirroring each other. "It won't be easy for either one of you to quit."

What?

"The good news is that the stock contractor has the bulls out to pasture for a long rest before bringing most of them back."

"The bad?"

"Thundering Bunny can't come back until we know the fate of the sheriff. And Sheriff Bubba Taylor is in a coma." Red released his hold on me and sat back in his chair. Stubble peppered his cheeks and chin. It made him look old. I knew he was tired.

"The doctors say you shouldn't ride again."

Red's jaw churned like he was ruminating on a huge mouthful. "I mean, you don't have to. Not with the settlement. Since the sheriff's incapacitated and all. And you probably won't have time to. Not with the ranch needing so much work."

His eyebrows lunged at each other. The caterpillars squared off. "I don't think you should ride anyway, because, you know."

"What?" I didn't know if I was relieved Red knew, or if I was angry that the rules wouldn't allow me to ride now that he knew. "Who else knows?"

"Well, I've known all this time, Chris. You're my sister's kid. How could I not know?" He squirmed in the chair like he was sitting on a hot plate and someone had turned the temperature up high. "I couldn't be closely associated with you because I didn't want anyone asking me any questions."

My temper reared. "Why would anyone ask you questions?"

"I'm your mother's brother. Uncle, if you'd like." He sucked in a deep breath, then sighed long and low. "Your daddy stopped bringing you around after he'd lost your mother, my sister, to that cancer." He scrubbed at his face. The callouses on his palm made a raspy sound, as if he scratched sandpaper against his chin. "I let it go. I let you all go. I told myself that I was letting him grieve. Back then, I was nursing my own grief."

Red drew in a big breath. "Well, then your daddy remarried. His new wife didn't want your mama's side intruding." Red's shoulders slumped with his next sigh. His expression, however, remained tight. "Things were never the same after that."

Got that right.

"Folks didn't think it was odd that we remained strangers. I mean, it was true. I didn't really know you. Too many years had passed." He settled into his chair.

"So yeah. What do you think? Maybe don't ride again. Then it'll be our secret." He winked.

Our secret? It isn't our secret. I'm sure half the town already knows. I was lying in the hospital in a johnny for chrissakes. Laney knows. Michael knows. The doctor lady is sure to have held a press conference by now.

"It's a small town," Red said. "While they're willing to accept you as Chris Taylor, they're not ready to think on, well, the entire issue."

Issue?

I'm not an issue. "I am Chris. This is me. No one has to think any further."

Red beamed a disarming smile that brightened his tense face. "Brought you something," he said in changing the subject.

The bells clanked a familiar peculiar sound even before he freed them from a new gear bag. "I gave Buckshot that dented set you've been using. I'd like you to have these."

CHAPTER TWENTY

I asked the hospital nurse for an Ace bandage. After she left, I threw it in the sink. Too skinny. It wouldn't work. She hadn't understood.

I searched through my belongings. What was left of my stuff, from that night a week ago, had been dumped inside a plastic sack marked with my patient identification. Most everything had been cut from me on arrival at the emergency room. A few tattered remnants of my six-inch-wide binding hid inside the wad of my filthy shirt and rumpled jeans. I upended the bag into the sink.

My Wranglers were usable.

I was contemplating their amount of filth and stench when, outside the bathroom, someone had entered my room.

I thrust my legs into my jeans and zipped up. For a second, their familiarity felt like home. My home. When Daddy was alive and we headed to the barn on a bright sunny morning to buck bulls. The rays had warmed my cheeks even though my breath could be seen in the winter air. He'd slapped my back like I was one of the guys. I walked taller and emulated his long easy stride.

Out in my hospital room, someone sniffled. I cracked the door to peer through. *My aunt.* I wondered if she'd ever let me call her that?

I stepped from the bathroom.

Mary Langdon hugged me. *She's family. She's my family. I hoped.*

"I miss him horribly. Every second of every day." She let go and set me at arm's length, but still held on. Tears pooled on her lower lids. "He had been pulling away. I thought it was part of growing up.

I thought he was becoming a man. That maybe he didn't need his mother brooding over him so much."

I didn't know what to say. I didn't know what to do.

Mary Langdon took a folded Kleenex from her pocket and blew her nose. "I've made so many mistakes." She sniffled and walked to the bed where a duffel now sat on the balled sheet.

"I couldn't bear to look at you. When Devyn told me your name. I just couldn't." She wiped her nose with the crumpled Kleenex. "You're the spitting image of your father. So handsome." She clutched on to the duffel. "But I couldn't look at him either. Not after I left."

Please let there be clothes in that duffel. I held the opening of my johnny closed behind my back. It hung to my knees, otherwise I could have tucked it in like a shirt on backwards. Not that I've ever worn a button-down backwards.

"Buckshot reminded me of my own father and what he did to me over the years." Mary Langdon shook her head as if warding off an apparition. "My father's face still visits me in my nightmares." She shivered.

"But I see *you* now. I see Chris. You're kind and gentle and generous like my Devyn was." She started to cry. "And that makes you nothing like my father."

I hugged her to me and patted her back.

"I should have given Buck a chance," she said into my shoulder. Her arms came around me. She drooped against me. "He was always good to me. He was good to Devyn though I never let them meet."

I rubbed her back, smoothing the wrinkles from her jacket. "My daddy always said, 'Don't should all over yourself. Leave the shoulda, woulda, coulda in the past. Start fresh.'"

"I don't know how I can," she said. "I've made too many mistakes."

I didn't know how she could either. I didn't know how *I* could. How to move forward from here?

She broke away as if embarrassed. "I brought you a few things." She unzipped the duffel. "Devyn would want you to have them."

Her hands shook as she took a stack of clothes from the bag. She handed me a button-down shirt. Rolled socks and a pair of boxer briefs sat on top. When I took the clothes, she propped a set of boots on the bed.

She rummaged in the bag and took out one more thing. "And this was in my laundry," she said.

It was one of my Ace bandages.

"Thank you." I scurried into the bathroom with my arms full. The string-tied johnny flapped open in my wake. Cool hospital air rushed against my bare skin.

It only took minutes to dress.

I emerged from the bathroom a new man.

Mary Langdon's hands fluttered to her open mouth.

What's wrong? I felt for the bathroom door handle then swung the door back open, ready to retreat.

"Oh, Chris," she said behind her hands. Her eyes brightened with delight.

I dared a smile.

"So handsome. The spitting image of your daddy. I think he'd be proud." She smoothed the crispness of the shirt flat to my shoulders. "I know I'm proud of you."

"Thank you..."

"Aunt Mary." She filled in the words when mine trailed off. "And you'll need this." She took a turkey feather from her purse. I hadn't noticed before, but the feather in my hat's band had been snapped in two. "Devyn had told me it was a 'thing.'" Aunt Mary smiled. "He said it was your thing. You and Devyn."

In the hospital parking lot, I folded my long legs into Aunt Mary's two-door Datsun. "Where are we going?" I asked. It was a good question. I didn't have a home. I wasn't going back to the County Boys' Home.

My truck. I could live in my truck. "Do you know where my truck is?"

"That's where we're going."

Through the window, I watched the town fly by. Most folks had deserted the streets for church. Maybe they were home already. Back in the day, we would have been seated around our formal dining room table, in our Sunday finest, for a large midday meal.

My stomach growled.

The long highway was bleak and lonely. Miles upon miles of nothingness sped by.

We turned off the road at four half-buried wagon wheels. They lined the entrance to a drive that wasn't much more than a cattle path through scrub land. It didn't look like there was anything out this way to speak of.

A random post leaned over here and there. Rusted barbed wire coiled along the ground to claw at downed wood posts. I imagined the cattle had escaped the property decades ago.

Over a rise stood a defiant, two-story farmhouse. It was flanked by various outbuildings. There were the makings of corrals, but many of the panels slumped in stacked heaps. Some of the holding pens were intact. In fact, it appeared work was being done to resurrect all of them.

We passed a John Deere tractor that had been left idle next to a dry stock tank. The windmill towering over them had lost several blades. I doubted even a Texas twister could have stirred it to work.

The first thing I homed in on was my three-quarter-ton truck. *Why is it out here?* It didn't matter. As long as I had my truck I was safe.

A long sigh escaped my lips. The stiffness I hadn't known I held, relaxed. I slumped low in the small seat.

I wanted to jump from the moving car and run to my truck. Wrench the door open to listen to its groan. Sit behind the wheel on the cracked vinyl bench. Roll down the window, if I was lucky enough that the handle didn't fall off first. And crank the engine over just to hear her complain. My truck. For me, a safe port in a storm.

Aunt Mary slowed her car down, I think so I could read the sign.

BOYS' RANCH was painted in large black letters on a white background. The paint hadn't had time to dry before the sign had been propped up. Wet paint ran in trails from the Y and the H.

Luce stood on the wraparound porch of the two-story farmhouse, between Rupert and Margaret.

When the car stopped and I stepped from it, my monkey girl ran down and threw herself into my arms.

"Chris! Chris! Guess who I was for trick-or-treating last night?"

She was wearing a protective vest over a small replica logo shirt. "I was you, Chris!" She wiggled from my arms. "Is it true? Is it true? This is your ranch?"

"It's true, Lucine," Red said from behind me. "This is the Taylor family ranch. Been in your family for generations. Now it's Chris's turn to take its reins."

Red clapped me on the back. Rupert shook my hand. Margaret helped Mary carry tinfoil-covered trays indoors.

Devyn's practice equipment had been moved from his garage into two open bays of an equipment shed. A side wall was lined with a panel to hang bull ropes. The back wall had been fortified with cubbies for gear bags and protective vests. Boots, shirts, and hats already waited. It was all there. *A Disney World for bull riders.*

"It's going to need a lot more work," Red said. "But the boys have been eager."

A small patch of lawn around the house was mowed. Sprinklers fed its thirst. A couple of chickens dodged the sweeping spray and dashed back again to peck in the wet grass.

"Michael," Red said in answer to my questioning look.

A blue bus rumbled along the drive, jolting and jumping over erupted boulders. It led a caravan of several trucks and stock trailers.

Before the bus came to a complete stop, the door opened. Boys tumbled out. Most ran by. Mullet-head drifted only far enough away not to be the center of my focus. Michael slammed into my chest and gripped me in a fierce embrace. "I missed you, man." He pushed away, then chucked me in the shoulder.

He wore a new hoodie against the chill but had his favorite baggy shorts on. His twiggy legs were tan from hours in the fall sun. He shucked his loafers and wiggled his newly freed toes.

"Isn't this place a kick? I could probably have my pick of the rooms, but I'd much prefer the attic. If that's okay with you." His face was made up. Any hint of leftover bruising was hidden by a foundation that blended seamlessly beneath his jawline. Mary Kay had nothing on him. He could teach their classes. I'd bet he'd sell enough product to be given one of those pink cars.

Michael was gorgeous. I tried not to stare.

"Earth to Chris. All right with you if I do up the attic?" He fluttered his thick eyelashes at me.

I wondered if they were fake. Not the cheesy fake. The I've-got-a-right-to-make-a-big-deal-of-myself fake.

"Yeah, sure," I said without registering what I was committing to.

Mullet-head hung around in the background.

I bobbed a curt nod.

He jumped forward to join us.

Michael placed a hand on Mullet-head's shoulder. The slight squeeze didn't go unnoticed by me. Guess I couldn't call him Mullet-head any longer. *Jimmy.*

"Scuzz-cut went back to jail. This time as an adult." Jimmy's face was bright and shiny. His clothes were washed. His mullet had been fluffed by a blow dryer. But he hadn't lacquered the do. He looked softer somehow. Relaxed. Happier.

Mullet—Jimmy—excused himself, then scampered toward the house. Michael followed me to where a stock trailer had already backed up to the holding pens made of heavy steel panels.

"I almost forgot," he said, then trotted off.

The trailer's door swung open until it crashed into the pen rails. Thundering Bunny took his time about stepping off. He wasn't slow. But he wasn't in any hurry. He was confident. Determined. Like he owned the place.

I heard my daddy in my head. "Some of the bulls are mean. Some are nice. They all have their own personalities. Just like people. Treat them well. As you would want to be treated."

"The bulls are yours," Red said from behind me. "Maybe you could teach some of these boys how to stay on 'em."

"Thunder." I think I sniffled. I wasn't crying. It was probably the sharp noon sun in my eyes, or a speck of dust.

"I'll leave you two to catch up. I'm gonna go find out who makes the best fried chicken. You come up when you're ready, son."

I rubbed my eyes.

"Brought you something." Michael unzipped the old duffel and held it open by its handles.

My jaw dropped. My breath hitched.

"I counted it once. It's more than most folks around here get paid in a year."

"What the what? Why—"

"It's yours. I told you I had placed that bet on you when you wanted me to do my thing." He handed me the duffel. "I'll always bet on you."

"What are you two smiling about?" Laney asked.

My heart about flopped into my stomach when I saw her. My stomach somersaulted to my throat. I felt giddy and sick all at once. And I wanted to stay like that. To feel this way every second of every day for the rest of my life.

I zipped the bag and let if fall to the ground.

"Nothing," Michael and I said in unison.

"Jinx." Michael punched me in the arm. His grin showed almost every pearly white tooth in his head. "Hang tough," he said with a big wink of his lashes before running toward the house where everyone was gathering for lunch.

"Be dangerous," I replied.

I couldn't get enough of looking at her. She stood on one foot and crooked the other knee up. That foot rested on its toe, canted inward. She ever so slightly twisted back and forth.

Laney clutched her hat in her hands, and I didn't know if I wished I was the one tortured in her grip or if I wouldn't want to suffer as much as that crushed brim.

"I thought I'd never get you alone," I said. I pinched the bottom edge of Laney's jacket and dragged her to me.

She tossed her hat onto the duffel bag.

I hadn't seen her for a week. Not really. She had visited me in the hospital. But we were never without company.

Speaking of which… "How's your sister?" I hugged my arms around her and crossed them at her lower back. She placed her palms flat to my chest.

Mm. She smelled so good. Ivory soap freshness and sunshine. There was a hint of horses—like she had groomed Gold Rush with products. There was also the scent of pine shavings. How could I resist a girl who smelled as if she'd rolled in clean pine shavings?

"My sister's working in the ER, or she'd have been here." Laney's hands cupped my face. They instantly heated my chilled cheeks. She had the darkest, deepest, prettiest eyes.

"Uh-huh," I said, staring into them. "You don't have to do that."

"What?" she asked. She took her gaze from my eyes to study

my lips as she settled against me. Her warmth tingled to my booted toes.

"You don't have to spare my feelings. I know where your sister and I stand. It's not like most of the town doesn't secretly share her vehemence."

Laney traced her thumb across my bottom lip. She replaced her caress with a kiss that was more like a whisper.

It wasn't enough. *Would it ever be enough?*

A strand of her silky black hair swept over her cheek. I resettled it behind her ear. Her lobe was so soft, I couldn't help but trace its shape.

She leaned her head to my hand. "Mmm," escaped her lips.

I kissed her forehead. I kissed over her left eyebrow. I kissed over her right one.

Laney dropped her hands to my chest and gently pushed.

We stared into each other's eyes.

I could see a future with Laney. I could let myself love her deeply and completely. I rubbed the tip of her nose with mine.

When I finally kissed her, it was with all of my soul.

Her lips parted. I tasted her tongue.

The dinner triangle clanged.

We pulled apart.

"So what do you think?" Laney asked.

"You're beautiful," I said. "Or did you mean the kissing? Because I think I'd have to have more to decide." I just wanted to kiss on her all afternoon.

Laney laughed and shoved me from her. "No. This?" She panned with her arm. "What do you think about the Boys' Ranch?"

"I think I'm the luckiest man alive," I said without taking my stare from her.

Laney took my hand. Our fingers entwined.

Perfect fit.

I held her hand to my lips, closed my eyes, and gently pressed a kiss to her knuckles.

CHAPTER TWENTY-ONE

December 1994

"I promised Luce I'd say good-bye to you before you got shipped off to the state institution. So here I am."

A nurse came in to offer me a chair. I shook my head. I wasn't staying.

My stepmama looked as white as the fresh sheet tucked under her armpits. She was off life support. Monitors had been minimized. It was like she was in cold storage. *Fine by me.*

"Want you to know, Luce is happy. And I'm thrilled you're not ruining her life any longer."

I saw no change in her placid face. Her quiet breathing remained constant, barely moving the light sheet up and down.

"I inherited my daddy's family ranch. It won't be official until I turn eighteen in a couple of months. But your boyfriend, my uncle, Bubba, is in the next room. Coma. The doctors don't know when he'll wake, if ever. Same as you. So, without him and without a guardian, it's all mine now. Well, as soon as I'm emancipated or come of age. And trust me, there's no one now to stand in my way."

I leaned forward and patted my stepmama's frigid hand. "I won't be coming around to see your face again. So, enjoy the institution."

And there was one more thing my stepmama needed to know.

"Luce and me? We don't need you."

I took my hand from hers.

Her eyelids snapped open.

About the Author

R Kent hides out during the winter months in New England attempting to blend. Still can't shuck the boots. But has managed to trade the cowboy Gus for a baseball cap. R Kent is the author of *The Mail Order Bride*, a traditional western, published by Bold Strokes Books, 2020.